Still Worlds Turning

Still Worlds Turning
New Short Fiction

EDITED BY EMMA WARNOCK

NO ALIBIS PRESS

First published in 2019
by No Alibis Press
Belfast

Printed and bound by TJ International, Padstow

Cover design: Bob Price
Typesetting: Stephen Connolly

A CIP record for this book
is available from the British Library

ISBN 978-1999882259

2 4 6 8 10 9 7 5 3 1

CONTENTS

Introduction *June Caldwell* 1

Introduction

June Caldwell

My favourite description of a short story, as scribbled by me in a battered notebook in a Claire Keegan workshop one cold, miserable November: 'A black cat in a thick hedge in the dark of night ... you know (or think) it's there, but you're not sure.' Whatever the form is, or claims to be, or warps itself into for our sequestered reading pleasure, a short story is a tricky distillation that's notoriously hard to pull off. It needs to make sense, to retain plausibility from beginning to pretend end; it should scratch the subconscious in a leisurely but maddening way; a good story will leave you with niggling questions. Really, it's a form not intended to satisfy. One moment in a person's life that leads to significant change. A Polaroid shot The night love died. A buried secret. It doesn't have to be overly dramatic or an intricate untangling of the whys and hows; that's a job for the novel. It should, however, provide some greater understanding of the commonplace complexity of simply being alive. And don't expect anyone to gift you the rules. It's all a bit Masons with MacBooks out there.

I'm not inclined to sully the great dead bearded males, they did very well for themselves after all. But on every university course I snored through, and plenty more courses outside of the standard curriculum, that was usually what was on offer. You know who they are. And you know the stories. So brilliant and exact and detailed and philosophical and head scratchy and finger waggy, they don't need to be fussed over further. A near biblical sizzle to them that's supposed to mollify and amaze and have you walk off and shut up and never dare write one yourself. I didn't question why there weren't more women writers either. There were, of course, but their stories weren't making it onto reading lists. Mostly I craved something modern and relevant. Stories that spoke to me about my own experience of trundling through, what I failed to understand about life. Stories that were a bit more psychologically exciting. Ones that could rattle a repressed self. Trajectories of desire. The politics of havoc. Action, inaction, too much action. Tales of immigration, displacement, loneliness, love. Narratives that flailed and fell, dazed and surprised, provoked an emotional reaction. Show me what matters, point out to me the things that are missing.

I found them by chance in Janice Galloway's *Blood*, a 1991 collection of fragmented short stories about geriatric suicides, burning cats and eavesdroppers. I devoured it in one afternoon in the university library and took myself off for some pints to recover. I moved on to Lorrie Moore's *Self Help*; *The Penguin Book of Modern British Short Stories*, edited by Malcolm Bradbury; stories by Katherine Mansfield, Alice

Munro, John Cheever, Ian McEwan and Raymond Carver. Then I stopped reading them for fifteen years.

There is a lot of gabble about the golden age of the short story nowadays. It sounds like a fat hen sunning herself before the neck break. We may even be at peak, they say. Prize after prize and who could beat that last collection out of the traps ... it was bloody phenomenal! A gamechanger! Everyone is writing them now! Holy hell, when will it stop?! Yet still the most inventive, captivating, weird, astounding and disparaging collections and anthologies land in the bookshop brass windows and in review pages of glossy newspaper supplements on weekends, upping the ante, driving us to commotion. Darker and more disparaging themes. Crazier formats and structures. The short story is on fire! No, the planet is on fire. Let's not get hellish with embellish. Is it true that short stories don't pay? Oh hey. The average collection written in Ireland sells on (usually to the UK first, and if ever beyond) for around one thousand pounds. Fling a collection out and you'll soon have a tasty deal for a novel. For each person this happens to, there are two dozen it doesn't. But let's not let that scupper the delusions, they keep firing like funky labour pains. You're well on your way! It'll be festival invitations to Portugal and Canada next! The Booker might even change its own rules soon, look what happened to yer one with the seven-figure deal!

One of the most painful misconceptions is that short

stories are no longer *that* difficult to write … thanks to more incongruent modes of communication. Write as you see it, as you use it, in the way you consume it. The recipient will then have to make sense of it, like a mound of drunken texts. We are now faced with meaning as a colourful pick 'n' mix, compared to the more traditional grey methods of writing short stories, balancing the outer acerbity of the world with the inner sensitivity of the person. The craft is at risk, the traditionalists say. So what, the neo-experimentalists shout back: you're no longer going to dictate how we express ourselves. This fairground mirror is freeing and fun in one sense, but deeply annoying if the simple act of telling an *actual* story is compromised. Rather than being at peak per se, the short story—like the taxi service—has been deregulated. Everyone can get a licence effortlessly now and have themselves a go, with the lights gleaming on the roof and the radio blaring. It's no longer the sculptured art with the emphasis on the unsaid, the selectness of discretion. The weft and warp between the curvature of lines we were told was the mainstay of the short story. In place of the delicate subliminal message, you may just get a bale of briquettes over the head instead. And what, after all, is wrong with that?

Another of the criticisms about the modern short story is that there seems to be no allegiance to plot, no guidelines. The farming out of ideas is forcing the reader to do too much work. We must slog harder to figure out what's really going on. The writer is quite often living the very opposite kind of life to the one they're choosing to write about. You can walk far-flung cities on Instant Street View instead of burrowing from memory or picking through research. Newbies are choosing to write on bigger, bulkier themes. Work is bashed out quickly. There are so many Masters programmes, a glut of courses, online how-tos, tips, and roadmaps, resulting in butter mountains of good stories. The publishing industry might want to take some of the blame. Collections are usually gone off the shelves in six months, while novels will hang around like the last goon at the party.

McGahorn, by contrast, produced at least twenty drafts of each story. He only wrote about the environment he was familiar with. Stories either directly relating to his life or the lives of others around him. Lucia Berlin wrote from her own life, a mix of auto-fiction and memoir, characters so layered that even the most hateful still managed to elicit empathy from the reader. And Kevin Barry 'writes for the drawer', leaving stories to stew for weeks at a time, before rubbing over the material to look for the hot spots. The reader is not stupid. The reader, in fact, is a narky customer with well-rounded expectations. Good fiction should take time. It is a lure, a revenue of persuasion. Story is a portage for what's really going on in our lives; the plunge into love and the lower registers of shame when we get it disastrously wrong. A conduit for understanding catastrophic elements of self. I say all this because for every fast-turned collection, we may perhaps need to slow down.

When I read the twenty stories in this collection, I was struck by how wide-ranging and speckled they are. Rife with euphemism, surrealism, fabulism, humour, calamity. Several capture rising panic in the workplace (aside from George Saunders, I've rarely read short stories based in the workplace) and the hyperrealism of what it means to get through a day in the artificial intelligence age. A woman communicating sweet nothings with a lover in a bedroom via mobile phone contemplates the psychogeography of 'a whole town stretched between us ... the surface of our separate skins blued or bluewn or bluesed by pixel-light as we typed against our own private darknesses'. In another, a son tries to communicate with his mother who is directly in front of him, but lost in a black hole of disease. He deploys the technology of music, nostalgia, birdsong, to try to bring her back. Stories that range from the abjectly lonely to the couldn't-care-less out of control. Characters are forced out of shitty situations into even shittier ones. Andy Warhol's assistant tries desperately to get a grip on a new internship in New York in 1964 but ends up on a random road trip. Others grapple for small truths in settings that feel almost too big to handle. Really cheeky ones sometimes end without resolution at all. A teenage girl in a 'loony bin' dreams of becoming a mermaid. 'I see my lost sisters with their pale lips smiling with their ladybird backpacks and their buckets and spades. They are holding hands.'

Reading these stories felt like having a good long goo at a corkboard of curious Post-its. Starting from somewhere in the here and now, heading just far enough off into the future to be realisable. And yes, some of the age-old themes of the short story are here: pain, frustration, carelessness in intimate relationships leading to rot, basic needs not being met, dreams snuffed out. The self, losing itself, while trying to find itself again. Sexual frustration, sexual desire, the guilt that desire harvests. A woman on a beach ponders her clandestine lover's sexual competence, inside the architecture of a children's story. The form is deliberately contradictory with the adult theme. A child bears witness to the crumbling mental health of a bereaved woman after a tragedy, finding her friend's incapacitated mother strangely repulsive but irresistible to look at. Ordinary despair, so ordinary it sets off to blast its own boundaries out of existence. These are disembodied voices and outlandish characters who unselfconsciously rant, then push the reader away again. 'Flicks a duster across shelves. Boils a pot of beans add a spoonful of bi-carbonate soda for the green.'

There is a lot of experimentation and playing around with form and style. A drunk hallucinates hellishly in eerie grassland, while an angsty mother contemplates the nature of female friendships, as an antidote to the stress experienced by an ill son. Powerlessness is captured in the zaniest of ways. Time warp and introspection jumble with the reader's head. 'He thinks of Molly and how he didn't tell her that he ordered shark at lunch.' Others nag with manic interiority. There are dangerously funny stories and awkwardly cloister phobic set-ups to wander through. An editor who makes 'air quotes' with his fingers in a newspaper with a dwindling readership, sends a reporter out to investigate a notorious brawler, now living in a dump. '"The dump, the dump ... The dump, the dump, the dump" to the tune of *The Pink Panther*. My memories of the place were fond. The stench incongruously nostalgic ... It reminded me of simpler times, before I had a mindset.'

In creative writing workshops participants are asked to face some difficult questions. Why do first person voices sound so similar? Who or what is that universal voice and how can be it switched off? How does a character negotiate being in the world? How much of what anyone says is true or supposed to be true? In a story about working in a 'premier nightclub'—most likely a strip club—a woman scales her own potted history by reading the staff rules handed to them by their boss decades ago. Each of the stated regulations are interspersed by memories of how the guidelines were broken by the staff they were designed for. But can we fully believe her version of the truth all these years later? Is the second person narrator more apt to talk back to a younger self after a gap of years? How can point of view be manipulated to make more complicated and dependable characters?

A young man who 'lacks the vocabulary' to communicate

with a woman he fancies, attends Marxist meetings to find some common ground. 'He went to the meetings because he knew she went to the meetings, and listening to her voice was like listening to Duke Ellington. He had no idea what any of it meant, but it made his heart pump sunshine.' He gets subsumed by heaps of theory and philosophy, when all he really wants is just to hold her hand. Is the third person narrator, with its CCTV coldness, a more astute way to narrate a story where action carries more meaning than thought? Or will the reader yearn for more? In one of the most fantastical stories, realist dialogue is used to sucker the reader into thinking it's credible for two gangsters to kidnap a woman and introduce her to an abused tiger in a park. It's not an easy task to suspend disbelief for six thousand words. Yet this story does exactly that and more. It's a lovely feeling, for the reader to be strategically fooled, to burst out laughing, spit your tea out.

If writing itself is a form of lunacy—you hear this kind of guff all the time—finding out how you're supposed to do it *right* will send you all the way over the edge and onto the sand. There really is no covert set of rules. All you can do is keep reading and writing short stories, savouring, quarrelling with, trying to understand them. Who is telling the story and why? I came back to short stories in my late thirties—both as a reader and writer—when I felt properly ready for what they might do to me. Now I can't imagine a day without letting at least one dirty up my head. And I will always prefer writing them to anything else.

The scribblers of these stories understand the compulsion for dreaming up peculiar places, restless worlds, still worlds. It is obvious they read short stories as well as write them. They've put in the hours, daring as well as playful. Some are already well known. They have an instinct for what works, they are in control. And that's what we do with fiction, we control what characters do, to give readers what they want. Others are new and excitable, digging through the processes for the first time, and the giddiness is tangible. But all of them succeed in what they set out to do: tell a story while entertaining the reader to the finishing line. Characters are stopped from too much navel-gazing, in order to make things happen, to push action on. We are dragged into the middle of a mess and shown how thorny life is. Loss is measured in various ways, tension fiddled with, consequence dished out. If, as Claire Keegan says, short stories are the closest thing to silence before expression, the writers in this anthology have earned what they've put on the page.

NOTES FOR THE ATTENTION OF THOSE WORKING IN THE XANADU NIGHTCLUB, THE HENNESSY COURT HOTEL, BELFAST, 1983, found in the pocket of an old handbag when clearing a roof space, 2018

Wendy Erskine

The Xanadu, Belfast's premier nightclub, attracts guests wishing to relax in a congenial environment. It is therefore imperative that you recognise the high standards you must meet, and which herewith are laid out in some detail for you.

I was already in the taxi home and didn't hear about him until the morning after. In the paper they said he was a barman. Wouldn't have liked that, wouldn't have liked that at all. Picture they used was one from years ago, handsome, young, but he looked like he was standing on the bank of a river. Never really ever thought of him surrounded by water and grass.

But yeah, imperative, herewith. You can just hear him. You can just hear Frank.

You are not employed by the Hennessy Court Hotel. All queries, therefore, should be directed to me at the Xanadu, F J Hanna. You will be required to arrive at least twenty minutes before your shift begins. Under no circumstances should you use the main entrance to the Hennessy Court. Please gain admittance at the rear of the hotel (green door next to the kitchen exit).

Sweet reek of bins, especially in the summer. Doors closed slowly on that service lift and I was always surprised when it actually started moving. Going to the top floor, are you? If they asked that, they'd clocked immediately that you were one of the Ooh La La girls.

Shifts run from 10.00 pm to 2.30 am, Monday to Saturday. The Xanadu is closed on Sundays. These hours may change depending on circumstances and it is imperative that you check the rota.

That rota, typed up, sello-ed to the wall of the changing room and signed at the bottom by Frank, scratchy fountain-pen writing. As well as evening shifts, I came in some mornings because Frank said I had a flair for admin. Thanks for that one, Frank. If I wanted, I could come in the front door then, use the main lift. Main lift had red carpet halfway up its sides.

You are provided with a changing room and toilet and it is incumbent on you to keep it tidy. I take no responsibility for any items left in the changing room.

That changing room, mirrors in a row, one cracked, one with Hollywood lightbulbs, box of tissues, everybody's coats in a pile in the corner. Rhonda always hogging the Hollywood mirror: I'll be finished in a minute I said, did you not fucking hear me, I'll be finished in a minute! Empty crisp packets, mints, a couple of mugs, a calendar, everybody stripping off where they could find a spot. Be wondering

12

the next day why my knickers were tight and I'd realise it was because they were somebody else's. Home shoes all in a row, tired and scuffed. Remains of a cake there sometimes because Simone's ma worked in a bakery. Anna, known as Delphine, ate apples peeled with a knife. I would watch her slowly circling the apple with the knife, then slicing off pieces one by one. Hey, why do you eat it like that? I says. Never seen anybody put that much effort into an apple. But she just pared off another piece. She was English, could've been an English way of eating an apple. Came over to be in a play at the Lyric Theatre, but when it ended she stayed on. Loo never flushed properly, big sod of pink paper by the end of the night. A customer's lost bottle of Youth Dew sat on top of the cistern for a while, but the meaty fug of the bogs held its own against the Youth Dew.

You are instructed not to reveal any of your own personal details to the patrons You must only be known by your working name.

One time Leondra asked Frank where Xanadu actually was. I do believe it's in China, he said. Visited, so I've heard, by Marco Polo in the thirteenth century or so. It's in a poem as well. I thought it was in France, Leondra said No, it's most certainly not in France, Frank said. Well why in the name of Jesus do we need to wear all this French shit then? she asked. You wear that French shit because, my sweetheart, it is alluring and sexy unlike, I would imagine, the garb of a thirteenth-century Chinese person. I doubt that would draw in the crowds. And those outfits, I have to say, were extortionate so less of your cheek and your language, thank you very much, Leondra.

Jackie was Leondra. Tracey was Simone. I was Marie-France. Lorna was Brigitte. Kay was Celine. Leanne was Antoinette. Rhonda was Alouette but that just never stuck. She was always Rhonda. Anna was Delphine. Gimme the Delphine. I need a squirt of the Delphine. Sounded like something you'd clean a sink with. There were the few other girls. Joanne Creighton. Claire McGrath. Monica Harper. Ghost girls. The fakes.

Your uniform must be worn exactly as intended. It is your responsibility to keep it in pristine condition. You are expected to wear shoes of this specification: black, court style, leather (patent leather permitted), stiletto heel, at least three inches, preferably more. Tights must be black fishnet.

Frank got the outfits from somewhere that had closed down. Certainly weren't new. The all-in-one suit had high-cut black satin pants, Playboy bunny style, attached to a stripy strapless bodice so wired that it could stand up by itself when there was no one in it. The previous wearers must have been super-constructed cos only a handful of us Ooh La La girls could manage to fill it out. Balled-up toilet roll padded out the boob area if you could stand the scratchiness. Socks were better. The outfit wasn't comfortable cos the pants were cut so your arse was always hanging out of them. The gusset was that narrow you couldn't wear knickers. Tights and black satin with no knickers wasn't, you know, hygienic, but the outfits weren't ever dry-cleaned and there wasn't any way you'd put them in the washing machine. I just rubbed at the stains with a damp cloth and let the thing dry in front of a heater. The beret always had to be angled over to the right.

Could still rank everyone's legs for you: Simone might have been a dancer, but her legs were too thick with muscle; Rhonda's were pretty good although kind of bandy; wee Leondra's were the most like the picture on a box of tights. Anna's legs were really long because she was nearly six foot but they were too skinny and me, me in the heels, I never walked that well. Mind the pigs that go up on their hind legs when they take over that farm? Always felt like that kind of. *It is expected that you will maintain a high standard of personal grooming. Extremely short hairstyles and anything of the 'punk' variety should be avoided. Make-up should be skilfully applied. No dark lipstick. No glitter. Recommended is Helena Rubinstein cosmetics available in Anderson and McAuley's at a reduced price for employees of the Xanadu. Ask for Margaret. Nails should be manicured. Minimum jewellery. Please remove wedding/engagement rings.*

I went in to see Margaret one time. Tooted foundations on my hand. You might need something heavier, she said. What way do you mean? Well, that one you're looking at there, it's got very little coverage. It's for people with a naturally very fresh complexion. Cheeky bitch but they were all like that in those places. I'm a friend of Frank, I said. He said I could get something off. You know, Frank from the Xanadu.

Your duties involve the following: serving drinks, on some occasions serving food (food preparation not required—food will be ordered from the hotel kitchen), collecting glasses, hosting our guests, ensuring that there is a welcoming atmosphere. Further explication of duties is provided below.

Nothing better than illicit food, the steal of a chip or a chicken drumstick. I would always snaffle something if I had to bring in the food from the lift. Never that appetising though Monday to Thursday because the chef on those nights never fried anything for long enough, and who wants a too pale chicken wing? Who does? I could be trusted though. My other duties, my extra duties, included working through the invoices, the till receipts, the records of how many people had come through the doors on which nights. I took the money to the bank. I never mentioned to the others the extras that I did. I liked Frank's office. The strip light and the chipped table, the smell of the money when we counted it and put it in the safe. In the daylight the big blooms of the carpet in the club were patchy.

At all times guests should be treated with courtesy. It is imperative that you are highly discreet in your dealings with guests, many of whom may be involved in activities deemed 'sensitive'. You should not inquire about patrons' occupations or home lives and any details which may be inadvertently divulged to you should be kept confidential.

One of the top guys from the Castlereagh Holding Centre, he was in every week, but I only ever asked him about his dogs, the two golden retrievers. Some men were keen to tell all: the fella who ran a shirt factory and the number of people he employed and where he exported the shirts to; the building contractor, the story of his firm from his great-grandfather to the present day. Noticed mouths, crowded teeth climbing over each other, mean little incisors, the metal curve between a cap and a receding gum, the regularity of false teeth. And eyes: tired and worried, lost, sometimes kind. I nodded my head a lot, said 'I see' a lot. Didn't laugh much. Somebody like Celine never stopped laughing.

Some men didn't really want women about and they were only there because of the late licence. Would've been happier in a plain Formica bar, a serious drinking bar. There were the guys that were indeed very interested in women, that slide of the hand up the inside of your thigh as you put down the tray on the table, the whisper in your ear, I'm just imagining what I'd like to do to you, sweetheart.

The foreign correspondents liked to stick together round the bar. There were sometimes a few actors in from whatever theatre show was on in the town. I got the two groups mixed up sometimes. The correspondents always let you know what paper they were working for and they were usually at pains to say what a shit-hole they found Belfast. But then they had been to other shit-holes too: Beirut,

Saigon, Biafra. But for shit-holes, they seemed to spend a lot of time reminiscing about them. This city, one of them said, the whole place stinks of chip fat. I didn't mind the Dutch guys when they came in, the ones who ran places like Enkalon, they were really well mannered. For a while a crowd of hairdressers came in every Sunday night and they always wanted ice buckets. Women came too. Some wives, some girlfriends. They looked at our legs, our tits, our hips, finding relief in imperfections, a too big nose or thick ankles. The pitiless gaze of other women. Sisterhood shit is very overrated.

The Xanadu was owned by Mr Mahood. He came in every week on one of the quiet nights, usually with a big fella in tow. He talked to Frank in the office or had a drink at the bar. He would wipe along a table and then look at his fingertip. There was one morning he came when we were in the office because he wanted to put something in the safe. Mr Mahood, as he always had to be called, asked who I was. She's just offering some assistance, Frank said. Mr Mahood didn't even look anywhere near me when he said you'll be keeping that fat mouth of yours shut or you'll know about it. *There will usually be at least eight girls working. Two will be solely in the bar area and will be required to restock and replenish bar inventory and supplies. They will ensure that all cash, float and till procedures are carried out accordingly. A further two girls will serve food if it is ordered and clear tables. And a further four girls will circulate the room, joining our patrons for conversation at the tables.*

Girls are permitted to dance.

Behind the bar was my favourite spot, preferably with Leondra because she was always prepared to do half the work. Everybody that was there, wasn't all that, according to Leondra. Your woman over there, well she wasn't all that. That guy in the suit wasn't all that. That politician in the corner wasn't all that. They could order the most expensive whiskey in the place, but they were making themselves look like fools, because the drink wasn't all that. Didn't like working with Anna at all. If someone had a complicated drinks order, meaning an order of more than four drinks, she would widen her eyes and look at me, as if to say, how can you possibly expect me to deal with this? And so I would have to do it, or Rhonda or Leondra, if it happened to be them. There were always crisps and nuts behind the bar. Nobody really noticed if you ate them. We were full every night, even on slow nights the takings at the door never dropped. Our receipts showed that we were always at capacity. How many people there knew the Xanadu was laundering Mahood's money I don't know. Maybe they all did.

If patrons' behaviour becomes overly spirited please seek assistance.

Guy on the door was Gary McGoldrick and some of the others said he was a kung fu master. The Leeds top he always wore under his white shirt made it a yellow gold. On their way in he was invisible to people, the man in a black suit standing in the shadow, but they would know about it if they started something because he could move fast. Wee guys, wee bantam cocks were always a problem, puffing out their chests, flashing their money around.

Please be discreet if you encounter patrons outside the environs of the Xanadu.

Frank, did you think we actually wanted to say hello to the punters? How's it going, pal? Tell me about your day so far. There was no one I wanted to see. You'd sometimes turn on the telly and see someone being interviewed, sober shirt and tie, grim face, and you'd think briefly about the sixth, seventh whiskey, the stupid game with the beer mats, the tie undone. I was unrecognisable on the street anyway. I went up and down my road with no make-up and my hair in a ponytail, worked some mornings in the fruit and veg shop where I needed to be muffled up because there was an open storefront. Most of the girls would barely have said hello to each other. I saw Leondra in a neat little pencil skirt one time, going into the cafe opposite where I worked. I thought I could see someone rise to kiss her. I knew that if I'd gone in she would have looked at the sugar, looked at the salt and pepper, lifted the menu to her face. Way it was, wouldn't have taken offence.

Funny walking along beside Frank outside the Xanadu, although that would happen sometimes if we went to the bank. In the daylight he seemed smaller and his hair was suspiciously jet. One time we were passing Marshalls and I said, You time for a cup of tea? He looked at Marshalls as though it had just been teleported there from outer space. In here? he said. Marshalls was quite empty but I still leaned across the table. You need to be careful, I said. I know what you're doing. And what, pray, would that be? You know what. No I don't. He took a sip of his tea, put in a spoonful of sugar. These non-existent girls whose wages you're taking, you know what I'm talking about. Joanne Creighton and co. Frank laughed. Mahood finds out, you're dead, I said. He stirred the tea, reached in his inside pocket for his fags. Very touching that you should be concerned. Don't think you need worry though. This place, he said, looking around Marshalls, is what I would call modest in its charms. What you're doing is stupid, I said. And so spoke the genius from the fruit and vegetable shop. He smiled and lit his cigarette. Don't worry.

It is absolutely forbidden for employees to visit the hotel rooms of guests, or to arrange assignations with guests. Such activity will result in instant dismissal. It is also forbidden that employees receive gifts of any kind from guests. Tips, however, should be handed to myself, and I will take responsibility for dividing these between all workers.

Of course it happened, parties back in the rooms, drinking the minibar dry. There were nights when Belfast was the most exciting place on Earth, a ripped, blasted adrenalin high. Or people might head to another hotel, the Europa maybe. Brigitte had a weekend in London with some fella that she never saw ever again. It wasn't that nice men didn't come to the Xanadu, they did, some were alright, but nice men on the whole would not want to meet a future partner there. Anna's lanky looks had a minority appeal among the Xanadu clientele but there was a certain type of person, a not nice fella, who could smell the need for attention. She did everything as though there was somebody watching her, and there was but it was only me and I wanted to say you're not on the stage now, love, and nobody cares about those big smudged eyes. Went back to a house on the Lisburn Road with a man who came into the Xanadu, and then his two mates turned up. Told me this as she dabbed concealer on a tear at the side of her mouth. She was in her tights for only a few seconds before the costume went on but I saw the green and purple bruise on her left breast, the crescents of teeth in the bite mark. Appalled me really because her breasts were so tiny there was nothing much to take a bite of. What the hell happened? I asked. I spoke to Rhonda about it. You must know people. People that can—you know. You know what I'm on about. You're connected. Rhonda was putting on her mascara, eyes and mouth wide open. I mean even just to have a word. Rhonda turned around to face me. Harden her. She won't do that again in a hurry. Well, I said, that's very harsh, Rhonda. She shrugged. Think what you like. I don't care. She's not even from here anyway. I tried Frank. It's completely forbidden for you girls to arrange assignations with guests, he said. It's meant to result in instant dismissal.

But sure isn't everybody here breaking the rules, I said, one way or another? *Drinking anything beyond soft drinks while working is not permitted. Please encourage patrons to buy the house champagne.* Well of course people sneaked drinks because it was easy, although nobody liked that house champagne that tasted of pish. It came in boxes for brake discs and other car parts. But the label on the bottles was fancy, gold foil and curly writing. Frank himself never drank. When he ordered drinks for everyone he always made sure that he poured himself a glass of cold tea, amber as whiskey. I saw him doing it. He looked at me. What? Nothing. What? Nothing, I said I need to have my wits about me, Frank began. As do you. So lay off whatever it is you are drinking there. And do not help yourself to another packet of nuts or it is going to be curtains for you, my friend. You can hardly get that zip up as it is. *Payment will be made to you on a Friday and that payment will be in cash. In the unlikely event that payment has not been calculated correctly, please put your contention in writing and it will be dealt with at my earliest convenience. Please do not ask for wages in advance.*

Little brown envelopes, glued with Frank's smoky spit. If people weren't in on Friday they were able to pick it up on the Saturday. We were meant to get the division of the tips on the Friday as well, although we always had to remind Frank about that. He put the tips in an old marmalade jar but there was never as much as we thought there would be. A fella came in one evening. He took a spot at the bar but he didn't talk to anyone, not the other two scrotes who were laughing about something that had happened to a mutual friend of theirs on holiday. He ordered a vodka tonic, sipped it in an unhurried way. I tried to make conversation a couple of times but he wasn't interested. Frank was at a table with the business crowd. Every so often there was a peal of laughter and people leaned back in their seats. They'd ordered food and I watched Leondra and Brigitte manoeuvre the trolley out of the lift. Gary McGoldrick came in from the door. He didn't say anything but he nodded in the direction of the man at the bar. I shrugged. What was the problem. Fella seemed no trouble. There was only me behind the bar. Simone had phoned in sick. I asked the man if he wanted another drink. Sure, he said. He took his money out of a leather wallet with long, pale fingers. What's your name, love? he said. Marie-France, I said. He sighed slowly and turned in his chair to briefly look round the club. I mean your real name, he said. It's Marie-France, I said. Okay, Marie-France, he said. You're not Joanne Creighton then? I said that I didn't know everybody's names. No? What about Claire McGrath? Not sure, I said. Claire McGrath around tonight? he asked. I don't know, I said. You don't seem to know too much, love, do you? Don't seem to know too much at all. I wondered how much it would have cost me to say, that's me, I'm Claire McGrath. My daddy's McGrath and my mummy's McGrath and I'm Claire McGrath. Well alright, love, that's me leaving anyway, he said. He hadn't finished his drink.

There will usually be two taxis to service those requiring a lift home. The taxi fare is the responsibility of those who are travelling.

I was usually the last to get out of the car on the journeys home and I had to pass to the driver the handful of coins that everyone had given me. Why not just pay me in bottle tops, huh, sweetheart? Streets were always deserted at that time of night. Everyone wore a long coat because no one could be bothered taking off their outfit at the end of the shift. The Ooh La La disguise coat. I said to Frank about the man. No need to worry, because those girls have disappeared for good, he said.

Please ensure that your language is at all times ladylike.

Me and her seen yous in town. Her and me seen yous in town. She and me seen yousuns in the town. What's the thing we're not meant to say again? Simone asked. Yous. I'll stop saying yous when some of them English fellas start saying er. Tinker. Drinker. Not tinka, drinka. They not see the er or what? Well, Frank said, the difference is that while you are here because you are paid to be here, they are here because they are paying. Therefore the gentlemen in question are entitled to speak howsoever they wish. Because, you know, the customer is king. I think what you mean, Frank, Simone said, is custome.

There should be absolutely no smoking by employees. It is not in keeping with the image of our hostesses and that of the club.

The only people who didn't smoke were Anna and the girl who used to be a dancer. The ashtrays on the tables were made of onyx and like rocks. Frank always used to say, the *onyx* ashtrays, never just the ashtrays. He really thought they were something. They were too heavy to be washed properly so they just got wiped out.

If you decide to terminate your employment at the Xanadu club, at least two weeks' notice is required. You will be required to return your uniform in the condition in which you received it. All repairs will be deducted from final wages. Any further questions you may have about your employment in the Xanadu, please do not hesitate to ask myself and I shall try to furnish you with the detail you require. F. J. Hanna.

I was the only one who went to the funeral mass, although I only stood outside. It took me two buses to get to where Frank was from. Two buses and a walk. It was raining on and off the whole time. After, the people who weren't away to the burial headed to a little bar with a wagon wheel on either side of the door. I recognised Margaret in there, Margaret from Helena Rubinstein. You won't remember me, I said. You sold me a foundation once. You were a friend of Frank's? Well, I worked with him, I said.

Mahood brought in someone else, a guy who had run a bar in London. This fella appointed Rhonda to be a floor manager and she didn't need to wear the costume anymore. She was wearing a tight black suit and white courts when she told me that I was late. People need to arrive on time, she said. Seriously, Rhonda? Is that the case? Mahood was in with a couple of friends, Rhonda slinking around them, clicking her fingers for drinks and food. Mahood had split with his wife and was living in the top suite in the hotel. Let's face it, Rhonda said later on when we both happened to be in the changing room, it's not the same for you without Frank, is it? You two were thick as thieves really, weren't you? No, I said. I wouldn't say that at all. New girls starting next week, Rhonda said. We're junking all the outfits. Getting something classy. Everybody looks like shit in the outfits anyway. It's going to be an American theme from next month, Gatsby's, total refurb, and new girls starting.

I didn't want to stay. I was an Ooh La La girl. I was Xanadu.

Detachment

Gerard McKeown

The job was a mistake, the sort you make when you're on autopilot: a spilled cup of coffee; a typo in an email, Mr instead of Mrs. Only this was much more drastic, like falling asleep at the wheel, drifting off-road unaware, only to wake in a crushed car and wonder how you survived.

It was an office job, administration based—Microsoft Office: Outlook, Word, Excel. Scanning, photocopying, filing, monotony, rinse, repeat, wait for Friday, stress until Monday, stay on the cycle and one day, hopefully, you'll be alive at the end. Squeeze the assets. That's what these jobs do. Squeeze them like spots. And when one pops: well, that was sad.

Mr Fleming, my boss, dragged me into a meeting room one Monday morning, telling me my miserable face sapped my colleagues' morale; a customer had even complained I sounded glum on the phone. My boss loved work, but then he earned more than me, and took regular holidays, playing golf in exotic locations. Though I don't know where he found the energy to even swing his clubs, never mind walk between holes. Mr Fleming's breath reeked of battered fried-egg sandwiches with melted cheese. He had the build to match. With a wheeze, like an asthmatic climbing a flight of stairs, he reached into the pocket of his two sizes too small blazer, which he'd either bought when leaner or to inspire him to lose weight, and brought out a folded-up sheet of A4 paper.

'This,' he said, 'is a P-I-P. Pip.'

His voice held the pride of the long-forgotten caveman, who not only invented the wheel, but named it too. When I didn't react with awe, he proceeded to explain what PIP meant: Performance Improvement Plan. The sheet of paper detailed how I was expected to smile while speaking on the phone, ask clients what I could be doing to improve their customer experience, ask for extra work every morning, all that HR stuff that's lovely in theory but not in practice.

The kicker was when he said, almost as an afterthought, that I needed to start shaving every day. He had big plans for the business and wanted me to look the part.

'Can't have you looking like a member of WHAM!' he said, with a laugh, as though Wham! was the most edgy, dangerous band out there. Not some cheery popstars from yesteryear, who—much as I'll admit to letting loose on the dancefloor to *Wake Me Up Before You Go-Go* when hammered—have never been synonymous with rebellion.

I would have killed to tell Mr Fleming to stick his job up his arse, but I needed the money. I took the page back to my desk and thought about pinning it up on the partition between me and the grumpy old fucker who sat opposite. Only, Mr Fleming would have clocked it for sarcasm. I spoke to my dad about it. He'd endured years of sweating towards old age in a photocopier factory and had managed to come home every day happy as a bouncy ball. I'd grown up suspecting he was simple. I only asked him because I was desperate.

'You know,' he said, wagging his finger, as though the questionable fact he was about to reveal would be worth listening to. 'Stephen Hawking said that when we discover the secret of time travel, we'll only be able to go forward, but not back. That's why we've never been visited by anyone from the future.'

'Get to the point,' I said.

That's when he told me about detachment.

If you're stuck in a job and there's no way of finding happiness in your work, or finding something better, then detachment is the best action to take. It takes time to master. To start, you need to pause every evening as you leave the office. Notice how your shoulders warm as they release the tension holding them ever so slightly up. If you wear a tie, loosen it; open your top button. Give your eyes a few seconds to find their focus, now they're no longer staring at a blaring bright screen less than a foot in front of your face. Take in the evening as you leave the office. Tie those good feelings to that image. Focus on it throughout your working day. Go in every day. Sick or stressed it doesn't matter, be at your desk enduring everything: chewings from the boss over glum phone calls; emails that come in when your inbox is already overflowing; paperwork dumped on your desk and monotonously explained. You need every ball in the air, crashing down aimed straight at your head. Put up with it, picturing that image of home time as you go. You'll struggle at first but soon find you start to miss out chunks of the day. Don't fight it, and one day you will walk into the office at ten to nine, and with what feels like the next step, walk out again at six. It sounds like time travel, but it isn't. You'll still experience, just not consciously acknowledge, those chunks of days you've sold to your employer.

I followed Dad's instructions. Not complaining, but smiling, as I waited for the day detachment would occur. Soon enough it did. I got off the train one morning and hurried to the office, only to find myself standing outside in the rain at six o'clock. I didn't even have an umbrella. I walked to the station, peeping at my watch every few steps, like a child who's just learnt to tell the time. Sneezing and sniffling through the packed commute home on the cold train, I grinned so hard my cheeks hurt.

After that, I never had any conscious experience of my time at work. I could go in tired, sick, hungover, it didn't matter. Once I detached at the office door, it was as if someone else took over and suffered the drudge of the working day, without me having to so much as smell it.

That first weekend I got up at seven; I'm one of those

people who wake at the same time regardless of whether they're working or not. After leaving the house, I found myself wandering round at six in the evening, carrying bags of shopping I couldn't remember buying. The next morning, I planted myself in front of the Xbox after breakfast. I was still there come evening.

I began to notice people in other professions, mostly catering or retail, detaching too. They had a way with them: an energy that ticked over, a carefree adeptness, giving the impression that they liked you, but would forget you as soon as you left their sight.

That first year passed in what felt like a month. No clock watching, and no work stress following me home to waste my free time. The stream of evenings and nights were mine to enjoy. The second year went even faster. The third faster still. During the fourth year, I started to worry. A bald spot on my crown that had been the size of a two-pound coin before I started detachment, had by now taken over the top of my skull. I started shaving my head every morning. Crow's feet had settled at the sides of my eyes. Would I wake in a few months, ready to retire, wondering where my life had gone? I stopped savouring the view at home time, hoping that would break detachment, but the dark evergreen trees across the street, each potted inside the space of a removed paving slab, continued to sway in the evening breeze. They seemed to be waving at me, as if they wanted to tell me this approach wouldn't work. I started drinking strong coffee—

double espressos on the way to the train, another double at the station, only to find myself standing back outside the office at six o'clock, the work day an unknown adventure behind me. A couple of evenings I turned and walked back into the office, only to find myself standing back outside again ten minutes later. It seemed I couldn't consciously acknowledge any time spent, not just during working hours, but also in the physical space of the office.

One day, on the train home, I noticed a spot of blood on my cuff. The next day detachment wore off in a dark room. My ass cheeks rested on a hard, wooden bench. I tried to look at my watch, which lit up when you pressed a button on the side. But it was missing. Along the bottom of a door, a seam of yellow light indicated a brighter world outside. The low hum of voices in the near distance suggested this building was used for work. As I heard the succession of heavy bolts sliding back, I realised I was in a cell. As I stood up, I had to grab my trousers to stop them sliding down Where was my belt? A light came on. In the doorway stood a policeman, his stern face confirming this was serious. Once he had me in an interview room, I asked for a solicitor, even before asking why I was there. Money was tight, so I needed legal aid.

Sitting opposite the policeman in silence, I rolled down my sleeves. No blood on them. But I never roll my sleeves up. When did I start doing that? The back of my left hand, my strong hand, was bruised, but it didn't hurt unless I pressed on it.

My solicitor walked in, enveloped in that friendly, professional, half-glazed look. In that moment, I wondered how many people I encountered every day were detached; maybe more than were ever present. Maybe no one was aware of me in their conscious moments. If only. Then there would be a chance for me to escape and become forgotten.

'Do you know why you're here?' the policeman asked.

I looked at the solicitor, who nodded it was okay to answer.

'No,' I said, shaking my head.

'How come?' he said. 'Do you suffer blackouts?'

'No.' I *experienced* blackouts: they actually eased my suffering.

'Would you like to see a doctor?' he asked.

I thumped the desk. 'I want you to tell me what the fuck I'm doing here.'

'I have to ask you not to raise your voice like that. You're in enough trouble as it is.'

'What did I do?'

The policeman opened the thin paper folder in front of him and proceeded to read the events of, not only yesterday and today, but their build up over the past two months. My boss, Mr Fleming, had retired; the same boss whose complaints started this. His son, Mr Fleming Jnr, had taken over the business. Apparently, I'd been expecting a promotion that never came. He saw me as part of a set of old-fashioned employees who never joined in the fun. He wanted work to be fun. After giving me ample chance to engage with new company policies—dress down Friday, after work drinks, et cetera—all of which I hadn't bothered with, he gave me one month's notice. That notice concluded two days ago. When I showed up on the first day, HR asked me to leave. When I sat at my desk, Mr Fleming Jnr tried to manhandle me out of the building. That's when I hit him. The police were called, and I got sent home with a warning. When I showed up this morning, Mr Fleming Jnr fancied a rematch, only I beat him to death. I protested that this was ridiculous I hadn't been in a fight since school, and even back then I lost most of them.

'One punch,' the policeman said. 'You killed him with one punch.'

That's why there was no blood on me. My teenage playground pastings popped into my head, and despite the shock of having killed someone, I felt a strange sense of pride at winning so easily. The news of what I'd done brought a different kind of detachment with it, like hearing about the death of a character in a film you haven't seen: I'd never consciously met Mr Fleming Jnr; he joined the company after I started detachment. A colleague told me years ago that he had worked there summers while at university, and he was a prick. That was nothing to go on. The changes he'd made were all things I'd have approved of, if I'd known.

All this time I'd thought it was me sleepwalking through

the working hours. Now it seemed another person had taken over my body and done what he liked. A person I had no knowledge of, or frame of reference for. I'd liked to have met him and asked why he did this to us.

I refused to sign the statement the policeman put in front of me. He wouldn't accept my plea of self-defence, not when I'd so freely walked into my former workplace and beaten a respectable, well-liked businessman to death.

By the time detachment ended the following day, I'd signed the statement, confessing to maliciously killing Mr Fleming Jnr in a fit of ego-fuelled rage. Fresh cuts and bruises had appeared on me. The court refused bail, and I was held on remand until my trial.

When my dad visited me, he warned me against mentioning detachment in my defence. No official medical body recognised it. Everyone who practised it, denied it if asked. There was a tacit code: tell the wrong people and we'll have your balls.

'Why didn't you read your diary?' Dad asked.

'Diary?'

'You were supposed to write a diary entry every day before you left work. To stay informed about what's happening?'

'You never mentioned a diary.'

'I must have. Didn't I? Well, I meant to.'

And that was it. Simpleton. When I mentioned detachment to my solicitor, he offered to arrange a psychiatric evaluation. That never happened. What did happen was a series of nightly beatings and warnings from prison staff, that if I mentioned detachment in court I'd be dead before the trial finished. The trial ended up being heard over a series of afternoons. I missed the whole thing.

Upon snapping back into myself one evening, I was told by my new cellmate, a four-hundred-pound serial killer called Clive, that I'd been given a life sentence with no prospect of release. To celebrate, he put me in the prison hospital, just to show me whose cell it was. As I lay on the floor of our cell, twisted and bleeding, he held a razor to my throat and told me what would happen if I reported him to the guards. My jaw had to be wired shut, so I couldn't tell them anything. I wrote down that I'd fallen off my bunk. The guards knew the truth, but they didn't care. They were nice enough to put me back in with Clive.

Every night, Clive talks in his sleep. There's no linearity to what he says; it's just snatches of odd, mostly violent, images. I sleep very little. I still lose the hours of nine to six to detachment, which is when I get to mix with the other inmates, so I have no conscious experience of them. I often wonder if I was placed with the most unhinged, dangerous prisoner as punishment for mentioning detachment. My only hope is that Clive's morbid obesity will cut his life short. I imagine him lying on the floor clutching his chest, appealing for me to get help. I'd stand on his windpipe, give him a taste of the rough stuff. But until that happens,

society has decreed that I can fend for myself. Every time
Clive so much as looks at me, I flinch. I wish I could go
numb, or detach from those moments, but my brain won't
let me. Some things, it seems, you're supposed to endure.

Fine

Joanna Walsh

I have a friend who always offers me a choice. I arrive at her apartment and she offers me tea, which I accept. Then she says if I prefer I could have coffee, and I no longer know whether I would prefer tea, which had seemed such a fine choice. When I ask my friend what she would prefer, she professes no preference, and tells me she will have what I would prefer. I am no longer able to prefer either tea or coffee.

Then she offers me wine.

I sit having tea on her sofa, the tea that seems no longer satisfactory because it is not wine, or coffee, when she asks me how my son is doing. I do not like to lie so I say, not well. She draws in breath. To say someone is not well is something she does not want to hear, although she has no sick relatives or friends. The answer she expects is 'fine', which is not an answer I want to give. 'Not well' is not the answer she likes, though it is likely that she knows this is an answer she might expect from me. My answer must be brought round from 'not well' to 'fine' by way of further choices, which she suffers the burden of providing. In order to make him fine, she must first find what makes him sick. Could my son be suffering from this, she asks, or that? He has been checked, I say, by the doctor. But do I think, she asks, that he might be suffering from a third, or fourth condition? He has been checked, I say, at the hospital. But what about this, or the other? I'm sure, I say, that if the doctor or the hospital thought these possibilities worth considering, they would have checked them too. Perhaps they did.

She must know that to offer me these choices is not a matter for laypersons. And that is why I don't listen to my friend. Not listening makes me draw back from my friend, physically, into her sofa, and she must see this drawing-back. I do not know, at first, that what I have, sitting here on my friend's sofa, is a headache. Because I am not prone to headaches, a headache is a thing other people have. Therefore this bad feeling cannot be a headache. I do not know why I don't like my friend's suggestions. I know she must mean well because she is my friend, or at least I can't not think that she means well or she would no longer be my friend. Perhaps I should listen to my friend. Perhaps, though she may desire only the luxury of having been right—and this possibility disgusts me—she may be right. Perhaps I will sacrifice my son to disgust. It is always a possibility.

What *is* wrong with my son? He tires easily. He frequently gets ill. Everything about him revolves around the possibility of his having something wrong with him. This is all I know, and I do not want this to be the way he knows himself. Because I do not want him to know himself that way, I do not want to know him this way. To prevent myself from knowing him this way, I refuse to consider his illness a topic of conversation. Because I refuse to consider his illness a topic of conversation, I refuse to consider his illness. And I am not sure about this choice thing.

'My friend Zdanevitch' writes Viktor Shklovsky in his book, *Zoo*, of his comrade in the war of 1916. My friend and I are not at war, so friendship is no more than a leisure pursuit. For what reasons did we make friends, my friend and I? Because we had children at the same time. My friend goes into another room to talk to her stepdaughter, who lives in Australia, on Skype. This is not a room I have been into as she does not invite me into all the rooms of her apartment. I cannot hear what she is saying but I can hear that she is cheerful in a way she is not with me. My friend's stepdaughter, perhaps, accepts her offers of choice, so their conversation may go on.

'My friend Zdanevitch,' Shklovsky writes, at the moment he sees that '*on both sides of the road lay Turkish soldiers hacked to death*' at their moment of surrender in Erzerum.

As a friend, my friend is tedious, gossipy and ignorant. Perhaps, as my enemy, she would be more interesting.

Still I sit on her sofa and wait for her, refusing to take one choice or another, not even the choice to leave.

Sing to Me

Louise Farr

When I was fifteen, I stopped speaking. When they told me, my lips formed an O and sucked out all the breath. My hand went over my mouth to keep the words in. It was due to a life changing event, so according to The Therapist I have two lives instead of one, which are BEFORE and AFTER. He draws a diagram on a piece of paper because I am apparently a very visual person. This is a tactful way of saying that I am Helen Keller meets *Girl Interrupted*. I see the two fleshy halves of my life splitting open like a post-mortem.

I'm sixteen now, but life isn't exactly sweet because I live in Bluebird House, which sounds like a Disney castle but is in fact a ~~loony bin~~ child and adolescent inpatient psychiatric unit which is where they sent me after that night. The lights reflected on the water and I could hear the mermaids singing.

'The Little Mermaid' was Katie's favourite bedtime story. *Tuck me in, Natty.* She sucked her thumb in her pink and white nest, surrounded by an adoring audience of stuffed animals. *Tell me about the castle, Natty.* The castle, I said, had open windows and the fish swam in and out like birds. It was made of pearly shells that burned in the blue light. The little mermaid had the most beautiful voice of all her sisters. I'm allowed visitors but I don't want them. This is AVOIDANCE. The Therapist gives me homework like calling my dad to say HI, or writing a letter to dead people. Something to think about, he says. He has a face like a kindly moon and says take care, Natalie. He uses my name a lot to show that I am a real person.

Frankie is my best friend in Bluebird House, although technically she is my only friend on account of everyone in here being socially challenged and not right in the head, although that's not a helpful definition according to Dr Freud, and can lead to STIGMA. Frankie weighs approximately five stone. I have big bones, she says.

I have named my psychiatrist Dr Freud. He has black hair like Elvis that he greases back on his huge head into a mini ponytail, and shrunken trousers that show off his hairy ankles and his bright red socks. I have a fat yellow file with my name on the front. Natalie Daisy Margaret Maloney. Sixteen years old and highly confidential. He is also my dealer. There are tiny peachy pills and plastic capsules half green and half white. There are bitter white tablets that knock me out at night and give me a mouth full of metal and violent dreams. There are storms with waves as big as supermarket malls, and boats splintering into tiny pieces. There are medication times.

No one calls me Natalie. I've been Natty for as long as

I can remember, mainly because Katie couldn't pronounce it when she was little and then it just stuck. Katie was short for Katherine because she was only four. She loved animals, especially dogs, and her favourite colour was yellow.

Melissa was Lissa or Liss to rhyme with kiss. She thought snogging was the same as swallowing dead slugs, but she was only nine. She liked butterflies and ballet, and once she made a mermaid castle from a cereal box with turrets that were empty toilet rolls. They did a butterfly release at her school, or maybe it was paper lanterns or those balloons filled with helium gas that make you sound like Minnie Mouse. There were prayers in the local church, and some people came on buses and coaches to pay their respects. The school put a statement on their website, offering their deepest condolences.

Natalie means Christmas Day, but I was born in April, which is the cruellest month according to a dead poet called TS Eliot on account of spring being a slap in the face when you haven't showered in days and want to crawl back into the earth instead of all that bursting, budding growth. He also wrote a poem about measuring out his life in coffee spoons, and the mermaids not bothering to sing to him which means he was not a Happy Bunny.

I am the eldest of three.

The Therapist wants to know more about me. He wonders if I could write it down. He slides a yellow pad towards me that says Fluoxetine in the corner, which is another word for Prozac, and they should give me a GCSE in crazy meds because I've taken nearly all of them, and once at the same time. I write GOOGLE IT and put my pen down like I've finished an exam. The pharmaceutical clock ticks. The plane disappeared. One moment it was crackling over and out on the radar and the next minute it was gone. There was an explosion or a hijacking or maybe there was an act of God. There was just white noise.

Frankie is sixteen, but she looks older on account of not eating. She moves slowly and carefully like an old woman, and her bones are a hundred years old. She has to drink gallons of milk. Frankie says CHIN UP, CHICK because I'm stuck here whether I like it or not, and there are worse places to be like adult wards with old men wanking through their dressing gowns. She doesn't eat and I don't speak. These things are who we are.

I speak to my sisters when no one is listening. I tell them stories.

The little mermaid was a teenager who didn't appreciate her beautiful castle or her father or her five supportive older sisters and ended up buying drugs from a sea witch in order to snare a prince who only LIKED HER AS A FRIEND. Men will always let you down. Like my dad, for example, who left us for a woman called Sue. Is it short for Susan, I asked, and he said he didn't know. He said he loved us very much.

My sisters live under the sea, fathoms deep. They are best

friends with brightly coloured fish and they wear starfish in their hair and necklaces made of sea pearls. They have their own mermaid gardens and Katie has sunflowers and Lissa has pink-tipped anemones that open and close like they are saying hello and goodbye. When they are fifteen, they will swim to the surface and they will sing to me.

Dr Freud thinks I could benefit from some therapeutic input which means that he wants me to TALK and PROCESS my feelings because apparently I have my whole life ahead of me. I see a road stretching into the distance like an American road trip.

I hated flying. Planes are very safe, they say. You have more chance of being killed by a falling coconut. They tell you what to do in the case of an emergency, as if anyone listens to a whistle in the arse end of the ocean. They show you pictures of people adopting the brace position like crash test dummies and how to put on an oxygen mask. Adults with children are supposed to put them on first.

I was on a school trip to visit the war graves in France. *Dulce et decorum est.* The boat smelt of diesel and old fish, and Dylan Stewart won £100 on the slot machines. We filed past pale lozenges with name and rank and date. There were unknown soldiers too, which is a way of saying there is not much to put in a grave. The bus was quiet on the way back and Courtney cried. The police were already at the hotel with bad news faces. Miss Horner said there was no easy way to tell me this.

I wasn't supposed to read the news but I did. The search was ongoing and the cause unknown. It was presumed there were no survivors. There were 170 fatalities including two children.

The Therapist understands this is difficult for me.

Frankie's head becomes a skull. She sobs through the night as staff hush and soothe, and she leaves in an ambulance for the hospital where a long tube will snake down from her nose into her belly. Will it make me fat, she says, over and over again.

The other patients come and go and sometimes they acknowledge me but mostly they are huddled up in their own personal hells unless we have GROUP or COMMUNITY MEETING. They have wrists ringed with scars that are bright pink ridges or fading and half hidden with ratty plaits of thread. They complain about the staff or the food or Big Lauren who doesn't wash or Megan who hides food in the curtains. They don't ask why I never speak. They leave but they don't always get better.

I see The Therapist on Wednesdays. I sit on a soft chair with hard elbows and he asks me what I'm thinking. I think about the harbour with the boats clinking together like ice cubes and the long pier with nothing at the side to keep you from falling in. I think about the long slipway, slippery with sea moss and walking until I can't feel my feet any more. I think about falling down like Alice until I see my sisters swimming towards me, reaching out their hands. I can see the turret tips of the castle. The Therapist waits patiently for me to speak. He says take all the time I need.

My dad wants to get to know me again. He sends me letters that I don't read. Sue sends me a card that urges me to smile through the rain. Her handwriting is small and neat, and there are no spelling mistakes because she is a teacher. Dear Jim, I write. I tell him that I am not interested in getting to know Sue, who is a very nice person despite being a home wrecker and the member of a golf club. I imagine Sue in a pale yellow sweater and putting my dad on a low cholesterol diet. She drives a Mini with a personalised number plate and heated leather seats. There is a sticker at the back that says JESUS IS MY ANCHOR.

There were seventeen seconds between the distress call and the loss of transmission. The text said I love you Natalie. My Mum wanted me to use my real name when I grew up. There were three kisses. Lissa, Katie and Me.

I would like to be a mermaid now, watching the ships go by. I would ride icebergs like chariots in icy storms, singing to sailors who watched the gathering clouds with a sense of dread. I would hold their heads above the waves as they cried for their mothers. I would swim with my sisters far out in the ocean where the water is as blue as cornflowers and as clear as glass, and it is very, very deep like church steeples stacked on top of each other.

If I had a bottle, I would write a letter in it and send it

down to the bottom of the sea. I would send a message with the seagulls, and they would cry out your names as the wind buffets them about. I would say that I love you and I miss you and I won't forget you. I imagine you down there my mother, my sea queen. I see my lost sisters with their pale lips smiling with their ladybird backpacks and their buckets and spades. They are holding hands. They will sing to me.

Seafront Gothic

Sam Thompson

Off season and not a soul on the promenade. Shuttered ice cream parlours, chains on turnstiles, arcade machines frilling their lights for no one. Driving all day makes things less than real. The hotel was out on its own, a shabby hulk with unlit windows, and as I tried the door I was already telling myself I had wasted a journey.

The young man standing at the check-in desk was watching me, glassy-eyed and rigid, as if I had dropped a coin in a slot to have my fortune told. He looked capable of standing like that forever. But at length a smile stiffened his face.

'Hiya, Tobes,' he said. 'Welcome to the Seafront Gothic.'

*

I woke to the screaming of gulls and a splattered skylight. Niall had put me at the top of the hotel in a room barely wide enough for the single bed. I threw off a sheet speckled with black mould, then got dressed and found my way down to the dining room. The tables were set but no one was around. I lifted a fork: it was coated with dust.

'There he is,' Niall said, behind me. 'Have a seat, wherever you can find one.'

He disappeared through a swing door before I could answer. He'd always had a knack for getting me tongue-tied.

I had tracked him down through mutual acquaintances—not that there were many of those. None of his friends had seen him, but I heard from someone that he had left London, and from someone else that he'd gone practically off the grid. Finally one of his old girlfriends had given me the name of this place.

Niall returned with a tray and set out my breakfast.

'Enjoy,' he said, and whisked away.

White specks rotated on the surface of the liquid in the teacup. On the plate lay two strips of grey fat, two carbonised triangles and a clump of pale matter, jelly in the middle and burned around the edges.

I found him in the lobby, behind the desk, pretending to scribble in a notebook. He looked up, blank-faced.

'Can I help you?'

Two elderly men were sitting in a pair of armchairs. The lenses of their spectacles matched the lobby's windows: opaque with smears, scratches, dust. One of the men lifted an enormous grey handkerchief to his mouth and convulsed in silence. Niall put down his pencil and walked away from me.

'What are you doing here?'

I followed him down the corridor and into the bar room, where as I entered I had the impression that two figures were leaving by two separate doors. Then I saw a mirror on the wall and understood that one of the figures had been the reflection of the other. Niall reappeared behind the bar and began to wipe it down with a cloth.

I said: 'It's about Allie.'

*

She was the youngest of the three of us, and naturally we were protective. I was, at least. Niall pretended not to have any feelings of that kind, and it was true he had never been as close with her as I was, but I knew he cared in his way. I knew that when he understood the situation he would put rivalry aside.

I had been worried about her for a long time now. For years she had been drifting away: she seldom answered her phone, her replies to my emails were terse if they came at all, and once when I called to her flat unannounced she looked almost frightened to see me. She stood in the entrance with the door half-closed. I knew something was going on, and I was not surprised when, the next time I phoned, she admitted her boyfriend was making her life difficult. His name was Sol. It was the first I had heard of him. The situation was hard to explain, she said.

With a sick feeling in my chest I asked whether this man

had hurt or threatened her, whether she was in danger, where she was right now. I told her to leave at once and come straight to my place, or that I'd fetch her if she preferred, but she laughed and told me not to worry. I'm fine, she said. It's not like that. We just can't be in touch for a while, all right?

When you've always been someone's big brother, it doesn't feel right to leave her to fend for herself, but Allie had her own life. I told myself that if she needed help she would let me know, but after several weeks of silence I decided it could not go on. Her safety outweighed other considerations, so I went back to her flat. If this Sol was there and he wanted to make trouble, so be it. I had a right to visit my sister.

The door to her flat was answered by a woman I had never seen before. She told me she had been living there for three weeks, and she didn't know where the previous tenant had gone. Perplexed, I tried Allie's phone, but it rang out. The second time it went straight to voicemail.

I was seriously concerned. Allie might be hard to reach sometimes, but it wasn't like her to vanish. I sought out everyone she knew, however slightly, but none of them could tell me anything. I had been asking around her friends for almost a month when she phoned from a withheld number and told me we needed to meet.

We both arrived early at the place she had named, the cafe of an arthouse cinema on the other side of the city. I knew what she was going to say: things had gone bad with

Sol, and she had moved to get away from him. She needed to be where he couldn't find her. Can you imagine it? Seeing the girl you've known since her infancy sitting at an aluminium table, an adult, worn by her life, hurting in ways you can't help or understand. She had kept her overcoat on and put her bag on the floor. She wore her hair in a loose ponytail. There were fine creases at the corners of her eyes and mouth. I reached for her hand in a reflex of affection. I had never noticed them before, those creases, and they made me feel, as sharply as ever, that I did not yet know her completely: that there would always be more to discover. I felt as if we were children again, a boy of thirteen years and a girl of eight.

She drew her hand out of reach and told me she had come to a decision. She was moving away for good, and this time not just south of the river but to another hemisphere. She wasn't going to tell me anything more about her plans: she had to feel sure that no one could trace her. I begged her to see sense, arguing that she couldn't let herself be terrorised. I got angry, thinking about this faceless criminal who had invaded her life. He mustn't win, I told her. Men like that must not be allowed to win. I don't know what he's done, but you mustn't run away. We'll protect you, I said. We'll teach him a lesson.

When I ran out of steam I was glaring at her across the table, breathing hard, and I knew her mind was made up.

★

I walked along the promenade, the wind going through my shirt. My patience with Niall was running out. I had told him everything and he had acted as if it wasn't his concern. A woman watched me from the entrance of a shop. She wore a sheaf of necklaces decorated with metal discs like tiny coins. Her shop window contained a few bits of hippy junk: dreamcatchers, incense burners, crystal balls, pewter goblins. I nodded a greeting as I passed, but she stared back as if she had never seen such a gesture before.

Back at the hotel I noticed that all four of my car's tyres were flat. Three boys, ten or eleven years old, were sitting on the concrete wall, watching me with big grins on their faces. A mongrel nosed at their feet, then danced up on its hind legs to try and grab something that one of the boys was holding out of its reach. The boy threw the object into the air, and the dog leaped and caught it. It was a stone: I heard the teeth clack.

I climbed stairs and walked along corridors. At the top of the hotel, I found an open door. The room was the same size and shape as the one I had slept in last night. In front of a cathode-ray television set a Sega Mega Drive nestled in its own wires. A big silver portable stereo with two built-in speakers stood at the foot of the bed, and cassette tapes were stacked in crazy towers against the wall. The cassettes were home-copied, like the ones we used to make, with the album titles and track listings written on the inlay cards in ballpoint. Looking closer, I saw they actually were the ones we had made. Many were in my own handwriting.

I looked out of the window. Across an angle of the roof, I saw the heads and upper bodies of two people talking in front of the hotel. One was Niall. The other had her back to me, but the curve of her hair and shoulder gave me an idea I could not ignore. I pressed my forehead to the glass, then ran down a flight of stairs and found another window on a landing.

Here I could see that the young woman wasn't Allie, after all. Of course not. She was in profile now, and she was really nothing like my sister. She was a rather unfortunate-looking woman, in fact, who at best resembled Allie got up in a grotesque disguise. Her nose was a lumpy snub and she squinted through thick spectacles. Her hair was dry and ratty, and she wore canvas overalls that Allie would never have considered.

I carried on down to the lobby, intending to catch Niall, but when I reached the front of the hotel he and the young woman were gone. The only people in sight were a mature couple, his hair silver, hers brass, walking on the seafront in matching vermilion shell suits. They stared at me, astonished, until I went back inside.

*

I found Niall lying on his side in the empty fireplace of the dining room, with one arm up the chimney. His face was smutted with soot. The unfortunate-looking woman was standing over him. She turned away from me, dragging her hair across her face.

'Hello,' I said, noting again how unlike Allie she was. Her hand repeated the fitful movement through her hair, and she hurried past me, almost breaking into a run as she left the room.

Niall scowled.

'Was that necessary?'

He was trying to sidetrack me again, but I was not going to allow it.

'We need to leave,' I told him.

A clot of soot fell into his face.

'What are you supposed to be, anyway?' I said. 'The caretaker?'

He wiped his face with his free hand, smearing streaks across his forehead.

'If you like,' he said

He gave a cry of triumph and pulled his arm free of the chimney.

'Here, hold this.'

The object he passed me was dry. It weighed nothing, and smelled of nothing. It was a dead magpie. I swore and dropped it.

'There's more, I guarantee you,' Niall said.

He began to thread his arm back up the chimney, then paused and sat up in the hearth. His arm was black to the shoulder.

'You know she isn't going anywhere,' he said.

I was holding my hands away from my body like a scrubbed-up surgeon.

'I told you,' I said. 'He's forcing her.'

Niall shook his head. He was no longer smiling, but there was a kind of affection in his face.

'Look, Tobes. I'll say this much. There is no such person as Sol.'

All at once I pitied him. Something had gone wrong in his life, I realised: there must be a reason he had decided to make a bad joke of himself. I spoke as gently as I could.

'You're not making sense,' I said. 'Why would she tell me those things?'

Niall was settling back into the fireplace, reaching up the chimney again. Already the honest look had been replaced by a smirk.

*

I leaned on the promenade railing and watched the water, trying to get the fresh air through my head. The waves were small but violent, the water dark even where it was shallow. The waves had a gel quality in spite of their quickness: where they ran over rocks it was hard to see where the water ended and the rocks began.

I had spent an hour walking around the side streets, trying to find a tyre pump for the car. Eventually I had remembered my roadside assistance scheme and trailed along the seafront in search of a phone signal. With the sea to my left and the hotel behind me, I walked to where the town began to run out; or I thought I did, but I must have been distracted, because when I looked up I found that the hotel was ahead of me again, though the sea was still on my left. I tried a payphone outside an ice cream parlour, but the handset was dead. Now it was getting dark.

I knew what Niall's smirk was implying. I could unfold his whole fantasy. It was ridiculous to insinuate that Allic would invent the story of Sol; ridiculous that she would pretend to be abandoning her life. It showed a nastiness in Niall that surprised me, even now. He wanted me to think the worst of her and of myself. His lie had tiny hooks to it, but they weren't getting into me.

I turned away from the rail and looked up at the Seafront Gothic. In the failing light the hotel seemed larger but less substantial: a print on wet sky. Light showed in an attic window.

A figure was coming along the promenade. I knew it well. I knew her proportions, the way she held her head, the way she placed one foot in front of the other, the unstudied pendulum swing that made the simple action of her walking not just fascinating but nourishing to watch. There was no mistaking her. Not trying to explain it to myself, I hurried forward, and I saw what should have been obvious all along though it had seemed too irrational to consider. If she looked like Allie in disguise, this was because it *was* a disguise: I saw the falsity of the teeth, the cheapness of the wig, the joke-shop distortion of the oversized spectacles, the rubbery pallor of the putty on her nose. I didn't care why she had done it. I only wanted to embrace her.

When she saw me she turned back the way she had come. I followed. She picked up her pace and I did the same. I called out her name, but she didn't stop. Instead she ran and I ran after her. Without intending it I was in full pursuit, hearing her quick breathing and her feet slapping on the paving slabs. I asked her to stop, pleading with her not to be afraid. Another voice was shouting too, somewhere above me, but now she had come to a place where a flight of steps led down to the strand. She took them dangerously fast, stumbled at the bottom and kept running towards the sea. The tide was halfway out and the beach was a treacherous landscape of shingle, mud, rocks draped in seaweed and drifts of plastic. She fell, but picked herself up before I could reach her. I slipped, cracked my knee on a rock and hauled myself forward without losing pace.

A voice called my name. Niall was leaping down the steps. I ignored him and kept going, because her ankle had turned on a rock and she had fallen full-length. When I caught up, she was sitting in wet sand. I dropped to my knees beside her and tried to catch my breath. The tide was out but the waves sounded close. She pushed the hair out of her face.

She was not Allie. Her features were not a disguise: she was a different person, with even less resemblance to my sister than I had thought to begin with. I mumbled an apology. She was gripping her ankle with both hands. Niall reached us and she let him help her back to the promenade, where, I now saw, other people had lined up along the railing. The woman with the coin necklaces was there, and the boys, and the couple, and others.

With the locals helping the young woman to limp away along the promenade, Niall came back. My knee was already too stiff to bend. I let him haul me upright. We walked up the beach and climbed the steps.

As we started back towards the hotel I tried to say something, but I was oddly short of breath. Most of the sea was shadowed but the horizon was a rod of bright silver. I leaned on Niall and he held me steady. He touched my shoulder as if to say that as long as I was here, I need not worry about making myself understood

Scrimshaw

Eley Williams

And again we were messaging late at night until the early hours of the morning. I pressed my face closer to my phone screen and imagined you doing the same. A whole town stretched between us, and I considered the surface of our separate skins blued or bluewn or bluesed by pixel-light as we typed against our own private darknesses.

We dispatched small talk, sweet talk. Sweet nothings. Then your message said that you were feeling unhappy. *We're all feeling unhappy*, I thought but also flushed with responsibility for taking charge of your state of mind. I flexed my thumbs.

I couldn't ask you about your day because perhaps that had been the cause of your unhappiness and would just further it. I couldn't tell you about my day because it was the cause of my unhappiness and might exacerbate your own. I couldn't comment on the weather or the politics or the price of either and neither of those things because unhappiness *unhappiness* unhappiness. I kept typing the first letter of possible responses to you even though I know that this causes three rippling dots to appear on your phone screen. These dots change in character depending on your mood: ellipses,

Hansel and Gretel breadcrumbs, Polyphemus' sockets, the side of a rolled dice. As I trialled potential first responder letters, the trailing three dots must be shifting minutely on your phone screen. Three dots undulating while I dithered, modulating the colour of the blue light hitting your face as you waited for my message to materialise. I drafted a breath then deleted it.

The word *unhappy* implies something of a void. A state of *not-happiness*, sure, but not necessarily one featuring a person in an active participation in despair. I looked up synonyms for *unhappiness* and wondered where on the scale you might place yourself if given the option: *cheerlessness, desolation, despair, despondency, dolefulness, downheartedness, gloom, gloominess, glumness, malaise, wretchedness.* I would list them to you in alphabetical order like this so to not imply my own personal hierarchy in terms of the terms.

Perhaps best not to dwell on the word *unhappiness*. 'You cannot be in control of another person's feelings,' was a phrase I had once overheard on a bus. It spoke to me. It resonated, and I thought to save it to my Notes on my phone and embolden the text So: no need to draw attention to your unhappiness by querying it or requesting context: I cannot hope to lance that boil for you without first dragging out descriptions of the boil, handling the boil, prodding the boil and haranguing it unto carbuncles. This metaphor has run away with me to the fair. What I mean is: questions, as with boils, can cause irritation from direct pressure and over time the inflamed area enlarges. Better then to dwell apart from your unhappiness in my answer. *You cannot be in control of another person's feelings.* Undwell, antidwell, disdwell, dedwell.

I send you a link to an online live-feed of walruses. The page was a go-to site for me. I had it bookmarked, ready for whenever insomnia had me in its grip or its jaws or its jar or its spackle. The walrus live-feed is maintained by the Alaska Department of Fish & Game with their cameras trained 24/7 on the Walrus Islands State Game Sanctuary (*WISGS*), one of the largest gathering places in the world for Pacific Walruses. Whenever the season is right at any time of day or night you can click on to the live-stream and watch 15,000 walruses rolling about and sunning themselves. Puffy and hairy and taking stock of their walrus days. There is audio too which just adds to the charm: your phone or laptop speakers come alive with their huffing and puffing, moustacheod blurts and blusterings of no-foot never-footed scuffling.

I think walruses belong to that sub-set of animals that are twee but also somehow noble in their anatomical absurdity. They look like they were designed for the purposes of an Edward Lear poem. See also: penguins, pelicans, flamingos, koalas. Maybe that's a personal opinion. I should list them to you in alphabetical order so to not imply a hierarchy: *flamingos, koalas, pelicans, penguins, walruses.* Walruses look frustrated and benign. I thought that this might be an appropriate response to your unhappiness: I am sorry for frustrations, you were right to tell me, I can be your technique for distraction. I can never tell if we are flirting but I can help you. *I can distract you,* I draft. I delete. *I want to drive you to distraction,* I try typing. No. Dot dot dot. *I love you,* I draft in my text message, a word for each dot that must appear on your phone's screen. I delete the draft.

On idle instinct, I click the link that I sent to you. I want to check what was currently taking place at WISGS walrus colony. I could use the distraction too. The page begins to load: *REFRESHING STREAM* it reads. Soon, I think: walruses in a refreshing stream.

I give a pleased sigh and draw my phone closer to my face, twitching my thumb and reading facts about walruses in case my link acted as an opener for further conversation between us. In terms of taxonomy, the family name for walruses is *Odobenidae.* I think that's one of those words that has the same shape as its meaning. Another one of these words is bed. You can see what I mean in lowercase: *bed.* You can see the headboard and the footrest and a little plumping of duvet there. Maybe *llama* is another one: the shape of the word looks like a llama sitting down, its legs tucked beneath its body. Just so, *Odobenidae* is a walrus lying, merman aslant, on its side. I consider typing all this to you but want to make sure you have responded to the link first. Maybe it will take a while for you to work out what I've sent you. Perhaps your connection is poor. I thumb through more facts as a distraction technique.

Nobody seems to have a clear idea of the word *walrus'* etymology. Surely it's unlikely to be related to some notional 'horse-whale', a rearrangement of its aquequine parts through language. I skip along some bluish screens and read that 'a variety of walrus found in the North Pacific has sometimes received the distinct specific name *obesus'*. I roll in my bed and chew the cud of that fact. *You cannot be in control of another person's feelings.* Another site claims that a name given to the ivory of their tusks is *morse*. It shows small objects, crucifixes and jewellery made from sawn tuskbone. More. Cryptic and coded in their fatheadedness, *Odobenidae* morsey and moreish, their rubber faces standing up on wealthy white stilts.

You have not replied. It has been minutes. Usually you are quicker than this. My phone tells me it's 4:02 which doesn't look like the shape of anything. I check to see what is happening on the live-feed of walruses, relieved to see that the page has finally loaded. I would not have wanted to send you a dead link, down a dead-end.

The walruses on my screen are grey and pink. They are brawling. No, they are not brawling. They are roaring as they not-brawl.

I realise I have sent you a link to a live-stream of walruses mating. It is obscenely in High Definition, as obscene and absurd and rolling and violent and loafish as 4:02 on a clock face and I have never been more awake in my life.

I wait and wait. The walruses mate on. I draft an apology then delete and wait and wait and I am so unhappy, *dejected*, wretched. There are no three dots from you in answer, not even the beginning of an SOS because you have fallen asleep? Switched your phone off? Ceased to exist entirely? All three. I concentrate on ceasing to exist entirely but I do not know what you are thinking, *we cannot be in control of another person's feelings*, but I did not mean to send that to you, and I hope the thrill of error filled your state of not-happiness, and know there is a blue glow between my fingers, my fist over my screen, and the sound of braying, and lancing, remorseful, like something loud and long and clear.

Molly & Jack at the Seaside
Lauren Foley

Molly and Jack are lovers. His friends call him Jimmy. They go down, to the beach, close by the harbour, on Tuesday evenings, and wriggle in the sand. *Molly and Jack are close friends. His nickname is Jimmy. They play on the beach. They like to play in the sand. They like the seaside.* Well, then again now, he wriggles really, against her; and she lies there thinking of apple trees. *Jack acts the fool. Molly likes apple trees.* It may sound a biteen fucking silly to you, but apples on trees are her favourite thing to think about. She is in love with green, yellow, red, and freckled apples. *Do you like apple trees? Molly thinks about them all the time. Molly loves apples. Molly knows her colours.*

Molly would love to be like those girls, the ones she watches with all her concentration, off of the telly. *Molly watches naughty girls on television.* Those vase-figured girls— with their too bright teeth—who go chomp in through the skin and suck out the juices of the succulent flesh. *The girls on television have Extra® bright white teeth. The girls on television bite right into their apples.* Flesh that is usually white, sometimes yellowy, and quite often brown. *Apples are juicy.*

Her dog is always knocking over the vegetable tray where

she keeps her fruit tucked inside a brown paper bag. *Molly has a dog. Molly's dog runs. Molly's dog plays in her kitchen. Molly's dog makes the apples fall. Molly says 'bold boy, bold boy!'.* It keeps them fresh if not un-bruised. *Molly's apples get banged.*

She would love to have that kind of too bright personality, the one that has the ability to chomp teeth first into the flesh, the one that isn't quite so plain and dowdy and tubby. *Molly is a nice girl. She should like to be nicer. Molly should not think about biting. No. No. She should not. No nice girl should. Nice girls do not bite.* When you bite too much, they bite back.

It's just that when he lifts her skirt and pulls her knickers and draws her to him he's already inside before she's even felt the moisture or the warm hot breath and the sweet soft nothings she would expect for giving him what she's giving him. *Jack lifts Molly's skirt. Jack takes Molly's knickers off. That is a bold thing. Molly should not let him. Molly should keep her knickers on. That is what a good girl would do. Molly is dry. Molly lets Jack take her knickers off. Molly is not ready. Molly is very naughty. She is a bold girl. Molly likes Jack and dirty bold things. She does not love him. It isn't like she's handing it to him on a lace-topped platter. Molly is a good friend to Jack. She likes to share. Molly shares herself. Molly is easy. It is easy to be naughty. Molly is a naughty girl with boys. Molly will say she only knows two boys. Two boys are a lot of boys to know. How many boys do you know?* Good girls only know one boy. Remember that.

She's been seeing Jack for over seven months now. She does worry about her sons. They have been left before.

So, isn't it better for her to have her own little bit of adult privacy once a week than to be discommoding them for the sake of her wants. As she duly considers whether she does want this, she considers what it is she wants or needs for herself. *Molly thinks about herself with other people. Molly thinks about herself with other grown-ups. Grown-ups have special private times together. They are called kin-ky times. A kink is a twist like on a twisty drink straw. Twisty drink straws are a fun way to drink minerals. Kinky times are a fun way for grown-ups to play in private. They can play all kinds of secret kinky games. Molly always does what she is told when she plays kinky secret games. Molly plays by the rules. She is con-sid-er-ate. Considerate is nearly the same as kind.* A good girl is kind and well behaved.

She needs those limbs. *Molly wants Jack's arms and legs.*

It's not moist though, not an easy slide; but a slim fit. *It is dry.* 'It's hard.' *Put it in its place. Is it in the right place? Is it in the wrong place? Do you keep pushing something in when it does not fit? If you keep pushing will you break it? When you break something can you fix it? Should you think before you act? Is there always time to?*

Be they the limbs of a tree or the limbs of Jimmy ... 'JIM-MY!' 'Ouch.' JIM ... AAAHh ... EEEEE!!! *Molly likes branches. Apples grow on branches. Molly likes trees. Fruit trees are her favourite. Molly says she likes Jack's arms and legs. Molly calls Jack's name. Does she? Does she shout his name out?*

Molly's forty-eight and not a penny from the ex to keep her three boys going. *Molly is very old. Molly is ancient. Molly has some money. She would like to have more money. Molly has an old friend who owes her money.* He keeps his money tree for himself. *Molly thinks he should share.* Sharing is good. Girls should share. *Sharing is how you become a good girl.* Sharing is how a good girl shows her manners. *Do you share? If you share, do you like it?*

Most of all she'd love to go chomp—chomp, chomp, chomp—into the flesh; bite right into the skin, through to the soft fleshy inside, feel it, let herself go in the motion, let herself go in the rocking wriggling movement. In and out, in and out, in and out, in and out, in and out, in and out though it's never quite in. She wants to feel it. Really feel it. *Molly wants to bite. Bite. Bite. Bite. Molly would love that. Molly wants to move. She would love that a whole lot. Molly wants to move like 'it's playtime'. Things move in and out. It is not always easy to get things in. Molly wants ex-per-i-en-ces. Experiences are new feelings you make or do. Molly wants to be sin-cere. Sincere is almost like what honest means.* No sin. No, no. No full lies. Molly would love the exploration. She'd love to be idly touching him with her fingers, stroking him, licking him. *Molly wants to touch Jack (slowly). Molly wants to pat Jack. Molly wants to lick Jack.* 'Licking tastes nice.' 'Juicy apples.' 'Juicy fruits.' *Molly wants to eat the apples. Even though she knows it is naughty.* Bold girl. 'Bold boy! Bold boy!' 'Bold girl.' 'BAD DOG!' *Molly wants to lick Jack. Is Jack a dog?* She doubts she's the type of girl who'd go chomp; so she doesn't. *Molly does not touch Jack (slowly). Molly does not pat Jack. Molly does not lick*

Jack. 'Licking tastes nice.' *Is Jack the dog?*

Things haven't improved much from Molly's teenage years, stretched out flat on her back on the beach. *Molly is old now. Molly was young before. Molly does the exact same things now as then. Does Molly do them? Does Molly do these naughty things ...?* Wanting to succumb, wanting to fuck it all to hell. But Molly worries, keeps thinking she'll be 'caught'. *She lies /≠/ She wants to give in. Does she? She wants to go crazy. Is she? Is trouble scaring Molly ...?*

Someone will hear him grunting. *Jack makes pig noises.* 'Oink. Oink. Grunt. Grunt.' *Can you do that?* 'Oink. Oink. Grunt. Grunt.' *Should you do that?* Someone will see them leaving the pub. *Molly is scared.* A local could follow and watch them. 'Licking tastes nice.' An uncastrated male pig is called a boar. 'Juicy apples, Moll; juicy apples.' A boar is big and hairy. *Molly is a good girl.* 'Juicy Fruit®.' *Molly wants to play with Jack. Molly will play nicely.* Could be watching them right now. Molly wants to play with Jack. Alone. 'Molly tastes nice.' A big hairy pig. 'Molly wants to play alone when no one else is watching.' *Does Molly?* 'Molly knows how to play that game as well. Very well.' A big hairy fat pig. She can't relax. *Molly is a good girl. Molly knows how to play both games.* 'Molly is the best girl.' Molly can't see them with her eyes closed. 'Take Molly.' 'Molly is a good girl.' 'Molly is the best girl.' 'Take Molly.' She can't give herself to him. *Molly is scared. Jack is not a dog. / Jack is a pig. / Jack is a pig in an orchard.* A fat fat BOAR pig in the orchard full of apple trees. The boar will eat the apples. He'll eat the apples off the ground. He'll eat the apples that have already fallen. He'll shake the tree. He'll eat the apples he knocked down. He knocked them down / he knocked them down / heknockedthemdowntoeatthem *'Ouch / Ouch!' Brown paper all gone. 'Yow! YoW!'* He'll bruise the apples. There. *Brown.* There. *Brown down. 'There there.' 'Brown down there.' 'There there.'* Brown. 'Put paper down there.' Brown paper down down there. *'There there.' 'Hush.' 'Shush.'* tHE big FATfat pig will eat all the apples. *'Hush. Hush.'* A faTFat pig will munch his way right through them. Crunch. Crunch. *'Shush. Hush.'* FaTFat piggy will devour the core. *'All gone.'* FaTFat piggy will eat the bits that shouldn't be eaten. *'Here.' 'There.' 'Here. Here.'* A faTFat piggy is called a boar. *'Come here.'* A wild boar will keep eating the orchard's apples one on top of the other on top of the other on top of the other ontopofanother ontop of another ontopof the other on top of the other on top of another other another other another another another other/other/other/other/other/other/other/ other/other other other other other other other other other another … / Grunting as they go   : *'All gone.'* / *'All gone.' / 'Full up.' / 'Belly full.' / 'Tum tum yum yum.'* / *'JUICY apple, Juicy APPLE, Juicy Fruit®: ALLGONE'* / *'Put your knickers on.' Playing in the dark is scary. It can scare you stiff.* The gasps she makes owe themselves to the sharp stinging pains each time he jabs himself into her. *Molly puffs. Jack pokes Molly. Jack hurts Molly. Molly does not like it.* It's the secret she loves. *Molly loves secrets. Molly keeps secrets.* Molly knows good girls keep quiet. You have to stay still to play nicely.

Late on a Friday night watching Gay Byrne on the telly, with a rug over her feet, thinking of her tryst to come she stores the warmth—knowing that one night soon she'll be freezing her tits off down the harbour. *Molly stays up late on Friday nights. Molly watches TV. Molly watches The Late Late Show. Molly has a woolly blanket. Molly thinks about Jack. Molly keeps warm inside. Molly gets cold outside.*

'How do you keep warm?'

Molly's insides feel like outsides.

'What makes you hot?'

Molly always wears a skirt. *Molly wears a skirt to the beach. Molly likes skirts first. Trousers second.*

Oh! It's a pure cold wind that laps at her seams, but she thinks of the secret smiles it'll give her all week long, and that's something. Isn't it? Isn't it. 'Doesn't it? Doesn't it?' *It is windy. Molly thinks about smiling. Does she?*

She wants a shoulder to rest on for those few moments after. *Molly wants to lean.* She needs the comfort. *Molly wants to be mollycoddled.* She craves it. *She really really wants it.* 'Do you want?' *Do you want it?* 'You want it.' *You want it?* 'Take it.' 'You want it.'

Beach sex doesn't allow comfort. *Playing on the beach can be awkward=tricky.* 'The devil to pay.' There's always something jutting into her back and she's constantly tilting her head forward pretending to be huddling close when all that's really going on in her mind is: Please Jesus, don't let the sand get into my scalp. *Molly's back hurts. Molly's always bruising.* 'Brown.' *Molly leans into Jack. The sand is messy.* 'Down there.' The ends of your hair you can manage, but once it's in your scalp you're left with it for the rest of the week. *Sand is hard to wash out of hair.* 'Brown in hair down there.' 'It's scratchy.' *Scratchy?* 'It's dirty.' *It's dirty? It's hurty.* '*Hush-hush-there-there-put-paper-down-brown-paper-down-down-down-there.*' What's worse than that? Sand up her bum? Pah! Sure, that's nothing. You can shower that out of you. *Dirt gets all places, but you can wash it off. Can you?* 'Brown dirt gets all places, but you can wash it off. Can't you?' 'Down there.' 'Brown down there.' 'Therethere.' It stays there. Can you? Can you wash it off? 'Put your knickers on.'

She wishes she was the type of girl who'd go chomp. *Molly wants to bite. Molly dreams of biting.* Because then she'd take control of the johnny. *Molly wants to play with rubber.* She'd slowly tear the wrapper and slip it over his taut transparent skin, rolling it down, touching the vein as she'd go, she'd tease it on. And for the life of her she'd pay attention to what she was doing. *She would play carefully. We must play carefully.* 'When we are careful we can play how we like.' If only she'd reach over and take it out of his hand. That'd be something. *Molly thinks it would be a game for a brave girl.* On the nights when what's worst happens she couldn't give a shite that she's not moist, or a flying fuck about a shoulder respite as he pushes and pushes into her. The grains of sand rubbing against her insides. And how? How does he not feel it? 'This makes you hot, Moll.' God knows it's not an easy slide those times. *Molly likes to play on the beach. Not every night. The sand hurts. It gets everywhere. Jack does not mind it. Jack does not mind her. Jack does not mind Molly. He does not mind her. They do not mind her. No one minds her. Molly doesn't like it.* 'The dirt *inside her.*'

All of this bucking around on the beach amounts to nothing. She wants to feel the tension release from deep within her. She wants to breathe 'O!' and mean it. *Something is missing. Can you tell what it is? No, it is not apples. Try again. Molly wants excitement. Playing horses is OK. It is not great. Molly wants to let go. Molly wants a surprise.*

If only that eejit would travel deep within her. If only he would take her some other way. Make her another way. The thrusting never feels comfortable enough. She wants it hard and fast. She wants to want it. *Molly wants Jack to go on holiday. Molly wants Jack to take her with him. Molly wants to relax. Molly wants many things.* 'Is Molly greedy?' 'Moll has to *stay still* to play nicely.'

There is a clammy residue gathering on her top lip and in the crevice below. Molly shifts about on the sofa, wishing the wetness away. She can do it to herself. She knows she shouldn't take such pleasure in her own body. The way she does it, it's not venial, it's a mortal sin. There is a part of her she can reach quickly and deftly. It floods her face red and her brain fuzzy. Molly has a mantra she says to herself at her most personal of times:

Fuck me rough/ Fuck me hard/ Fuck me with urgent disregard.

¶

Good girls are not greedy.

Remember that.

Lullula

Niamh MacCabe

—Yes.

—And are you warm? Hmm? Are you warm?

—Yes.

—Yes-in-dee-dee. The sun warms the room something brilliant. Can you feel the sun? Here, give me your hands, they look cold, you're holding them fierce tight, looks like you're about to throw a punch, are you about to swing? Left jab? Right cross? A hook, hmm?

He taps her fingers, papery skin taut on bone. Her eyes are drawn, listless, to his touch. She stares at her hands as if seeing them for the first time. He waits. She unfurls fist in a leaden splay and watches the fingers flare slow, raw nails like ragged golden husks.

—Crikey, Ma, but these fingers are shocking cold, are you cold?

—Yes.

—Righto, I'll pull up your blinds, let in more of this sun I've been blabbing on about. Amn't I only marvellous? Here he is! Woohoo! MMA champ of the world! The Notorious!

He struts to her sitting-room window, bobbing his head like a boxer, swinging arms wide, kicking legs out. Her eyes follow, saliva thread hanging from lip. He is her yardstick. There is nothing but him, a middle-aged man of vague familiarity moving towards a brightness in the wall.

His phone bleats, stinging his stride. The girls. He jerks the blind and white sun rolls into the room.

—There now. Isn't that better, me lady?

—Yes.

He searches for something to do within her sight.

—Will I put some music on, Ma? What will I put on?

Strumming through her CD collection, he chooses an old favourite of hers: 'Dawn Chorus: A Recording of Woodland Birdsong'. He mutes his phone, burying it deep in the pocket of his combat cargo shorts. He settles cross-legged on the light-filled floor between her wheelchair and the empty black hearth, thin calves protruding from baggy camouflage fabric. He puts his hand in her outspread palm. She closes her fingers around it, displaying a physical intimacy she never would have when they were younger. She is of a poised generation, closed to indulgence. Bolted to her, his next hour is sealed. He will give no thought to the phone lost within the folds of his clothing, its memory laden with messages from his daughters, will give no thought to the charging desktop on his kitchen table back at home, give no thought to letting out the pup, no thought to clocking in on Instagram to like the girls' posts, picking them up later from school, bringing them to Supermac's, dropping them home.

'A Recording of Woodland Birdsong' begins. Coils of hissing white noise girdle a lone bird-call rising from the woods. He strains to hold on to the miniscule voice beneath the forest's muffled dawn.

The previous month, his mother had spent two weeks in St Phelim's nursing home. Respite for his stepfather, her occasional stays there have become routine in the past year as her condition deepens. Usually he drops by, taking a break from the desktop, turning up at lunchtime to feed her.

He had not been so vigilant on her very first day, arriving at the ward to find her bereft, chin and chest covered in mashed food, staring at the fork still clutched in her strong hand. He had stood looking at his sunken mother. Lousy guilt soldered an indelible mark onto him as he tut-tutted at no one in particular and changed her sodden paper bib.

Her form had been an erratic lag, folding and unfolding. Sometimes she would remember how to eat, sometimes she wouldn't and would just sit there, head back, mouth open like a nestling. Sometimes she would start off remembering then forget. Sometimes the reverse happened and she would try to wrestle the plastic fork back off him, scowling with the bearing of an old tabby cat. He had stayed ever-ready for either feeding approach, bird or cat, and wagered to himself which one she would be. His prize, if he got it right, was a KitKat with his nursing-home coffee. More often than not, he had slurped from the styrofoam cup minus KitKat.

Feeding time in the nursing home had always been

tricky. He would feed her, or watch her try to feed herself. He would warble merrily about anything that came to mind, always in the present. The variations of pastel on the ward walls. Is that green or blue? Maybe blue? Greeny-blue. The chart music on the radio. *I'm in love with the shape of you, we push and pull like a magnet do,* southpaw stance before her, striking the air to the tinny beat. The insistent lament of phones calling out from beneath plastic sacks of urine-drenched laundry, calling from within pockets, or from deep inside handbags under chairs. The wheelchair-accessible taxis ramping up and down, drivers making loud claims about the weather in contented country accents. That'll do. Not too bad. Could be worse. Grand stuff. I've seen better. The warmth of his hand in hers, her bloodless fingers closing tenderly around his like a Venus flytrap. The earth smell of parsnips. The sweetness of the yoghurt used to camouflage her pills. She had recently begun to crunch through them rather than swallow them whole. He thought the taste must be insufferable, whether she could name it or not.

Sometimes she would focus on one of the other women in her ward, as if she had just noticed them. Slowly she would raise her arm and point. Was she hoping that by singling out this elderly patient all would become clear? He would mumble an apology—sorry, so sorry, she doesn't mean—and try to distract her with Tweets he had bookmarked: the cockatoo who raps, the dog stuck in a tiny aquarium, the incident at Bellator 187. Or photos on his phone, the same ones he had enthused over the day before. 'And here's me, and here's me and the girls, and this is my new flat, it's got everything, look at the amount of shelving, Ma, and here's the girls last Christmas with their mother, and here's me with my Staffie pup Bantam in our block's garden. Featherweight and fearless, Ma. I'm teaching it to walk on the lead. It's not going well, but, no pressure no diamonds, isn't that right? Ya gotta show up at the gym, as they say.'

Usually, she would hold fast, ignoring the phone lifted up to her, gazing just above it. She would stare hard-mouthed at her neighbour on the other side. After a period of time, she would end the siege with a burst of schoolgirl laughter, as if one of them had got the joke. He would turn his back to the others to hide his smile. He would wink at his mother; I am complicit. If one of us goes to war, all of us go to war.

After lunch, he would wheel her out of the ward. They would trundle past the nurses' station, past jingling medicine trolleys, the occupational therapy room, the chapel, visitors' toilets, residents' hairdresser (always open, always empty), and the small tea shop stocked with a collection of chocolate bars and individually wrapped biscuits. They would emerge into the daylight and head for a patch of green beyond the car park where he would name the trees and the birds. He no longer gave her flowers to inspect because once, when he had turned around to face her after adjusting her wheelchair brakes, he had spotted the remains of a primrose dangling dainty from her mouth, her thin jaws rolling slow over the creamy petals like a cow at cud. Had he seen a sparse eyebrow rise as she stared through him?

One afternoon, they lingered beneath an oak at the car park's edge. He fell into silence, listening. Cars, laughter, traffic lights bleeping, the Main Entrance doors sliding politely open and shut for no one. Behind all of it, a songbird. He allowed the tenuous little trill to just be, without feeling the need to identify the bird for his mother. He looked at her. Her eyes were closed. Was she sleeping, or had she forgotten to open them? What's the difference? He closed his own, and leaned against her, breathing in hospital detergent from the hoodie he gave the staff to dress her in, one belonging to his eldest daughter, emblazoned with a flaking metallic NIRVANA.

The bird offered its air, ending each fragile verse with a melodic question mark, waiting, then repeating the same process. Soon he heard a soft low sound start at his side. He watched his mother purse her lips and try to mimic the birdcall. She whistled, imitating the sound almost flawlessly, and waited. The response came after a pause, the bird returning the song with the invitational question mark still at the end: do you hear me, yes I hear you, do you hear me? Back and forth the lyrical exchange went between woman and bird, never deviating from the short tune, until the pauses between them lengthened and finally the conversation expired. She closed her eyes.

They wove back over the crumbling tarmac, in through the sliding doors, and down to her ward. Dreading that moment when he'd feel her bewildered stare follow him as he walked away, he had devised a new leaving process. 'Now my fine girleen,' he would say, 'would you like to listen to some music after our walk? Hmm? Are you tired? I'll bet you're tired of the chit-chat and would love to close your eyes and listen to some music on the headphones. I brought your CD of Vaughan Williams with me. Look, 'The Lark Ascending'. You like this, Ma, remember? Remember 'The Lark Ascending'? Remember *Alauda arvensis*, the skylark? And the woodlark, Ma? The woodlark, *Lullula arborea*?'

She would eye her surroundings, gape at him, her jaw hanging.

'We're back here at your bed in the ward and you must be well tired. So you'll be glad to hear I'm going to leave you be for a wee while. You rest and listen to your Vaughan Williams. Wait'll you hear, you like this.'

He shuttered the headphones over her ears, settled his palm over her eyes. He heard the opening strains of the spiralling violin; the music an impression of a lark's unbroken song. The bird rises, circling high into the air until it is just a flickering dot in the sky, its quavering vocalisation still clear as a glass chime.

He felt her flutter and close her eyelids behind his hand. He left before she opened them again, knowing that when she did, she would have forgotten he was ever there.

As a child, she had taught him how to recognise every tree by leaf, every bird by song.

—Do you know the difference between a woodlark and a skylark?

—Course I do, Ma.

—Good. Do you know the difference between a call and a song?

—Is there one?

—Yes, there is, son.

—Oh.

—What do you call a group of larks, sky or wood?

—Sky.

—I'm serious.

—An exaltation.

—Well, now, as smart as you are, do you know you can take a picture of birdsong? You can actually see the song?

—What's it look like?

—They take the song, shake sound out and map it like colours in a rainbow. You can tell which bird is singing by the waviness. But you still can't tell what they're saying!

I could.

—Indeed. Do you know that parents teach the nestlings their very own secret language? And the young dream about it at night when they're tucked up asleep with their brothers and sisters all cosy in the nest.

—Cosy.

—Picture that, the little birdies singing away in bird

land dreams, getting it wrong, getting it right, bar by bar!

—I wonder do they teach birdy curses. That'd be good.

—Don't need curses. Just need to listen, to memorise, and, most of all, to recall. No point in memorising unless you can recall.

—Same thing.

—It's not. In time the young pass that very tune on to their own. Imagine the wee baton being passed from bird to bird like a teeny tin whistle!

—Sounds like Chinese whispers to me.

—Then you didn't listen, sonny. A bird's skinny wee brain is a whole universe of sparks. There's order to it all, there's a secret structure within it. Now guess: it's called the what system?

—The Chinese system.

—It's called the Song system. You didn't know that, me boyo, and you with your big brawny brain.

—I do now.

—All for one?

—And one for all.

—If one of us goes?

—All of us go.

His father had left them both when he was four years old. Stoic as she was, she never spoke about it, but even as a child he could see the scour of betrayal that etched her bearing. From then, she had raised him single-handedly, not marrying again until he was well in his twenties and paired up himself.

The week after his father left, she had enrolled him in the local boxing club, fearing defence was the one thing she could not teach him. He was the youngest in the club, but they made allowances. 'You need a backbone for battle, son. Life can be rough. You need to be a fighter.'

His after-school hours were spent bantamweight fighting when she was working, and on walks when she was off, probing Benbulben and Bricklieve Mountains, Rosses Point and Lissadell shorelines, Slish, Union, Hazelwood, forests both native and planted. Deep among the trees, she would pull a leaf in passing, thinking he hadn't noticed. Ten strides later she would put him to the test. 'Look at this leaf. Look carefully at the shape, the colour, the size. Do you remember which tree it comes from? Think back now, me buck. What trees did we pass? Do you remember? Birch? Rowan? Ash? Bet you don't remember, do you, me little warrior. Too busy looking to see, isn't that right!'

Hands clasped behind her, she was always ahead, talking back to him, knowing he was there. He followed, keeping pace, slowing or quickening, step by step. Often she would stop mid-stride, head cocked like the hunting beagles of her Monaghan youth. 'Wait a minute. Whisht.'

In the forest stillness, a meagre voice would make itself heard, calling out. She would answer the bird with a mimicking whistle, sometimes adding a twist to the tune, a figary she called it, to confuse either him or the bird, he was never sure. 'He's telling me get out of his way,' she would explain. Bird and woman would spar in the centre of the woods, his mother holding her own despite her retreat. On one of their last walks together, she sang for him; a lilting lullaby she had learnt from her mother. She kicked the loose earth at her feet as she struggled to recall the once familiar lyric. 'Doesn't matter, Ma, forget it,' he tried to steer her away from the song. 'But I know it,' she said, 'I know I remember it, what the hell.' Berating herself, she persevered through to the end, with many restarts, throat clearings and embarrassed snorts. 'Christ Almighty, I used to sing it word for word,' she said to the ground as he walked home behind her.

The lone bird-call on the CD curves through the scratch of white noise and rings around the two of them, her hand still firm around his. He looks at her. Her eyes are closed. He feels a cramp stirring in his thigh. Slouching to a stand, he is careful not to move the held hand. He stretches his limbs, looking over her shoulder at the framed pictures on the sitting-room wall. A photo of his ex-wife enveloped by their three daughters, Mickey-Moused and complete in Disneyland Paris.

A photo of his eight-year-old self, holding a giant amateur boxing belt above his head, his mother's hand appearing off frame. A photo of her with his stepfather, planting a tree together on some anniversary. A yellowing photo of her dead parents, his grandparents, on Ha'penny Bridge in Dublin, tawny arms about each other, their lips a strange and sensual pink against amber skin.

The walks are over now. A fixed silence shrouds her. It began with the forgetting of her lullaby then many more small things, increasing in peculiarity until there came a point when they could no longer be dismissed as the curious eccentricities of age. She folded steadfast inward.

First, she became fearful of driving, and had begun asking him to take her into Sligo town on occasional trips. 'Would you mind, real quick, I'm a bit, would you ever?'

On one of those journeys, they had stood at the counter after he pulled in to refuel at Ballinode Garage. Feeling indebted to him, her pride insisted she would pay. 'Hould yer whisht,' she said, as she picked three chocolate bars for the girls and pulled a credit card from her wallet with elegant flourish. 'Just a minute now, hold on,' she said when she tried to remember the card's pin number. A queue behind them, a cashier silent, she quick-tapped the edge of the card off the cash register. 'What is it again, what is it, the tip of my tongue, hold on now,' her voice getting quieter, her head hanging. The tapping stopped. He paid, she followed him out. 'What class of a figary was that, boss?' he said, to lighten her. 'It was on the tip of my tongue,' was all she replied. On the journey home, his headphoned girls eating the chocolate and tipping their phones on the backseat, he saw a tinge of shame bloom on her ears and cheekbones.

Then, after years of silence on the affair, she began asking after his ex-wife, his daughters' mother, the woman he had left a month after the birth of their third child. 'When will you bring her over? Or will I come to visit yous? I haven't seen her in an age! My only daughter-in-law! Come on now!'

He had worked hard over the years to get his mother to say she was happy for him. 'Whatever you think yourself,' she had finally conceded. It had taken a long time to break through her lived belief in fidelity and reach her deeper faith in her son. This acceptance was as far as she could go. He was grateful for it. Now, he willingly gave up trying to drag her back from her surreal dominions to the stark present where he lived alone, saw little of his ex-wife, and only knew his daughters from a self-imposed distance, a forum patrolled by Group WhatsApp, Skype, and Instagram.

He joined her in the guilt-free heaven where everything was exquisitely fine, and, yes, she's fine, Ma, all good at home, all good with the lovely wife, the better half, the missus, in fact she was asking for you and we will visit you together soon for sure, all five of us, we'll land in on you, yes, yes we will.

He began to look forward to these deviations into parallel universes; he began to count on them. Things took on a seductive slant. It was enthralling, if he just let go and went with her; an addictive through-the-looking-glass kind of off-beat. Yes, everything is fine, we've got our good things, you and me, you've got yours and I've got mine. If one of us goes, Ma, all of us go.

Slow and steady, she clocked these forays up, rooting deeper on each of her rambles. There was the time she had made her martinis. His stepfather was away for the evening, and because he had noted a strangeness seeping in, had asked him to come keep watch. 'Your mother can be quirky, you know what I mean. It's difficult. Say nothing but keep an eagle eye out.' He was amused by his stepfather's anxiety, and pleased by his secret new role as warden. He sat at her side by the splintering fire in the sitting room.

At dusk, as was her custom, she got up, declaring it was time for a pre-dinner drink. It was. Would he like one of her Martini Rossos? He certainly would. It was her regular drink and her regular time for drinking it. He listened to her murmuring, clinking, and clanging in the kitchen. He puzzled over doors opening and closing, soft sploshing punctuated with long pauses of inactivity. When she returned without the drinks, he asked her where her martinis were 'Martinis? Yes, where are my martinis Indeed.' She gazed at her hands. 'Indeedee.'

He went into the kitchen and followed the trail. Her Waterford Crystal closet was open, the glasses were untouched. The hall door was ajar and there was a thin track of lilac splashes leading from beyond the hall to the kitchen sink.

Into thin-stemmed glass vases she had poured lavender hand lotion. She had placed the vases among the household cleaners beneath the kitchen sink. He discarded them, made the martinis, and re-joined her by the fire. 'There y'are now, me lass, drink up.' She looked at him, then at the drinks. 'Indeedee-dee.'

He didn't question her, she didn't ask, but did he see a dawning veil of fear settle on her brow as she stared through her vermouth into the fire? They clinked drinks, and she applauded him on his martini-making skills, saying he had learnt from the best, and that it could be his job from now on, whenever he visited. He accepted, with solemnity, his appointment, and made several more Martini Rossos that night. Each time, they clinked anew. Each time, he accepted his appointment once again.

In the years between then and now she had wandered on shaky limbs into the forest behind her home, looking for her workplace: the secretarial job she had retired from years before. 'For feck sake, I have a meeting in five minutes, where are my bloody notes?' She strayed between the alder saplings, lifting skirts of foliage at the base of each one. 'Didn't you hear, Ma? Stupid meeting's been cancelled 'til tomorrow! Come on back into the house, let's have something to celebrate.'

A year later, reduced to a Charlie Chaplin shuffle, she had faltered down her long driveway clasping two plastic bags, one with his stepfather's scarf and hat, the other with her old wellies. When questioned, she revealed impatiently that she needed to be getting home, that the bus wouldn't wait for her, wouldn't wait for anyone. 'As lovely as it is, I'm booking out of here, I can't stay another night.'

'Just one more, we'll hit the road for home tomorrow, one more night for the craic. Come on, Ma. Please.' She hesitated, brow furrowing, and considered him standing before her. 'Righto. One more night.'

By the time they had walked back up the driveway, her anchor had shifted from her youth to her long-lost first marriage. On seeing her husband wringing his hands in the hallway, she had asked him who the hell he was, what did he think he was doing in her damn house, where was her husband? His stepfather hid in their bedroom and cried, after he first reassured his wife of twenty-five years that he would find her husband, that he would bring him back to her, not to worry, he was sure her husband would never leave her. Later, after putting his mother to bed, he showed his stepfather the plastic bag she had been clutching. On seeing his favourite scarf and hat folded with loving care inside, his stepfather smiled gratefully.

The years of her second marriage, though contented, were a period she now rarely hovered over. Her darkening mind favoured the bright spell of her youth. Her husband struggled to forgive her, and pressed his stepson to take over. From then, he began to spend more time with them, ready and eager as he was to stand unruffled alongside her in the shifting and fickle maze of her restless mind.

His wearied stepfather sleeping in the guest room, he set up his childhood camp bed on the floor beside her. He slept lightly, shoes ready beside him, sleeping bag unzipped.

Late one night, on one of his stays, she had glowered like a spoilt child when he told her she didn't own a dog, hadn't owned a dog since her schoolday beagles, so there was no point standing there with a torch at the open back door in her pyjamas, calling out for Brimsy, her favoured childhood beagle, calling out to the silence in the dark forest beyond the garden, her torch beam piercing the silver birch. 'Come back, Brimsy! Where are you? Come home, you wee runt!'

The scratchy white noise on the CD has receded, and is now just a faint hushing buzz. Unchained, the sound of the lone bird-call climbs through the tangled woods, and spirals around them sitting sidelong like a pair of spent vagrants by the empty black hearth in her sun-filled sitting room.

—Can you hear the woodland birdsong, Ma? Do you remember this CD? It's the Dawn Chorus. You like it. Do you remember, Ma? Hmm?

—Yes.

—Do you remember hearing the birdsong in the forests? Do you remember walking in the forests, Ma? Hazelwood and Deerpark? And the mad tests you'd give me with the leaves?

—Yes.

Yes. It's the only word left. He structures his questions so her affirmations make sense. Are you good. Yes. Am I good. Yes, yes. He isn't sure if she understands what he says. He doesn't test her, for fear of a truth. For as long as she can yes, he can hold on to her. Is everything grand. Yes. Yes it is.

—I'm here, Ma.

His silenced phone vibrates from inside his pocket. He looks down. Seeing the tiny mute light pulse desperate through the fabric's innards, he closes his eyes tight. Holding his breath, he counts down the pinging cry, seven, eight, nine, ten, out. The beat stops. He breathes in.

Kneeling in front of her, he grips her hand. Her eyes glide within a narrow space, searching slow. She finds him, locks on. The white noise has faded. The bird's call is clear.

—By cripes, I think that could be a lark singing on the CD. Wait, no, not a skylark. Is that a woodlark, Ma? Is that *Lullula arborea*?

—Yes.

Maybe it is, it could be. He settles back down beside her, closes his eyes again. One for all and all for one. He pictures them, the three of them, mother, lark, son, circling each other, following each other, watching each other, like swaggering cage fighters. He wonders how many generations have passed since the recording of that dawn, how many years the lone woodlark is dead, has it left any trace, are its hollow bones dissolved into nothing. *Lullula*

arborea. Lullula arborea. Lullula, Lullula, Lullula.
The little bird fills the sitting room with its soft questioning call, pauses, calls again. Soon, he hears the spittle-filled whistle begin at his side. His mother has taken up the call and is trying to respond. His phone begins to throb again; he feels it on his skin. He leans down towards the silent pulse. A small white window pleads behind the heavy cloth of his combat shorts. He touches the little screen through the material; a blurred photo of his smiling daughters, lined up side by side like Russian nesting dolls. A warmth seeps through to his fingertip. If one of us goes, all of us go. He pulls the phone out, puts the girls on speaker, places the phone face up on the floor in front of him, the bright young faces peering wide-eyed and open-mouthed up at the ceiling.

—Daddy? Dad!

His mother's whistle sharpens, lifting alongside the lark, the bridled air twirling from her lank mouth with a little figary at the end. *Lullula, Lullula.* The girls laugh, and try to imitate, blowing soundlessly through puckered mouths before turning to a la-la-lilting song. He joins his mother's call, pressing lips hard together, the two of them hands held, eyes closed, heads back, wet mouths pursed tight, giving it everything, their whistles mingling with the three tiny songs from the floor, all soaring together to the sitting-room ceiling.

From Andy Warhol's Assistant, 1964

Michael Holloway

The year is 1964.

'Andy, do you feel that the public has insulted your art?'

'Uh, no.'

'Why not?'

'Uh, I hadn't thought about it.'

'It doesn't bother you at all then?'

'Uh, no.'

'Do you think that they've shown a lack of appreciation for what pop art means?'

'Uh no.'

'Andy, do you think that pop art has sort of reached the point where it's becoming repetitious now?'

'Uh, yes.'

'Do you think it could break away from being pop art?'

'Uh, no.'

'Are you just going to carry on?'

'Uh, yes.'

The interview comes to a close. Five out of the thirty people here stand up to leave the room but no one else gets up. All those twenty-five people don't know it's over. But it's over. Andy is still here. His thin mouth looks disinterested now, he's the only person I know that can look disinterested with his mouth. Someone asks about the *Nine Jackies* but the interview has finished and Andy comes over to me and tells me he wants to talk about *The American Supermarket* next time and we leave.

We drive for about fifteen minutes across town and the noise is incredible. I think my head will explode. It's giving me a headache. I'm squashed in the back seat of a car next to Andy, his skinny legs pressed into mine while another two people are pressed on the other side of him. A woman is driving, but I don't know who she is. When we get inside a number of people fill the place up and I can smell them and I can smell the alcohol and paint and I can smell the chemical smell of amphetamines and the chemical smell of his artwork. We are at 231 East 47th Street, Midtown Manhattan. We are on the fifth floor. There are reporters here, there are always reporters here, they click and flash and call his name, 'Andy', as if he's a dog and he looks anyway and they tell him to smile but he doesn't smile and they take it as some sort of smile and their *click-crack* noises nauseate me, I feel nauseous, and so I go to the other room which has no reporters but there are people in here and here I meet Baby Jane who has a huge build of hair like a giant bonnet and she is smoking next to a man wearing a striped jumper who looks a lot like Andy but then almost every man who is white and has white or blonde hair wants to look like Andy, and so Baby Jane waves to me and I sit next to her and she asks me my name and I tell her and she tells me she's Baby Jane but I know who she is already.

'I was in *Soap Opera*,' she says.

'Which one?' I say.

'Not "which one". There's only one.'

'Which one's that?'

'Obviously you don't know.'

'About the soap opera?'

'Andy's *Soap Opera*. It's a movie. He made a movie and I was in it. It doesn't matter.' She turns away with the grace of a bird and the bonnet-shaped beehive on her head seems to carry too much weight and so she leans forward a bit, into the man in the striped jumper, and they either talk or kiss and Baby turns back to me and tells me there are reporters here who aren't really reporters, they're actually fake reporters who just want to see Andy. 'There's not even any film in their cameras,' she says.

'If they want to see him why not take a picture?'

'They want to *see* him, not snap photos. I mean, come on, it's Andy, what could you possibly do with a photo of Andy that Andy couldn't do?'

'I don't know.'

'Exactly, you don't know.'

A woman takes a man into another room, I'm told, to give him a blowjob for no reason, and the acidic smell of paint and ink is blanketed for a while by the man in the striped jumper who smokes a joint and he offers me some and I take it and Baby looks at me lovingly as I toke on it, as does the man, and I ask him his name and he tells me he's Superman. So Superman crosses his legs over Baby's legs and kisses her and he says, 'So what is it you do here? For Andy, I mean.'

'I'm just an assistant,' I say. 'A helper.'

'A helper?' Baby laughs. 'Just.'

'You're not *just* something. You're either something or you're not something. So I guess you *are* Andy's assistant.'

'Yeah.'

Superman kisses Baby and the woman and the man come back from the other room and some more people appear and Andy walks in talking to a woman who is writing something down and Superman tells me he's gay and he kisses Baby while looking at me.

Andy announces that he has something to tell everyone. Then he doesn't say anything. Two men rip their shirts off and smoke joints. Andy calls me over and we drink wine. Andy calls me darling. 'Hand me that bottle, would you, darling?' he says. I hand him the bottle of wine and I put out my glass so that he can fill it and I anticipate thanking him because he shouldn't be the one to fill *my* glass, I should be filling *his*. But it doesn't matter. He drops the bottle on the floor and it smashes and everyone looks over and they gasp as if no one's ever heard a bottle smash before. It's like Andy just invented the sound of smashed glass. The wine floods then thins and looks like blood and Andy, without smiling, although I know he is satisfied, says, 'There. I call it ... what do you call it?'

'Smashed ... smashed glass,' a girl says.

'Smashed glass ... A Bum's Nightcap,' he says, and everyone laughs.

'What's it about?' a reporter says.

'It's about a man,' Andy says. 'A Bum. He wants to make it big in Hollywood but he can't. He's surrounded by all this neo-conservative propaganda and is pushed over the edge. And he drinks. And he just wants to make it big. To be an actor or an artist. But Hollywood eats him alive. Spits him out. He lives on Skid Row and can no longer push the boundaries but is still pushing them but he just doesn't know.'

They applaud him and it sounds like rain and I expect there to be a rumble of thunder for some reason, as if they are all a storm and Andy is standing in the middle of it and he is laughing at the storm, and the tornado of television cameras recording and the hail of hand-held cameras snapping and clacking and eventually the sound fades and a silence builds and throbs from the guts of everyone in the room. Andy's mouth, the main visible part of his face, doesn't move. It looks like he's dead. He might be dead. I'm his assistant and Andy Warhol might be dead. I get up a little too quickly in this personal panic and they all look at me. For a second. They look at Andy again and I feel forgotten. Aah, that feeling, and aah, the other feeling as Andy turns and goes to talk to someone, the feeling of relief, and the sensation is slowly orgasmic as the sound of voices builds and washes over me. I'm sweating, I notice. I shouldn't sweat here, these people don't like nerves, they're dogs, they sense something is wrong with you and they pounce on you, make art of you, and you become something for them. I breathe and walk to the window to cool off.

I don't notice anything different over at the window; a lot of them are talking about the view for some reason but I just stand here cooling off in the small draught of chilly New York air which smells bad like car fumes. I hear a distant sound of car engines lulling us all into a cosmopolitan trance, no one seems to even hear the noise any more, they just let it all happen. Soon Baby Jane's next to me, pressing her breasts against my shoulder blades, head resting on my shoulder; the sharp of her chin digs matrimonially into the triangular space of my clavicle.

She says, 'Who or what are you looking at, Helper?'

'Nothing,' I say. 'And my name's not Helper, it's—'

'Please, tell me more about yourself, Helper, I'm very interested.'

'Obviously not.'

'Oh come on, you can't expect to work with Andy and hope that people find you interesting.'

'I didn't expect that.'

'Yes you did,' she says, putting her hands on my shoulders, her breasts pressed into me, her body merged with mine, her stomach taking the shape of my backside. 'You, I assume, took this job ecstatic that you could stand next to the infamous Andy Warhol, that others will look at you and say "Oh, who's that handsome young man standing next to Andy?" But you're very naive, Helper.'

'I don't think so, Baby.'

'It's okay, we're all naive at some point. We all grow out of it. I think being around Andy's made us less self-centred. We care more about other people's self-centredness. Isn't that interesting? I find you interesting, Helper. How someone thinks they can work *assisting* someone. Not just anyone. Andy. Who gave you this job anyway?'

'I found it.'

In this moment Superman enters the picture again and Baby moves her chin off my shoulder and I feel the air where her hands let go of me and I realise, from her slow touch, she's made me slightly aroused, and I'm trying not to think of her, but her voice is still close to my ear, erotic and young, and Superman tells her he's taken LSD and he's going to go sit down or else he might just leave and drive out to the countryside and find the nearest farm and talk to the animals. 'I've done that before, you know. I spoke to the pigs up in Ithaca.'

'How did you get so far?'

'I just kept driving.'

'Honey, go lie down before Andy has to go,' she says to Superman who sleepily hobbles away to a couch where two girls are sitting, talking to two men, and he lays down on them and they yell out in surprise but he is asleep already and far too heavy for them to push and so, within seconds of hearing his voice behind me, Superman now sleeps in a drug haze on top of two young girls who mother him blindly while talking to two other men on chairs who both have neatly cut and styled hair which, I believe, is very much five years too late.

'We're going out,' Baby Jane says. 'Come with us. It'll be fun.'

'I don't know. I need to be with Andy.'

'Oh he doesn't care. He hasn't even noticed you've been over here. Fuck, I bet he hasn't noticed you've even *been* here. He'll see you and say, "Who the hell are you?" and kick you out. Ha ha. I bet. I bet no one's noticed you, Helper Boy.'

'I should stay, I'm working.'

'We're all working,' she says. 'We're working on life.'

'What does that mean?' I say, and I go to write it down but next to me a reporter writes it down before I get the chance.

He's wearing a brown coat and a fedora and I think maybe he's warm, and he speaks quickly at Baby, not to her, *at* her, and he says, 'Miss Holzer, do you think you're all artists if you say you're *all* working?'

'On life.'

'Working on life.'

'To a degree. But Andy's the real deal.'

I feel less aroused now that I'm not in her attention anymore, but there's something subdued that I sense, a kind of sexual attraction lingering in the air and I want to get out. A number of people, I begin to assume, are reporters but I see a woman in her underwear walking with them. They are leaving. Andy. Where is Andy?

'He's left, honey,' Baby says. 'He went with Ultra Violet but I don't know *where* they went. It doesn't matter though. You'll see him again soon.'

'But I'm his assistant, I need to—'

'Hey, Helper, I told you he probably hasn't even noticed you're missing from the group. And besides, you're with me. I'll just tell him I was showing you around. Or you were showing me around. Whichever you prefer. I heard there's this young model called Edie who wants to come here. When she does I'll show her around too. I like to. It's part of *my* job. See. You have your job, I have mine.'

'I suppose,' I say. I feel an uneasiness deep inside my chest from the thick smell of paint and wine and there is a drugs smell, a chemical smell mixed with the paint, and Superman sleeps, and beside the Bum's Nightcap is a young woman in her underwear shooting heroin into her arm and she falls asleep sitting up with her legs open beneath Superman and near them another half-naked woman is painting. She has, it seems, begun on a canvas but has thrown paint on the floor and is mopping the colours with her hands and laughing hysterically and others look at her and smile but don't get involved with her. The picture on the canvas is of a face. I believe JFK's.

'No suppose,' Baby says. 'Come with me.' And we leave. She pulls me along by the hand as if *I* am her child, as if I am the baby not her, and I hear sex noises before we reach outside. It's slightly cold but it's bright. East 47th Street. I'm caged in by apartment buildings, criss-cross staircases weeping from windows, spikes, spires and Italian-smelling food, richly flavoured calzones making me hungry, my empty stomach talking to me now, telling me I haven't eaten and every food smell is so delicious and a hundred times more attractive to me. 'This way. I have a car.' I get in her car. It's a black Pontiac. It smells of leather and the now-familiar chemical drug smell and she says, 'Wait here,' and she slams the door and disappears.

Here it is finally quiet. I hear the buzz and honks of the traffic but nothing out of the ordinary. In fact, I'm glad to be able to breathe the fresh air. I'm glad to be cold and shivering almost. My armpits are damp and my palms are sweaty, they leave dark handprints on the dashboard and on my notepad. I fix my hair in the mirror. My eyes look tired and my skin has paled. How has my skin paled? Is this what they do to you? Andy looks pale. I wonder what they did to him. I don't want to be famous, it makes you ugly and you spend most of the time trying to be beautiful when you're not. I sit back and feel the leather seat soft against my back. My breath is a sound here. Where is she? People look at me because I'm sitting in the car. Why are they looking? Do they recognise me? I work with Andy Warhol, I want to tell them, make them know who I am. I am someone. I, I imagine saying, am a some*body*.

Baby Jane returns with Superman. She climbs in front with me. Superman slumps in the back. She starts the car and goes.

'Where are we going?' I say. She doesn't answer but grunts, trying to concentrate on the difficult obstacle of New York traffic and soon she has pulled out and is driving. I, for some reason, feel happy. I want to shout 'We're driving!' but I don't. I subdue myself. Who am I? I'm just an assistant. I've no right to be shouting things of excitement. I've no right to be *doing* things of excitement. 'Let me out of the car,' I say. 'Just stop here, I want to get out. I'm going back. I'll wait for Andy.'

'No, you can't do that, Helper,' Baby says. Superman sits silently in the back, his head lolled to one side but he's awake. He looks tired. He smiles now and again. Superman isn't as big as the actual Superman. He's tall but he's thin. He's more like Clark Kent. I want to start calling him Clark. The only thing he's missing is the thick-rimmed glasses and then he'd be Clark Kent for sure. Or maybe he knows this. Maybe he's just Superman ironically. I can't tell. Baby isn't really a baby. That's ironic. But she calls me Helper and I really am a helper. I write this down. I need to know these things if I am to be by Andy's side, working as his assistant for the next few years. To understand him I need to understand the people he's with.

We drive through New York. She picks up speed when she can. I realise no one is speaking as we drive through the Lincoln Tunnel, and soon buildings that once walled in the roads are sparse and short. A greenness appears and she picks up speed, fast and faster. Superman winds down the window and yells a noise of utter joy. He looks and sounds so happy and I wish I was him, just for a second, to experience what he is experiencing, someone who can go through life without fear and just hold on to a happiness as if there has never been a tragedy in his life. The sun rises. Then falls. It is past noon. I see fields now. A completely different world to New York City. I have no idea where I am.

'This is a four-hour drive, honey,' Baby says. 'You might want to calm down. You look as crazy as him.' She nods backwards at Superman's grin, showing all of his teeth, laughing silently at the wind.

Over the course of four hours Superman takes some more LSD until Baby tells him to stop and soon he falls asleep for the final hour and I stay fascinated with the countryside. I've not been this far north of New York. I've been so used to the city it seemed that was all New York was, as if there's no other part of the world to know about.

I tell Baby Jane about my life, for some reason. I don't think she asks. I just tell her. 'I wasn't born in the US,' I say, and she glances at me for a second and then back to the road and I smile at knowing she's listening to me. 'I was born in England. I have English parents. We moved here, to New York City, when I was five.'

'You have no accent,' she says. I don't know if she means I have no British accent or I have no accent at all. And how can someone not have an accent? Might as well say you have no voice.

'I can still speak,' I say.

'I know that. But you sound American now. I never would have guessed. Do your parents have accents?'

'I don't know.'

'Why not?'

'They're dead.'

'Oh.'

'I had friends back in England,' I say. 'There were three of them. I've not seen them in twenty years. They probably don't remember me anymore. We had a particular fashion sense that looks old now. But, I think, everything looks old now. Everything is so new all the time.'

'Ha ha, nothing will be new in the future. Everything will all be done and before you know it we'll be repeating ourselves. Don't you think?'

'I hope so.'

'You hope so?'

'It's funny, but I don't like new things. It kind of makes me feel lost. Like I know one thing but everyone else knows another. It's all fads and trends.'

'Life's a fad.'

'That's why I enjoy working with Andy.'

'You don't enjoy it. You're lost in the city. I can tell.'

'I do enjoy it.'

'What American friends do you have?'

'What?'

'Did you ever make any new friends the twenty years you've been here?'

'Yeah, sure.'

'No, I mean *actual* friends. Like the three friends you had when you were a child.'

'No.'

'Didn't think so, Helper. That's why I'm driving. I'm taking you away.'

'Why?'

'To get you out of the city. I just guessed you were uncomfortable. Besides, Superman needs to get out too. You ever seen Superman on acid in the city? Not pretty.'

'No, I've never seen that,' I say. 'Is he okay?'

'He's fine. He's just sleeping. I bet he's having some wild dreams.' She laughs.

Soon the sun is bright and white, its chalky colour now washing over the road and soon Baby Jane pulls into a dirt driveway and parks. Switches the engine off. She looks at me. 'Get out,' she says. I get out and stretch. Those four hours seemed like nothing compared with standing next to Andy Warhol in the Factory waiting for the reporters to finish asking questions. Superman gets out of the car. He is drowsy but he is less high than I thought. He really is tall. I never noticed before how tall he was. His head reaches far up into the sky blocking the sun and replacing it with his Georges Méliès moon. He walks ahead. Purposeful.

'Where is he going?' I say.

'He's going to see the pigs.'

'Where are we?'

'Ithaca. Superman just loves the pigs.'

Superman's chemical smell leaves us and we slowly follow behind as he vanishes round a corner and our feet begin to crunch under stones and a noise far from the city washes over us, an animal sound, a living sound, and we go round the corner and there is Superman and Baby Jane tells me to stop and she tells me that Superman is talking to the pigs.

'Why is he talking to the pigs?'

'Because he's on acid,' she says.

And so we wait for him and I regret to acknowledge my testicles are aching. I don't know what it is. I try to sense the need to urinate but it's not there. I look at Baby Jane and feel a tad aroused and I hate myself for it. I watch Superman talking to the pigs and try to forget about my penis, just for a minute, just to forget the urge to masturbate and hold it in.

'Isn't he strange? He always wants to do this.'

Oh God, her voice, I think to myself. I rest my shaking hands at my side. I say, 'I need to use the bathroom. Where is it?'

'I don't know. I don't know whose farm this is.'

'You don't?'

'You could probably find one, I guess.'

'You mean break in?'

'The doors are open, see?' She's right. There's an open door. 'If you gotta go, you gotta go.' So I do. I leave her and Superman and go inside. It is silent and no one is around. I hope no one's home. The first room is a kitchen. The smell is savoury somehow. There are knives hung on the wall. A stove. A sink. Things. I go through the next room and there are so many plants in plant pots that I now smell them, alkaline and wet. I feel like a burglar. My heart is beating hard and it hurts my chest. I find a bathroom upstairs. I go in. Lock the door. I unbuckle my belt and begin to masturbate. I'm thinking of Baby Jane and of the half-naked girls in the Factory. I do it fast before I have a full erection and then I come and my legs shake and I rest my hand against the wall. I spend a few minutes on my hands and knees wiping it off the bathroom floor with toilet paper, in a farm I've broken into, as a man named Superman is talking to the pigs outside because he's high on acid. I throw the tissue in the toilet and leave. I breathe a sigh of relief and feel emptied which is a good feeling, I think. Superman seems to have finished what he was doing and he is standing with Baby, talking, and they see me and look at me and smile.

'Finished?'

'Yeah,' I say, feeling guilty and wondering if they suspect what I did.

'Hey, what are you kids doing here?'

'Just came to see the pigs,' Superman says.

'Go on, off my property. Don't you know this is my property?'

'Woah, old man, it's a free country,' Superman says.

'Sorry,' I say. 'We're leaving now.'

When we get in the car Baby tells me I shouldn't have apologised. 'It's not really his property. He doesn't *own* anything. It *is* a free country. How can someone *own* a piece of the Earth? You shouldn't apologise to that fool, Helper, you don't need to.'

'Okay,' I say and we begin the four-hour drive back to New York City and it'll get dark soon as the day has quickly vanished. I say to Superman, 'So what did the pigs tell you?'

'Told me about life.'

'What about it?'

'Nothing. Just told me about it.'

'But what did they say?'

'Well there were no answers. They just *told* me about it.'

'Stuff you already knew?'

'Yeah,' he says. 'Pretty much. But I like to hear it. Helps me understand. I have a greater understanding of life now.'

'Oh.'

'Do you, Helper?' Baby Jane says.

'What?'

'Do you have a greater understanding of life?'

'I don't know,' I say. 'I didn't talk to the pigs. But I did masturbate in the bathroom.'

'Ha ha, you did?' she says.

'The old man's bathroom belongs to you now,' Superman says. 'And you should understand better how you feel about things.'

'I don't know,' I say. 'I don't know if I feel anything at all.'

'Have a think about it,' Baby says.

'Okay.'

I sleep the rest of the way and wake up in a bruised New York City and I get out of the car all drowsy and they passively say goodbye and disappear into the brightly lit-up world that lives constantly. I go inside the Factory and there are still people there. It smells of chemicals and paint. People are wearing sunglasses even though it's evening. Even though it's indoors. No one sees me. There is Andy in a crowd.

The World Ending in Fire
Jan Carson

Lyndsey's mother was no better than mine. She never left the living room. She slept there and didn't even shift when she needed to use the toilet. I saw this as laziness. I was not yet old enough to understand loss; the way it could sap the sense right out of a full grown woman. Laziness, I called it, and something like slovenliness, though I was too young to have acquired this particular word. Still, I considered Lyndsey's mother a sloppy creature; something like a pig or cow.

I would never have said this to Lyndsey. I was careful with her. I measured my words. My own mother had taught me how to spot the cracks in people. How easy it was to destroy a person; that it was equally easy to build people up I did not need my mother to tell me that Lyndsey was beginning to come apart.

'Your mam's like a mermaid,' I said. 'Your mam's a dolphin, a seal, a jellyfish.' I soon ran out of plausible creatures but never once said 'your mam's like a pig, ploughtering round in her own muck', though this was what I thought every time I passed their window and caught a glimpse of Mrs Agnew sitting in her paddling pool. The least a person could do was leave the room to piss. Even dogs went outside.

Even properly trained cats.

'She has a special chair in the corner,' Lyndsey explained. 'You lift up the seat and there's a bowl for going in, underneath.'

We were sitting on top of the wheelie bin when this revelation came out; all three of our backsides perched round the edge so the lid was beginning to bow in the middle. We were only up there for a better stare. Even from such a vantage point we couldn't see the pissing chair. I was glad of this, like when the camera goes to the roof during the scariest bits of a horror film. There were whole sections of the room lost to us, our vision restricted by the curtains and the unforgiving angle of Mrs Agnew's venetian blinds. There were some things I didn't want to see.

'My nan's in a home,' said Louise. 'She pisses in her chair too.'

Louise was trying to make Lyndsey feel better. Back then, Louise was *always* trying to make Lyndsey feel better. She'd tell her there'd been a mad woman—just like her mam—in last week's episode of *Casualty*, or that she'd heard, from her sister, you could get extra benefits if your mam was mental, or that the Social would probably sort Mrs Agnew out soon. God bless her, Louise Mackey was constantly trying. She only ever made the situation worse.

'Shut up, Louise,' I said. 'Lyndsey's mam isn't like your nan. Lyndsey's mam'll get better soon.'

I shouldered her sideways, off the bin.

'You're not to worry, Lyndsey,' I said.

I insisted that her mother was just poorly and lots of poorly people couldn't make it to the loo in time. I said I was sure she would soon be on the mend. I didn't mean a word of this. I didn't understand why Lyndsey's mother couldn't snap out of it and use the toilet like normal folk.

The Agnews were a cut above the rest of us. They'd had a second toilet built into their under-stairs cupboard. As in all our stuck-together houses, this cupboard was located just a few steps from the living room, right beside the kitchen door. The luxury of this was not wasted on me. I'd often sat in front of our TV holding the piss in my bladder till it went thin and slow, understanding that running upstairs to our own damp bathroom would cost me three full minutes of children's programmes.

Our under-stairs cupboard was just a cupboard. My ma kept the hoover in there, hockey sticks, umbrellas and the Christmas decorations, all tangled up in an orange box. Occasionally a child—myself or, more often, one of my brothers—would find themselves temporarily incarcerated inside this cupboard for giving cheek or refusing the last dry mouthful of boiled potatoes.

When the subject came up, my da always said that the Agnews hadn't got the good of their downstairs loo. Mr Agnew died just six weeks after it went in. Mrs Agnew's *wee problem* began the day after they buried him. My ma always said this wasn't a thing to be joking about, but I could see the smile nipping at the corners of her mouth. She'd flick a damp tea towel at Da's backside or touch his neck gently, like he was made of ornament china. She knew she was lucky to still have her man.

We never asked Lyndsey where her mother went at night. I presume she slept in the paddling pool. None of us had ever seen her out of the water, though once, Louise saw her standing up in it, the wetness licking round her lardy white shins like she was going for a paddle in her own front room. Louise told us this in the same way your woman tells the Bible Story in Sunday School. She used fancy words. Her hands went darting about all over the place. She pitched her voice at a pleading angle, like she was trying to convince us of something untrue.

When the need to nap came over Mrs Agnew she'd plump a cushion and slide it between the sofa and her grease-damped head. Then, she'd sleep for half an hour or so, mouth open and cocked towards the roof. Sometimes she'd leave the TV on. The people from *Neighbours* or *Home and Away* stared out at her as if she was the thing worth watching and they, for a change, the watching ones. It was easy to imagine her sleeping all night in a similar position. Somebody always drew the curtains early, so Louise and I could only speculate about her overnight arrangements and what stopped her from drowning in her sleep.

Louise thought there were angels looking out for her. She said God wouldn't be so cruel as to let anything more happen to that family. She was referring to Mr Agnew dying so suddenly, and one of the brothers who was in prison for drugs. I was more of a pragmatist. I said, 'You'd be hard pushed to drown in six inches of water, even if you were asleep.' I was not taking the drink into account. Later, I would wonder if Lyndsey's mum heard me through an open window; if I'd put the idea in her head.

The paddling pool was one of those cheap ones for children. It was barely deep enough to cover Mrs Agnew's belly and thighs. It did nothing to disguise the defeated lumps of her breasts, shrivelling inside a *Kay's* catalogue swimsuit: floral print with a hold-your-tummy-in panel, like the one my ma kept for holidays. The pool was seaside blue. The sides had been inflated with blowing air and worn thin where she'd leant her weight, and leant again, and kept on leaning for almost three years. The bottom was made of thin blue rubber like something you'd use to keep the rain off leaves.

A series of cartoon fish followed each other—nose to tail—around the sides, never quite catching up with the fish in front. They were too jolly by far. The bright Caribbean shades clashed with the sadness of Mrs Agnew's wallpaper, her lamps and her ancient carpet with its fleur-de-lis print. The paddling pool was a damp island, wedged between the sofa, the TV and the glass-topped coffee table where she kept her Bible and the TV remote. It was always the first thing you noticed when you were passing the house, even if you tried not to look in.

We stopped to stare at her every day. We watched her through the window, like a zoo animal, on our way home from school. Lyndsey never once said 'don't'. But, when I looked at her, I could see she wasn't watching herself. Her eyes were looking through her mother to the hearth and the photographs rectangling across the mantelpiece: weddings, babies, her ma and da smiling together; he punch-proud in his work uniform. You had to wonder if Mrs Agnew ever looked up; if she'd forgotten about all those people grinning down at her. None of us could remember her smiling. A smile would have looked wrong on her sunken face, like teeth in the mouth of a very young child.

One afternoon I was bored and sitting on our back doorstep, listening in on my parents, when the talk turned to Lyndsey's mam. My da said she wasn't all there anymore. The shock of losing Mr Agnew had tipped her over the edge. Over the edge of what exactly? I wondered if he meant the paddling pool. Then, my ma said, 'Uch now, Margaret's always been wild religious. She's a great one for the Hell fire and brimstone; sure wasn't she Free P, before she married John? It doesn't surprise me one wee bit that she's ended up like this. Too much talk of Hell and sin.'

I'd wanted to go into them then. I had all sorts of questions about Hell and sin and what on Earth any of this had to do with paddling pools. But I didn't dare open my mouth. In those days it was considered impertinent for a child to listen in on adult conversations. It wasn't worth risking the wooden spoon.

Eventually Lyndsey explained everything to us. I have to say, it made little sense. The Bible said the world was going to end in fire. It was all laid out in the Book of Revelation, which is the very last book of the Bible, and isn't really about Jesus at all. There'd be flames and smoke and volcanoes going off all over East Belfast. Lyndsey had heard this from her mother. The world was definitely going to end in fire. It was the only half-sensible thing Mrs Agnew ever said after she bought the paddling pool. She said it over and over again, like a sort of slogan. You could tell she liked the sound of it.

When Lyndsey's Aunty Myrtle came over from Liverpool, and asked if she wouldn't consider getting out of the pool and going back to her work in Boots, Mrs Agnew just stared at her sister like the woman had horns. 'No, thank you,' she said, and continued to sit there, up to her belly button in tepid water. 'The world is going to end in fire and I'm not for taking any risks.'

She was heart-feared of getting burnt up, said Lyndsey. She wouldn't have candles around the house. She wouldn't permit a fire to be lighted. Even the idea of fire terrified her. She'd made Lyndsey take the electric fire down to the dump, though it was only made of moulded plastic, with a wee light flickering to create an effect.

'The water's to stop her burning up,' explained Lyndsey. She needn't have said this for we'd worked it out ourselves.

I wanted to ask what would happen to the rest of us who didn't have paddling pools, and whether the lava from the volcanoes wouldn't melt the pool's plastic, and what about smoke inhalation (which I'd seen on an advert for fire alarms). But I didn't. There were only so many things Lyndsey could carry at once.

We never asked anything. Instead, we gathered outside Mrs Agnew's living-room window. Sometimes we stood. Sometimes we perched on the wheelie-bin lid. We watched her eat her dinner off a tray, and doze, and read the Bible, awkwardly at shoulder height, for fear of getting water on it.

She looked like a whale I'd once seen on the proper news. This whale had washed up on an English beach and died. It was too fat and heavy for the sea to sweep it away. I didn't feel sorry for Lyndsey's mother. She made a feeling inside me like when another person has been sick and the smell of it gets down the back of your throat and makes you gag. It was okay to look but I did not want to be in the same room as her.

I saved all my sympathy for Lyndsey who was only eight at the time, then nine and finally ten, far too young to take on so much responsibility. She didn't have a decent parent left and both her brothers were feckless eejits, or so said my da once—all mumbly-like, to mammy—when he thought I was concentrating on the TV. Boom, went Lyndsey's dad, burnt to a crisp with two other RUC officers in a bomb some bad men stuck under their car. Then, two days after the funeral, her mother's down in Woolworths, buying a paddling pool and blowing it up and sitting in it for three whole years. It was hard not to see the two things related. The end of the world was only an excuse.

I wanted to tell Lyndsey that none of this was her fault. I imagined myself waiting until the two of us were alone. I'd put an arm around her shoulders, or maybe I'd keep my hands to myself. I'd say, 'Listen, Lyndsey, I hope you know it's not your fault that your da got blown up and your mum's gone mental. It's pretty shit that all this happened. But you are definitely not to blame.'

But I was eight at the time, then nine and finally ten, too young to find the proper words. All I could do was let Lyndsey have half my Mars Bar and always be it for stick in the-mud and hope she'd see, in these childish gestures, something akin to sympathy. By the time I was old enough to be of any real use, Lyndsey had moved to Glasgow. The paddling pool was long gone and it was not the sort of thing you could bring up casually on the rare occasions when she came home. 'Here, Lyndo, remember when your mum spent three years squatting in a kiddies' pool and you basically had to fend for yourself? That was a bit mad, so it was. I'm just down the road if you want to talk about it.' I didn't know how to bring the paddling pool up. By then we were not even close.

When we were about nine, I asked my ma what was going to happen to Mrs Agnew. Drink bottles had appeared in her living room. They'd circled their way round the pool's edge like glassy soldiers standing guard. My mother laid her hand heavily upon my head, as if she was measuring how tall I was. She said, 'You be nice to Lyndsey now.' This was the answer to a question I had not thought to ask.

Another time when it was just me and Lyndsey sitting on our garden wall, I asked if her mammy was going to be alright. I waited till after I'd given her the first choice of ice pops. 'Whatever one you want, Lynds. You can even have both if you fancy.' I understood this to be a form of kindness. She chose the cola one. We both knew this was second best. There was a softness to Lyndsey which never firmed up.

'I don't know,' she said. 'The wrinkles in her skin won't come out. She's been in the water too long.'

I thought about this for most of the summer holidays. I wanted to know how long was too long, at what point your body quit trying to fix itself. As an experiment, I sank my hand in a bucket of water and left it there for a whole afternoon. I read comics. I listened to the radio. I tried to ignore the numbness creeping slowly up my wrist. Afterwards, my hand was a raisin, but the wrinkles came out in less than an hour.

Later, when she was dead, we all lined up to look at Mrs Agnew. I could see that her skin was flat again, like a used paper bag smoothed out with a finger. Her mouth was drawn up at the corners, somewhere between asleep and a smile. You wouldn't have known from looking at her that she'd been underwater all that time. My da said the undertaker had done a stellar job. You wouldn't have known there was anything wrong with her at all. If you looked closer though, you could see the paddling pool had left a mark on the living room carpet: a big damp circle spreading out all round the coffin. It was darker than the rest of the floor, and perfectly circular, and cold to the touch. It looked as if Lyndsey's mother had leaked, like she'd left an ugly stain behind.

Night Waking

Lucy Caldwell

Out of nowhere you are suddenly awake, heart pounding. Nothing. The baby is next to you in the bed, asleep. In the orange glow of the salt lamp, the room's shadows are still.

There is no noise from your son's room.

The baby whimpers. Sometimes you wake a second before her, as if your body knows. That's what the baby blogs say, the ones that say co-sleeping is fine. A mother's instincts will keep you both safe. Though maybe it's you that wakes her. The rustling of the duvet as you turn, the agitation of a dream. You lie completely motionless, waiting to see which way she'll go.

And that's when you hear it again.

It's the creak of a footstep in the wooden hallway, the sound of a footstep that's trying not to creak.

No.

You wait.

You know the ley lines of the flat, the trusted, navigable paths. The faulty joists in the timber flooring, guaranteed to wake a sleeping baby, even when that baby will sleep through the full blare of police sirens on the road outside.

Again, nothing—although now the nothing is charged.

It's summer, so the heating's off; it can't be the pipes or radiators clicking to life. It's summer, so the balcony door is open, to let air into your airless flat. You're on the third floor and the glass box of a balcony doesn't adjoin those of the neighbours, so it's always seemed safe enough.

Your breathing sounds noisy. Your heart, too, leaping like a trapped thing in your chest.

The baby snuffles and rustles and turns onto her tummy. Was that another footstep?

You listen with your fingertips, with every hair of your head.

You locked the door last night, you're sure of it. Or rather, didn't fully lock it, as the Chubb lock has been sticking, but flicked the snib downwards to disable the Yale. It's always been your husband's task, like the bins and the recycling and the washing of pans, in the wordless division of domestic labour. But he's away for two nights, of which this is the first; a symposium in Berlin. You don't always bother doing the blinds, with the evenings so long. Has someone been watching? You know more than you mean to about the families opposite, the dioramas of their lives. Has someone who knows you, knows your husband, seen on his Facebook or Instagram that he's away?

You listen, you listen. Your whole body aches with listening.

There was the man who came to rehang the front door, when it sagged on its hinges and kept jamming in the frame. For weeks afterwards you had missed calls from an unknown number. When you finally texted the number and said, Who is this? a message flashed back instantly, An admirer, followed by a smiley face, and then a second message, Wud u like 2 go 4 a drink?

I think you've got the wrong number, you texted.

I dont think so (another smiley face).

I'm sorry, but I don't know who you are.

Yes u do

You didn't reply, and showed the texts to your husband that night. Do you want me to text, he said, and say I'm your husband or something?

Oh what, like back off, this chattel's mine?

You both laughed, and it no longer seemed so sinister.

You were pregnant at the time, though not enough that it showed. You'd felt nauseous, blurry; the man's arrival had jolted you from a midday nap—that first trimester tiredness that leaches from your very bones. You'd been blank at the door, almost rude, then overcompensated by faking brightness, offering tea, coffee, your stash of ginger biscuits. When he'd said, What I'd really like is a nice cold beer, you'd laughed and said, Sounds good.

You thought it must be him, though you couldn't be sure enough to contact the company. Besides, it wasn't as if he'd changed the locks, only the hinges, and no more messages came.

There hasn't been another noise for a while, now: long enough that you allow yourself to think you must have imagined it, after all. Or maybe you didn't imagine, but misheard and it came from your son's room: a flung arm hitting the bedstead, a book falling to the floor.

You should check on your son. He begged and begged, this evening, to sleep in your bed, the way he used to until the baby came. You almost said yes. You half-wanted it yourself, the warmth of his smooth body, the way he cuddles right into you as if skin is no boundary. But you knew you'd all sleep badly if you did: the baby would wake him and he'd wake the baby; she'd see him and think it was morning and time to play, so you stayed firm.

Your son has been frightened of burglars, recently, and so you've been reading him the rhyming books of your own childhood from the library; the Robbers with names like Grabber Dan and Grandma Swag, thwarting and thwarted by Cops in an intricate, uneasy dance, the burglar who accidentally steals a baby and then goes straight, returning the things he's stolen.

You really should check on him, but somehow your body won't move. If there is someone in the flat—there isn't, you tell yourself, but if there is—then surely it's best you're all asleep, or seem that way? Let that person, or persons, take what they want and go swiftly. Your laptop is on the kitchen table, your bag's by the sofa. There's a ceramic apple of loose change on the bookshelf, mostly shrapnel. It shouldn't take long. It might be done already.

You try to remember whether the noises, if there were noises, were moving towards the bedrooms or into the living room: getting closer or further away.

There's a drug problem in the area, groups of addicts on the streets like some dystopian film, abandoned needles and scorched crack pipes. You sometimes watch the drug deals from your balcony; teenage boys standing look-out on corners, their mini-messenger bags wedged with thick rolls of cash. The cars speeding the wrong way up the one-way street, the shuffle-run of the addicts once the drop-off's made. There have been leaflets from the police about muggings in the street, about home security. But there was stealth, not urgency, in the movements you heard.

Would-be rapists who creep into houses late at night and lie in wait for their victims, listen to them breathe. Abductors who take children to order: a little boy, blond-haired, no older than three.

Stop it. Now. Get up and check, the way you make your son do. No burglars in the wardrobe, no monsters under the bed.

You sit up.

The French teacher who told you when walking at night to hold your housekeys in your fist, and poke a key through your first and second fingers, a makeshift weapon. A novel where someone thwarts attempted abduction by piercing her captor's eye with a hairpin. You cast around the room. An architect's pencil, the sort that pushes up refillable lead through a bright, sharp point? A paperclip?

A siren streams past on the road outside, shrill and discordant.

You quell the bubble of a sob.

Your phone is in the corridor. You read an article about the correlation between cellphone radiation and cancer, official public health guidance by the state of California on how to reduce exposure to radiofrequency energy. Ever since, you've insisted that phones aren't charged in the bedroom overnight; the plug socket in your cramped bedroom right by the baby's cot. And what would you do, anyway, missed-call your husband until he woke, then text that there might be someone in the flat? Message your family group, your sister thousands of miles away in another time zone, and ask her to phone the police?

What, the operator would say, is the nature of your emergency?

I woke, in the night.

You case the duvet off your legs and got out of bed. Once you have babies, they say, you'll never really sleep again, even after the babies finally do. Your feet on the floor like the herd of elephants you're always chastising your son about. If there's anyone in the flat, they'll have heard you now. Abandoning your plans to sidle along the wall, you go quickly into the corridor, grab your phone. You stand for a moment. Nothing. Into your son's room. He's sideways in bed, half hanging out. You lift him, tuck him back in, press your lips to his neck. He moans. The baby, as predicted, has started to cry. Back into your bedroom, and pick her up. She stops crying, starts to rootle, but you don't feed her yet, just put her down in the cot where she can't fall out. To the sound of her outrage, you go down the corridor the other way, past the front door and into the living room.

Nothing and everything looks amiss.

It was the venetian blinds hanging over the open door, clicking against the doorframe in the breeze. It was a block, and then another, toppling from your son's precarious tower, constructed with Duplo and cereal boxes and his baby sister's bricks, which he insisted you leave out overnight.

You slide the balcony door closed, twist the handle up.

You check the front door, move the buggy up against it, just in case.

The baby's cry is now at boiling point. Your son wakes up and calls out for you, too. Some tiny, shameful part of you is glad not to be awake alone.

You should go to them. Scoop up your son and bring him into your bed, feed the baby and then all lie down together, the way families must have for centuries, the way animals do.

The sirens again, outside. More of them, now, and louder,

shifting in pitch and frequency. There is something still tugging at the edges of your consciousness. A framed map in the hallway, askew on its picture-hook. You right it, and think: was the frame always cracked? For a moment, you feel gloved hands on your shoulder, hot breath down your neck. Why would the blinds rattle on an airless night, or a tower suddenly tumble?

Something is happening, somewhere, you tell yourself, but not here, not here, not now.

The Longford Chronicle
Daniel Hickey

One year into my role as reporter at the *Longford Chronicle*, the editor asked me to write a feature on Finbar Brogan. The name, in a kind of cascading flashback, returned me to my boyhood, and the Brawl for Mayor.

That's a blast from the past, I said.

Rumour has it he's planning a comeback. Well, when I say rumour. The editor smiled meaningfully and with his fingers made air quotes.

I pressed my left temple.

Don't play the fool, Conway, you've seen the latest circulation figures. Readership way down? Management breathing down my neck?

Yeah?

We need him.

Oh?

We need Finbar Brogan.

Oh.

It's like Paul McCartney said. Oh I believe—he winked—in yesterday.

In the library, a quiet anteroom, I read the *Chronicle*'s archives on Finbar 'Bloody' Brogan, surprised how many other names I'd remembered: Willie 'The Neck' Dempsey, Joe 'Sharp' Malone, Ambrose 'Agricultural' Browne... When I was six-seven-eight years old we tried them on, eleven o'clock break: I'm Willie 'The Neck' and *you're* Ambrose Browne no I'm Willie 'The Neck' *I'm* Willie 'The Neck'! Nobody wanting to be Finbar Brogan.

Last boy out the door—rotten egg—was Finbar Brogan—

—Finbar Brogan,
Mouth pure twisted and nose all broken,
If you punch him, he will fall,
Because he cannot fight at all.

I lifted my head from the paper. A window in the anteroom looked out on a car park where there was a solitary tree. In the wind the bare branches shook. A mother and son, the mother in an anorak, the son in duffel coat, hunched up against the gust, struggled from one end of the car park to the other. It was silent. The branches shook. It might not have actually happened.

Towards the arse-end of the Age of Plenty, Longford
Municipal Council decided by nine votes to one to replace
the mayoral election with a fistfight. The decision was
greeted with much public approval. There was talk of

a 'return to the primal night'. There was talk of the natural impulses, untethered by finicky forebrain. Others mentioned an unconscious collective desire to undo, like with a swipe, the more bewildering effects of the Agricultural Revolution.

Whatever the case, the mayor of the municipal district was decided by fistfight, every February, on St Bridget's Day.

'May the strongest man win!' they said—

We said.

Strongest man? The fuck does that even mean these days, Dimitri. I closed the book, I threw the book, the book landed limply on a leather chair.

Dimitri sipped on gin and tonic, and the rain fell on Longford town, where we were eating lunch in Mulligan's Public House.

Tony Soprano, he said.

Yeah?

Man with the biggest opinions.

I am sick of opinions.

Primal urges?

Them too.

I don't know, man, you're the journalist. The man who's not afraid of his primal urges?

The melody of 'Yesterday' played in my brain as I drove

to the municipal dump, where Brogan now lived, having relocated after his last attempt at success in the Brawl. I'd never actually met Brogan in the so-called flesh. Like most of the spectators I'd only ever seen him from the cheap seats, way up the back of the municipal stadium, where the ring was a mirage and we had to squint or borrow binoculars to be sure who'd knocked out who.

Five minutes later I was at the dump's gate. In the distance, on the horizon, a towering mountain of rubbish over which seagulls flocked, diving, like into the ocean, for the scraps of last week's TV dinner. The stench was nauseating. Inside the gate, in the little prefab office, I asked the manager where Finbar 'Bloody' Brogan lived.

The other side, he said. I didn't know if he was speaking literally or figuratively.

The other side?

Keep walking all the way to the back. When you see the fence turn left, and you'll see the nutjob's hut up ahead, on the right, up against the fence.

The last time I'd visited the dump this must've been the late 1980s — I was either eight or nine. That was around the time Brogan first fought in the Brawl. Every month, a Saturday afternoon, my father would drive there, with a boot full of rubbish, singing the words 'The dump, the dump... The dump, the dump, the dump' to the tune of *The Pink Panther*. My memories of the place were fond. The stench incongruously nostalgic. The squawk of seagulls, the mountain range of waste—it all reminded me of

go on, say it

simpler times, when

It reminded me of simpler times, before I had a mindset. And in probably the first instance of my calamitous identification with the man, I wondered if this was why Brogan had decided to relocate.

I wandered the dump. The DJ in my brain, sarcastic bastard, played Enigma's 'Return to Innocence'.

when men were men and words were magic, Tom. Before all this, before all. Dimitri waved his hand panoramically, including all of Mulligan's contents: the mahogany-panelled bar, the bottles of whiskey and vodka, the leather upholstered seats and stools, the paintings of nineteenth-century landlords and their upright hunting dogs. The Stone Age, Conway, the bloody fucking Stone Age, man.

Okay, Dimitri, message received, you're a fan of the Stone Age.

He sipped his gin and tonic. So you're heading out to the dump?

I nodded.

Love that place, Dimitri said.

At the fence I stopped and wiped away my tears. Beyond the fence rolled staccato fields. The path was muddy as a traumatic past; juices oozed into long greasy puddles. A grey-green vapour, odorous and ghostly, floated above the puddles. Through the vapour, about fifty metres ahead, the hut leaned against the fence.

I heard grunting and a dull thud. Brogan was standing outside the hut, dressed in a purple tank top, black Adidas shorts and Reebok trainers, throwing the ghost of a right-handed jab at a makeshift punchbag. The punchbag barely wobbling. The tank top was at least two or three sizes too big, hanging loose from his shoulders. He appeared to be in good spirits. Oblivious to my approach, he jabbed at the punchbag, which I later learned he'd made from a plastic Tesco bag stuffed with the innards of discarded fluffy toys; their outer skins lay in a soggy heap outside the hut. Sweat dripped from Brogan's bony arms. When it became clear he was so lost in his 'routine' that even if I stood there ten years he might not have noticed, I coughed, sharply, to alert the man to my presence.

He dropped his hands and turned his head. The lenses of his glasses fogged up I imagined myself through them, a blurred version. He removed the glasses, wiped the lenses with the hem of his sweaty tank top, and placed them back on.

Morning! he said.

It was a Tuesday afternoon.

In the hut Brogan lit candles.

Sit down, Mr Conway. He pointed at an empty beer crate.

I sat on the empty beer crate. Tom, I said.

Tom, said Brogan.

The hut, he explained, was constructed from discarded table tops, detached fibreglass panels from unwanted chests of drawers and doubled- or tripled-up black rubbish bags. The floor was an old carpet he'd discovered one October morning, scouring the mountain for salvage. Himself and the gulls. It had been damp. A few days under the sun dried the rug, which now filled the available floor space with faded mandala-type patterns. The roof was the hood of an old burnt-out Datsun that had, he whispered, been used as the getaway car in a gangland shooting.

At night, Brogan slept on a bed fabricated from an old mattress. For chairs there were two plastic beer-bottle crates.

Do you know how long it took me to construct it?

It's cosy, I said.

With a towel he mopped the sweat from his shoulders, neck and face. He placed his hands on his knees. He appeared refreshed.

I'll show you something.

From a cardboard box he lifted an A4-size book.

Dine your eyes on this, he said, feast your prying eyes on this historical document. He licked his lips and winked.

It was a scrapbook. Every page displayed clippings from newspapers, the *Chronicle* and *Express* and *Advertiser,* the *Telegraph* and *Sentinel.* Reports on previous Brawls for Mayor. Pictures of Finbar Brogan, a young man, bloodied and beaten. There was the pre-Brawl speculation, the post-Brawl analysis.

Why have you kept all these?

He was still standing above me, looking down, over my shoulder. He appeared eager, like a child showing his mother or father a painting he'd done at school that day. He smiled broadly.

I am a narcissist, he said.

That night, in my apartment, I replayed the interview.

A narcissist?

I am low on what do you call it? He coughed. Empathy.

I'd already transferred the audio files from my Dictaphone to my laptop and the waveforms produced by Brogan's voice now rose and fell, steep as slopes and valleys, across the screen; their Himalayan shape in judgmental unsettling contrast to the waveforms generated by my voice, which appeared, instead, like flat, oppressive, featureless land: the Conway Plains, where ideas go to die.

That's a strange thing for a town councillor to admit to, Mr Brogan?

Hasn't stopped me getting elected yet.

I paused the playback. I stared at the contrast between Brogan's voice and my own.

The Conway Plains.

Longford was famous for its gyms. Blow-ins from towns

and villages across the paradoxical bogs of the Socialist
Republic of Roscommon-Longford, and the other assorted
Federated Irish Counties (FIC), often crowded the town on
bank holidays to

go on, say it

witness the fitness. It was Wednesday morning. I was
in the most prestigious of the gyms, GYMNAUSEA®, on
Great Water Street, waiting for the current heavyweight
mayor, 'Quotable' Padraig Moore, to finish pumping what
appeared, from a cursory glance, to be iron.

GYMNAUSEA®'s selling point was the promise that
if its signature intense training regime failed to make you
literally sick, so that you had to actually puke, a full refund
would land in your bank account.

Their slogan? We're SICK!

So I sat in the waiting area, opposite the changing rooms,
where I could make out the muffled retching of men.

It was years since I'd entered a gym. Had I ever entered a
gym? I don't know, and I didn't know, how to sit or where
to look. A stack of magazines on the coffee table: *Men's
Health*, *Men's Fitness*, *Men's Crisis of Identity in the Early Years
of the 21st Century*. The pages threatened suggestions for a
better sex life. Pictures of shining muscular men driving
knives into my gut.

Moore strode up, his shadow creeping up my legs and
chest until I was entirely in the dark.

He was wearing the mayoral chain, a string of heavy

square plates of bronze, draped over his shoulders. A white T-shirt said in big black letters: RETAIN THE CHAIN!

I stood up.

Sit down, he said.

I sat down.

Moore used to play rugby, second row, for Encephalographic Athletic. That he had won a number of the rumbles through chicanery didn't bother his supporters. If anything, it elevated his status. The people loved a rogue; 'Quotable' Moore was well aware of this sneaking regard and knew how to play the role. When he winked at you, you winked back involuntarily, then questioned your proprioception. Now that is real control. He was, according to the bookies, odds-on favourite.

So, I said, tell me about your training regime?

I am an advocate of SHIIT, the mayor said.

An involuntary doubletake, on my part.

Seriously High Interval Intensity Training, the mayor explained. He cracked his thunderous knuckles.

Right.

Plyometrics, callisthenics, isometrics and yoga, weight-training and running. In the evenings I spar with Declan

My face gone blank.

Declan McCann? Chairman of the Chamber of Commerce?

I told the mayor that Finbar 'Bloody' Brogan was planning a comeback. He lifted his left hand. You see this?

I do, I said.

With his other hand's forefinger he pointed at the left hand. That's Brogan's face there, he said. And he punched his right hand into his left hand's palm. I'll break him, the mayor said, like a bar of chocolate.

Is this on the record?

Dairy Milk, said the mayor, fucken quote away. He fingered the mayoral chain. He wiped it. I guarantee you, he said, the only time Finbar 'Bloody' Brogan will get to wear this chain is when I wrap it round his withered little neck and I strangle the bastard.

That made the *Chronicle*'s front page. MAYOR SAYS: I'LL STRANGLE THE BASTARD

You don't have a hope, I told Brogan.

We were outside his hut. The dump glittered in the winter sun.

But he went all *Shawshank Redemption*. Hope, he said, is a good thing.

I sighed.

Maybe the best of things.

Fucking bullshit, I said. I flicked my cigarette away. Hope is going to have you paralysed. Hope has a brand-new name and it's 'Quotable' Padraig Moore and it's going to beat the living shit out of you. Hope, I said, spitting the word away.

Brogan strapped his gloves on.

Well, he said, that's your opinion.

He jabbed at the makeshift punchbag.

Did the punchbag move?

Do I need to ask?

That week the front page of the *Chronicle* splashed on the COMEBACK OF FINBAR 'BLOODY' BROGAN. Circulation doubled. A hundred thousand extra units shifted. The pressure off. The editor loosened his tie, opened a bottle of champagne and said, What did I tell you, Conway, what did I bloody well tell you.

The cork rebounding off the ceiling; me flinching.

And look, he said, lifting the edition, the smell of fresh ink, your first front-page byline! Ha? Byline Boy at last! He slapped me in the back. My glasses fell off. You should be over the bloody moon, Conway. Cigars! he shouted at a phantom assistant. Where are the bloody cigars?

I searched the floor for my glasses.

At Longford's Civic Offices, the municipal council gathered for its monthly meeting. I sat in the public gallery, where journalists from the *Sentinel* and *Telegraph* were also present. Brogan's seat was empty; his glass of water, pardon the pun, full. Part of me hoped he'd suddenly seen sense and decided to retire.

Right, said the mayor, I'll open.

Will we wait for Finbar?

Look, if he can't be here on time. Moore scanned the councillors' faces. Agreed?

The councillors nodded.

But fifteen minutes into the meeting Brogan arrived. He was wearing the same ragged Adidas tank top and mouldy Reebok trainers. When he noticed me, he winked, as if we were in this together.

Sentinel and Telegraph smirked.

I wanted to sink in the chair.

Sorry, Brogan said. He was drenched in sweat, breathing heavily.

Councillor Michael 'Slaughterhouse' Fahy held his nose.

What's on the agenda? Brogan said.

The dump, said the mayor, and the other councillors, and Sentinel and Telegraph, laughed.

Up for discussion, said the mayor, is colours for the Brawl, who's wearing what. I have here eight little cards, put together by Eileen. He nodded appreciatively at Eileen, who nodded back, as if the cards were only part of some larger favour. Moore displayed the cards. You know the drill, on each of them she's written a colour. Red, blue, green, black, white, yellow, orange, and. He paused. His eyes kind of bouncing off Finbar Brogan. Pink.

But Brogan was wiping his glasses, and did not notice.

Moore chose first. Doesn't matter what colour I'm in, he said. I could be buck fucken naked I'd still steamroll the lot of ye.

He turned his card over. Orange, he said.

We wrote that in our notebooks.

Every year, the *Chronicle* devoted a full two-page spread to the topic. In the hierarchy of meaning, connotation had replaced denotation.

Brogan lifted a limp hand. He pushed his glasses up the long bridge of his nose and turned his card over. Black, he said.

Will you be doing the haka? said Councillor Malone.

But Brogan's mind was busy, his brain racing away, rejecting millennia of symbolism; he looked at black, and he saw the light. He'd never worn black before, and he'd never won a Brawl before. It was like doing your sums. It wasn't correlation, it was causation. A redeployed conjunction, linking unrelated phenomena, would one day justify the fundamentals of a new religion.

When do I get my kit?

Moore groaned. You know full well when you get your kit. He waved away the question. You'll get your kit the morning of the Brawl, same as the rest of us.

You can't make an exception?

The mayor shook his head.

But?

Moore lifted a finger. No buts, now moving on. Anti-social behaviour, he said.

Brogan stared at the table and shrugged, sulking.

Ah will you grow up, whined Councillor Malone. I am

wearing bloody pink and do you see me sulking?

Anti-social behaviour, said the mayor, has become an issue in some of our how do I put it? He flicked what might have been a particle of dust from his shoulder. Less well-off neighbourhoods. There have been reports, I am sure you have read in the *Chronicle* or *Sentinel*—

Or *Telegraph*, Councillor Eugene 'Fingertips' O'Toole said.

The mayor ignored him. Reports of gangs of teenagers on bikes, like some manner of posse from a Western film, causing absolute havoc.

Absolute havoc, Councillor Fahy said.

And it has come to my attention, I won't say by what means, that these teenagers have been observed wearing masks of our likenesses. That there are rival gangs, and that they call themselves after us, and that they wear masks representing our faces. There is the Fahy Gang. There is the O'Toole Gang. There is, of course, the Moore Gang.

Brogan wiped his forehead. Is there a Brogan Gang?

The other councillors glanced at one another. There was a silent interlude. Then cans of laughter burst open, filling the room.

No? No Brogan Gang?

In the Omniplex, watching another reboot of the Superman Dooperman franchise, I could not concentrate. My attention was elsewhere. It was in the dump, the hut, with Finbar

Brogan. He could not possibly win the brawl. The man hadn't a hope. Moore would floor him, five seconds; the bookies weren't even taking bets on that outcome. And yet he had, again, convinced himself he could win. What was that quote about insanity? I saw him in the hut, talking to himself, encouraging words. The others in the cinema laughed. For half a second I thought they were laughing not at some joke onscreen, a joke I'd missed, but at what I was seeing, in my head.

Good morning!

It was a Tuesday afternoon.

Three-quarters into the movie, I left and walked along Bridge Street in a panic. Was I was about to die? I had to stand against a wall and take deep breaths.

I needed to convince the man to give up. Failing that I would, I'd, I didn't know what I would do.

In my apartment I watched footage of the previous Brawls. Someone with sadistic tendencies had edited a compilation of Brogan's defeats. The video was almost three minutes. It opened on a black screen, before the video's title, RESILIENCE, appeared in white capital letters. The video was a montage of footage from previous mayoral Brawls, quickly edited, so that the editing itself resembled, in accelerating staccato cuts, a series of punches. Punch after punch after disenchanting punch. A blizzard of images of Finbar Brogan falling against the ropes, collapsing to the floor. Freezeframed closeups of his face mangled in what could have been either agony or ecstasy. I watched the man grow older. Meanwhile the song playing over the montage was 'Don't Stop Thinking About Tomorrow' by Fleetwood Mac. The editing of the punches timed to match the rhythm of the music: Don't—*punch!*—stop—*punch!*—thinking about tomorrow. Punch after punch after disenchanting punch. Yesterday's gone, yesterday's gone.

On Friday morning, in the dump, I showed the video to Brogan.

He held the phone and squinted. Good one isn't it, he said.

What?

Nicely edited, if I do say so myself.

I stared dumbly.

Lovely juxtapositions.

I wanted to run away.

He's not well, I said.

I was in the editor's office.

He needs help, psychological help, I said. What he doesn't need, the one thing he doesn't need, Jim, is another punch to the head.

The BBC called this morning. They were asking for you.

The BBC?

The editor nodded. The BBC, he said.

What do they want?

They want a documentary. They want you in the documentary. He pointed a fat finger at me. The BBC.

And here's where my thoughts mounted a pair of estranged horses and galloped off madly in opposite directions.

The BBC—

In my apartment, watching with horror on the laptop my voice's flatly rolling waveforms, the Conway Plains, I catch myself blinking in a manner eerily similar to Finbar Brogan. It's a mirror image of a Brogan facial tic, an involuntary impersonation. Did I just do that?

I close my laptop, I sit up.

Hello?

The rain, hissing like an old record, falls on Longford town. People talk of the Brawl. On the sides of the roads T-shirts supporting the candidates are sold, and masks are worn. The Brawl. The Municipal Rumble. Teenagers on bicycles in the masks of 'Quotable' Moore burn down houses on the outskirts. In the schoolyards, 11 o'clock break, the children pick roles, one boy is 'Quotable' Moore another 'Slaughterhouse' Fahy, while some unfortunate teen is designated Finbar 'Bloody' Brogan, and they mock-fight, egged on, and the children sing:

Finbar Brogan, Finbar Brogan,
Mouth all twisted and nose pure broken,
He can't punch, he can't thump,
And now he lives in the local dump!

A large electronic clock, with bright crimson digits, hangs on the Post Office's facade, counting down the hours, minutes and seconds to the Brawl's opening bell. Sometimes, at night, when the streets are empty, I stand there, drunk, listening with headphones to sad, crackly, repetitive music, watching the clock.

It was the night before the Brawl. I stumbled from the pub, bag of cans, and flagged a taxi.

The dump? Is that what you said?

That's what I said.

The taxi driver switched on the windscreen wipers. Out to gawp at Brogan I suppose?

He'll be well gawped at tomorrow, I said.

This is it. Will you go?

I wanted to say, Do you not know who I am? Do you not read the *Chronicle*? But I nodded and cradled my bag of cans.

If it wasn't for the Brawl, the taxi driver said, I don't know what I'd do. He rolled down the window, spat phlegm through the gap.

I was drunk and loose. I read signs wrong. Mother Insurance, Oriental Fire Brigade—

I don't know what I'd do, he said.

The dump's gate was locked. Fence dripping wet. In the slippery dark a cow groaned. Other shuffles, disembodied by the dark, were transformed by my mind into phantoms. I wrapped myself in a bubble of light from my phone and stumbled in the dark around the perimeter, shining the phone's flashlight on the mud and grass, until I found a gap in the fence. I put my phone in my mouth and on all fours crawled under the fence in the mud, panting like an animal.

Even though it was dark and wet, Brogan was up, jabbing at the Tesco punchbag.

I stood up, dripping with mud, phone still in my gob, glowing.

Brogan hadn't noticed me yet. I observed him a minute before I sprang from the dark singing

> *Finbar Brogan, Finbar Brogan,*
> *Mouth all twisted and nose pure broken,*
> *He can't punch, he can't—*

Stunned, Brogan spun round and swung a punch, clocking Tom Conway on the lower jaw. I spun and spun, pirouetting in the slippery mud when a filthy puddle rushing up smacked my face.

Oh my God. Tom?

Mud on my tongue, I sat up. I believe, I said, I am the

first poor fucker you have ever floored with a punch. I wiped the mud from my face.

Conway, he said.

Am I?

Not the first, no, he said.

Not the first?

He reached out a hand. It hung there, like judgment, in the drizzle and blue light.

He pulled me up.

There was Eddie 'The Fiend' Fallon, the Brawl of 87, do you remember that one? I landed a lovely uppercut. He went down like a sack of.

Shite, I said.

Spuds, said Brogan.

No, I said, you are mixing yourself up with Joe Dempsey.

Dempsey?

It was Joe 'The Neck' Dempsey knocked out 'The Fiend'. First Brawl I ever went to. I remember it like it was—

Brogan slowly untied his gloves. Tom, he said, it is a Friday night. What are you doing here?

They're singing songs about you in town, I said. They're taking the piss.

Brogan switched on the kettle. There's only one thing worse than being talked about, he said.

Yeah?

He rattled an iron cup.

Shrugging, I extracted the Dictaphone from my coat

pocket. Here you are now so, I said, being talked about.

The hiss of rolling cassette tape blending with the galvanised rattle of soft rain produced a disconcertingly womblike vibe, before 'Quotable' Moore's recorded voice filled the hut.

Brogan leaned in, listening.

I guarantee you, the only time Finbar 'Bloody' Brogan will get to wear this chain is when I wrap it round his withered little neck and I strangle the bastard.

I stopped the tape, rewound, played it again.

when I wrap it round his withered little neck and I strangle the bastard

And again.

strangle the bastard

Brogan blinking—

when I wrap it round his withered little neck and I strangle the bastard

You still like being talked about?

Brogan removed his glasses and wiped them with his T-shirt. This is 'Quotable' Moore, he said, the man is speaking metaphorically. He waved his hand, dismissing the threat. I wouldn't worry my head about that, Tom. I have a premium personalised horoscope.

Strangle you, that's what he said.

His language is figurative, Tom.

So.

So?

Aren't you living here in the dump? Is that not the same kind of thing?

Brogan removed his glasses and wiped them again. I've as good a chance as any man.

The next morning I woke up gasping, as if sleep was deep water, and scanned the *Chronicle*, *Sentinel* and *Telegraph* apps. Maybe Brogan had released a statement? Declaring his withdrawal from the Brawl?

Due to unforeseen circumstances, Mr Brogan stated, I have decided this year to—

But the headline failed to appear.

In the bathroom I surveyed my face. The lower jaw clicked interestingly. There was mild pain, Panadol, but no bruise. I performed a series of dramatic facial expressions: anger, happiness, shame.

Tell us, Mr Conway, how it feels to be the only man ever knocked out by Finbar 'Bloody' Brogan?

Thomas Conway, Thomas Conway,
Walks like a horse and talks like a cliché,
But listen to this one, mademoiselle,
Brogan punched him and he fell!

I stirred coffee and splashed a dram of whiskey in. Shannonside FM all talk of the Brawl. None of the pundits could see past 'Quotable' Moore. It was easier to imagine the end of the world than the demise of the heavyweight mayor.

I switched off the radio. I threw my Dictaphone, notebook and pen into a satchel and left the apartment.

The rain still fell on the town. Hawkers sold flags and banners on the wet grey streets. Vendors set up barbecues under awnings. The drizzle sprinkled the hot coals, hissing. Under umbrellas, in anoraks and caps, the people streamed toward the municipal stadium.

Inside the arena a distracted headset-clad woman directed me to a desk marked Media. Sentinel and Telegraph already present, the Impartial picking his nose. Around the ring and along the aisle there were TV cameramen, soft omnivorous microphones. I tripped into the empty seat marked *Chronicle*.

Look, it's the pro-Brogan camp. Sentinel smirking.

I slid my hand into my pocket, found a middle finger and showed it pure deadpan to Sentinel. Go fuck yourself, I said.

Oh? Chronicle got out of the wrong side of the bed this morning? Nervous?

At 2:45 the house lights shuddered off and the crowd suddenly hushed, the stadium dark.

A spotlight rocked on, shone on the ring, and in the dead centre a shining black suit and silver dicky bow, and a dangling microphone—dropped by what?—slipping into the whitely gloved hand.

The man lifted the mic.

Our pens poised.

He opened his mouth. Let's get ready to rummmmbllllle!!!

And an explosion of roars, Eurodance, delirious cheers and multicoloured lights that flashed and strobed in complex patterns on the ring, the floor, the walkway.

Four thousand faces, grotesque and yelling, now turned towards the entrance.

The table reverberated. My pen shook and dropped off, rolling on the floor.

Deadly, Telegraph said.

One by one the candidates entered. Luminous dressing gowns. Heavy metal. Prowling prancing the aisle to the ring.

They played air guitar.

They made faces.

The MC announcing the names:

Willie 'The Neck' Dempsey! Michael 'Slaughterhouse' Fahy! And Padraig Moore, 'Quotable' Moore, hunched up jabbing at enemy phantoms.

The pen trembled in my liquid fingers. The MC announcing the names. But no Brogan. Not yet.

Pen poised, sweating.

The bass drum reverberated.

Seven candidates rolling their shoulders skipped invisible rope. The MC smiled. And now, he said, after five years' absence, after five years' seclusion in the municipal dump, making his bloody comeback, it's Finbar...

BLOODY BROGAN!

A furious roar.

From every angle, filling the void, Fleetwood Mac, the crowd aflame.

Don't PUNCH

stop PUNCH

thinking about tomorrow.

Men and women straining, children standing up and straining, leaning toward the entrance; the roar directed like a spell, a dark incantation, to conjure Finbar Brogan up, as if he didn't really exist in the flesh, but was a manifestation of some creepy region of the town's collective unconscious, and if they roared hard enough, for long enough, the man would appear.

The man appeared.

Yesterday's gone—

My hands trembling, I gripped the rim of the table. The backs of my hands, dripping onto the notebook's blank page.

You alright?

Telegraph's question.

Fine, just.

But I couldn't watch. My eyes roamed, searching for something, and I thought I was going to throw up, when I saw a cameraman—

Yesterday's gone—

—standing in the aisle midway between the entrance and the ring, lens aimed at Brogan's approach. The only part of his face that moved was his mouth, absently and silently singing

Don't stop thinking about tomorrow,

Don't stop, it'll soon be here—

There was, between body and consciousness, a fracture.

Yesterday's gone—

That year's Brawl played games with hope. If it taught me anything it was to be wary of faith in the future.

Not that Brogan didn't compete.

He did.

Or at least seemed to.

I mean, he swung punches, but the other councillors stood off him, ignored him, even when he punched them.

It was as if he didn't exist.

And one by one, one after another, in the gut, the chin, the jaw, the incumbent 'Quotable' Moore pummelled and punched, uppercuts and jabs, until only Brogan remained, and they stood in opposite corners of the ring.

The arena silent. Moore's shoulders rose and fell. He turned his menacing head and roared up at the crowd and his supporters began a chant—

Dairy Milk!

Clapping and stamping feet on the beat of the three syllables.

Dairy Milk!

I had stepped into an advertisement.

Brogan was the first to make a move.

No, I said, under my breath.

He lifted his arms, defensive stance, and danced, almost tripping himself up.

Something golden glinted.

A Dairy Milk, in its blue and gold wrapper, flung from the crowd, landing in the ring. Another. Another.

Rain of Dairy Milk.

Brogan lunging, landing a limp punch on Moore's lower jaw.

Moore wobbled, as if about to fall, and lifted a gloved fist to his face.

The crowd gasped. I leapt up, but involuntarily, and when I found myself standing, tense and electric, staring at the ring, with Sentinel boring holes in my brain with her glare, I blushed and swiftly sat back down.

Dairy Milk!

The mayor did not hold back. Jabs, uppercuts, hooks from left and right. It didn't matter that Brogan was no match. It was as if Moore had imagined every embarrassment he'd ever suffered and projected the shame onto the incongruous frame of Finbar Brogan. The crowd would be left in no doubt that Brogan's failure was total, there was no hope, no alternative, and Moore, mercilessly invincible, was the leader for our ambiguous times, at the arse-end of the Age of Plenty.

He tore off the orange gloves.

With bare fists he pummelled 'Bloody' Brogan, whose nickname now was far too sickeningly literal. Blood dripped from his nose. When he managed to stand up again, on wobbling legs, the crowd cheered, but with irony. Brogan seemed to interpret the irony as sincerity, though, and like a religious fanatic, motivated by the misinterpretation, lunged again at Moore, who stepped lightly aside, and Brogan bounced off the ropes, crumpling again, but into himself, the spectre of himself, on the floor on the ring, in the pile of broken chocolate.

His chest rising and falling.

Dairy Milk!

Later, I wandered the arena, empty now, searching for the seat I'd sat in as a boy. The stadium silent except the echoing squeaks of cleaners' shoes on the sticky floor, the old Coca-Cola. I walked across crumpled polystyrene cups, Choc Ice wrappers, torn programmes, a forgotten or discarded Polaroid photo of a group of 'Slaughterhouse' Fahy fans...

When I found what I thought was probably the seat, although my memory was uncertain, I sat there, and I squinted at the distant ring. There were cleaners mopping Brogan's blood from the floor and wiping it from the ropes.

Can I have the binoculars, Dad?

Don't drop them, good boy.

The heft. I lifted the binoculars and fitted them in front of my eyes.

How's it looking down there?

I focused. Brogan had collapsed. Willie 'The Neck' Dempsey standing above.

Brogan's on the floor, I said.

Of course he is, of course he's on the floor. My dad laughed.

Tap on the shoulder. Security guard.

Time to go, he says.

I nod.

He steps away, into the sloping aisle.

But I don't move. I can't. I don't want to leave the stadium now. Shadows will do, the world outside is turning: Brogan, comatose, in a wailing St John's ambulance; 'Quotable' Moore from a gleaming SUV throwing broken squares of Dairy Milk—

I squint at the distant ring.

Sir?

The security guard again, standing in the aisle, calling. He points at his wrist, at a make-believe watch.

Time, he says.

The Seaview Hundred and Fifty-Two

Dawn Watson

'The hatchet is gianter than you,' said Tommy Hillis, and I
believed him. He was standing outside Lou's corner shop in
Queen Victoria Gardens. It was half past eight on a Friday
morning.

'But how giant exactly?' I asked.

'About this size,' he said. The tip of his white Hi-Tec
trainer touched the shop's pebbledash wall. His fingers
stretched halfway up the window. I wrote 'bigger than me'
in my notebook.

He stood up and took a Mars Bar from his pocket, opened
it. He threw the wrapper on the ground. It blew flat against
the wall. 'Way gianter,' he said, and took a bite. I sketched
the wall and the window, drew a double-headed arrow in
between. I wrote 'hatchet diameter' underneath. Tommy
walked off down the alley towards Seaview Primary School.
It didn't have a view of the sea.

At breaktime outside the toilets, a crowd of girls were
skipping with a long rope. I leaned on the red brick wall
and watched Janet Chowbury finish a run of one hundred
and thirteen skips. She could skip more than Bridget Willets

who was celebrated for her skipping. She owned two dogs, both called Biscuit.

Janet joined our school last year in P6. She moved from East Belfast because her mum was told to. Janet told me five times she missed her old best friend Cherry Fenton. Her school uniform was navy, ours was grey. Her mum made her wear it anyway. When she joined the back of the skipping queue, I asked her what she knew about the Hatchet Man. Janet pushed her clear plastic glasses up her nose. She said he kept it in the hedge.

'In the hedge?' I asked. 'What hedge? Front or back?'

'The yellow one,' she said.

I wrote 'kept in the front hedge' in my notebook. Janet tugged at the waist of her blue pleated skirt. 'Thanks for your help,' I said. 'You were a good skipper today.' She squinted at me. Her mouth hung open slightly.

I walked around the back of the school, sat on the ground beside the football pitch. It took ninety-four steps. I liked it was an even number. The grass was empty apart from three blackbirds. No one was allowed on the pitch. I opened my notebook, drew the hedge. It had a dip in the middle and sagged towards the pavement. It was wildly overgrown. The house was a gable end, the hedge crept around the side. It was patched in parts with fencing and turned green around the back. I wrote the colours, drew an arrow pointing to the front hedge. I wrote 'hatchet kept here' and an asterisk.

I stared at the page, tapped it with the pencil. I tucked

my hair behind my left ear. One of the birds took off, landed on the goal post. I underlined 'here' twice and turned the page. I fixed it flat with a crease. The bell went for the end of break. A dog outside the school gates barked my name. It went 'Sam Black-wood. Sam Black-wood.' I touched my forehead eight times, put the notebook in my backpack. It was denim and had planets on it.

No one had ever seen the Hatchet Man. Everyone knew he was there. He lived almost exactly halfway down Seaview Drive. His house was on the left as you came from Premier Drive. I had to walk past it every day to get to school. Everyone always made sure to stay on the right. People would tell you, stay on the right. If you were on your own, you would run fast past it. If people were in a gang, sometimes they played dares to see who would go closest. Big boys from Castle High.

After school, I went to Lou's to get a Curly Wurly. I went there at least two times every day. If we needed bread, my mum would say: 'Go get a loaf, tell Lou to put it down.' If there was a queue, I'd always re-join at the back. To make sure nobody heard me. At the counter, Lou would never speak. She would take her pencil from behind her ear, jot the amount in her book with the grid squares. Then, she'd look over my head at the person behind me. Smile at them, say hello, take their money. Our tick list went over all the pages. I wondered if she would ever get angry. Getting bread made my heart beat very fast.

Janet's sister Heather just got a job there. It meant she knew about the list. That made two people apart from me, my mum and dad. I set the Curly Wurly on the counter. Heather flipped to our most recent entry and made a note of the price with a stub pencil. I counted twenty-six plastic tubs of sweets on the shelf behind her. Midget Gems, Choc Lick, Floral Gums, Strawberry Bonbons, Chocolate Raisins, Chewing Nuts. Without looking up, she said: 'By the way, did you hear Henry Rooney touched the Hatchet Man's hedge?' Henry had three older brothers and once kissed Shauna Langley in the park. He wore a Karate Kid sweat band and was expelled from Castle High for hitting the teacher on the head with a typewriter. His dad was in jail for shooting a man dead in the Waterworks. I put the Curly Wurly in my coat pocket, took out my notebook.

'When?'

'Yesterday,' she said.

'Which hedge? Front or back?'

'The yellow one.'

'Was he seen?'

'Was he seen, says you? Well, it was after school,' she said. 'Henry was kept in detention by Mrs Clayton, so it was really dark. Andrew Wilson dared him. Henry was all, "Aye, come on then". There was nobody about, so he crossed Seaview Drive.' A woman in a green coat handed

Heather the right money for a Veda. 'Anyway, he walks over the street and doesn't he reach out to touch the hedge?' Heather straightened a box of 10p mix-ups with the tip of her index finger.

I'd been electrocuted. 'Then what happened?'

'What happened, says you? Well,' said Heather, 'all the fucking windows opened at once. They all flew up in a big slam, all of them. And the front door as well.' She rolled the pencil between her finger and thumb. Her eyes were like liquorice wheels. 'It was a trap.'

'Did the Hatchet Man come out?'

I wrote 'TRAP' in capital letters.

Lou shouted from the back store for Heather to restock the fridge. She dropped the pencil. It was attached to a string and disappeared behind the counter. 'No,' she whispered. 'The Hatchet Man stayed in the hall. Henry said his eyes were black, and his head reached the ceiling.' She picked up a crate of silver-topped milk bottles. 'The hatchet had blood all over it,' she said. 'Andrew shit himself. The two of them ran like fuck.' When I opened the door to leave the shop, a tiny bell jangled.

I sat on the wall outside. I drew a house with an open door. Then a man with a hatchet filling the frame. I scribbled in his eyes with heavy pencil. I thought about Janet's statement. 'Hatchet inside the house?' I wrote. 'Another one in the hedge?' I drew three question marks the same size as the door. I closed the book, reopened it, traced over the question marks again. Then, I closed the book and went home.

I lived a hundred and eleven steps away—in flat 35a, 175 Skegoneill Avenue. It was a big box of brown built for old people. We were packed in there by the Housing Executive when my dad got sacked from the shipyard. He worked in the pencil department and tried to burn down a grain store. I heard mum tell someone on the phone we were going to lose our house on Shore Road. Then we moved to the flat. My dad never went out after that. We had lots of boxes of pencils.

There is a concrete yard out the back. Red metal washing-line poles are everywhere. There's never any clothes on them. They stand there out of place like trees on the moon. Like telephone masts in a duck pond. A sprung metal gate swings shut when men come to the flats at night. There is a bow-legged trellis. I don't invite my friends round after school.

I've a page at the back of my notebook for things I find in the yard. I go out when my mum and dad shout. Last night, there were eight light-bleached beer cans, two hundred and thirty-nine small green cubes of broken windscreen glass, one Star Bar wrapper and an upside-down pram. There was an empty wet paper bag as well, falling apart. It didn't feel complete, but I noted it anyway. Wrote 'pick and mix' with a question mark. It could have held anything though. Crumbed ham, or grapes. It was impossible to know. I drew two circles around 'pick and mix'.

Someone had wound cassette tape around the poles.

Brown, glossy threads. I didn't know how to categorise them. I drew a picture. Underneath, I wrote 'cassette tape tape'. It went *phut phut* in the wind.

Monday mornings were worst. It was hard to be in the world again after spending the weekend pretending you weren't. I slept in my school uniform, so I only had to wash my face. It was ten steps from my bed to the bathroom. I flattened my hair with water. The door of my parents' bedroom was open. My mum was curled on the floor. Her white dressing gown was untied. It was seven steps to the living room. I edged past my dad, sleeping on the sofa. He had been sick on the carpet. There were eleven opened cans of Stryke beer. Two had been crumpled up. One was sitting on the TV. I looked inside. It had a cigarette butt floating in it.

It took me a long time to walk anywhere. When I went to school I left early. I had to look at my shoe soles each time I took a step. To make sure I hadn't stood in dogs' dirt. It was hard in autumn when there were leaves. They hid everything. I took a step, looked at my sole, took a step, looked at my sole.

That morning, it took me a hundred and thirteen steps to get to Lou's—two longer than was okay. I ran back home. On the second attempt I made a hundred and eleven. At least two of those were jumps. I pulled my eyelids down as far as they would go and counted to thirty. Lou put down two Dairy Milk.

Seaview Drive is long. It's three hundred and seventy-nine steps to the school steps. After a hundred and fifty-two, a dog ran in front of me. It darted from behind a parked car and disappeared into the Hatchet Man's garden. The house was dark blue in the early light. Seven crows sat on the telephone wires, one on a lamp post. The bulb was broken, glowing red. All the others threw yellow circles. I went to walk on, but I'd forgotten my step count. I thought about Janet's glasses. They were really big. I wondered was the dog okay. I couldn't see a hatchet in the front hedge. The yellow leaves were thin. I stuck two fingers down my shirt collar and pulled, took a deep breath. I held it for fifteen seconds. A bird darted over my head in a line. It looped up and over the roof. I waited for the windows to slam open. A sparrow fled a bush next door. It skittered onto the grey guttering. The windows stayed closed.

I walked across the road and stood in front of the hedge. I saw the golden retriever lying on a flattened patch of grass in the overgrown front garden. Its muzzle was grey. I whispered: 'Do you live here?' It didn't reply.

I touched my forehead eight times, then walked up the path. One—two—three—four—I crouched beside the dog. I took a Dairy Milk from my pocket, broke a piece off and set it beside the animal. It lifted its head to look, then lay back down. The crow on the lamp post flew off with a yawp.

I heard my dad shout: 'Sam? Come back here now.

Come. Here. Now.'

I heard my mum shout: 'Sam! Stop writing in that fucking book, go and get me a loaf of bread.'

I heard Lou shout: 'Sam, put that milk down and get out of my shop. Don't come back until you pay me what you owe.'

I heard Heather shout: 'Sam! You're so poor! I feel sorry for you!'

I pushed open the letter box. Through the flap, I saw woodchip walls and a brown phone chair. A very tall man sat on it. He was sharpening a hatchet on a grindstone. The sparks lit the hall up bright. He asked me: 'How many steps from there to here?' All the windows and doors slammed open. All the dogs were barking.

I looked from my feet to his. 'I think twelve.'

Then, I was nine and the man was my dad in his blue workman overalls. He was telling me a joke. 'Why are graveyards so popular?' he said. 'Because people are dying to get into them.' His eyes filled up when he laughed.

Then, I was five and the man was my mum. She was holding my hands above my head, dancing to Eddy Grant in our sunlit Shore Road kitchen. Her blonde hair a wild halo of light.

I pressed my hands over my ears, counted my heartbeat. On the street, the lamp posts flickered and went out. The school bell rang. The sun came up. I started my steps from one.

Twinkle

Judyth Emanuel

Hurry. Say Amen. For fuck's sake. Say it! For pity's sake *let me go.*

Little Herb head like a raisin, hics loud hiccups echoing through the stiff church, hics piercing unanswerable prayers crash like a pebble landing in a silent stream hic splash ripples. *Curse you my child. For you have the hiccups.* His mother lifts Little Herb and like a bride in reverse but dowdy, runs up the aisle as if removing Herbert from religion itself. She slaps. Be still. His hics pathetic hic hic hic the sympathy, oh poor little boy screams,

Don't wanna go outside and see the stupid stars.

Bless you my child. For you have screamed. The exhausted praying evaporates To some place. Nowhere. Impatient hush remains mostly empty pews. Parishioners bow heads yes statue of Christ as usual on the cross, a crown bless the thorns sticks in. Torture everyone takes for granted. Really. Praise the Lord. The faithful live in hope. Bless this meek 1972 hot Sunday evening Reverend Potter not praying predictable. Yet. *Say it.* Amen not fully fair dinkum dispensing paper cups communion grape juice disappointing Darlene prays,

Say amen. Blast it.

Not getting any younger. Skinny raucous her Nana harps,

Darlene! You aren't getting any younger!

Hallow be this girl for she must explode. Darlene's desperation for a cup of tea, slice of cake, sex. More of a sensitive girl Darlene believes Jesus Bid Us Shine. But. Darlene about to explode. She wishes. To hiccup. Let loose a thunderous fart. Burp cause earthquake. Flash boobs unladylike, unchristian smashing godliness straitlaced shell preventing any eruption of hums down there doesn't know what. Shudder of genitals must marry. Bible orders man woman become one flesh. Darlene thinks. Uncomfortable *and* unhygienic. Ugh! Fancy one blob of skin, thighs, stomachs, bums, spines overlapping. Scramble. Just a bloody mess. By God go on girl hook a husband quick. The girl a bomb ready to howl shrill as fuck. But Darlene never swears *shit fuck bugger.* She saves her swears like money. Swears best to keep. For later. Oh. Another tremble. In The Wrong Below. Stares at Stuart snoring four rows back. Creature man clutches his hymnal and testicles snug in his left hand unaware she scrutinises.

A second Darlene, the one to come, best keep her for. Well she wrinkles her nose urk gross a boy's balls.

The here and now Darlene decides. He will. *He will do.* Just because. The last man standing, cute knees and not much choice in Lightening Stone Ridge oh nasal blokes down the pub, brainless boys barefoot stub their toes, hang around the council pool. Others at eighteen go troppo get wasted searching for shinier lives run off to the city. Gold of wattle trees bloom as girls swipe the surplus left behind wondering how to get out of the damn Ridge boxed mindset, bang in the middle of nowhere. Thousands of miles to the nearest city beyond that. End of the world. Or everything big. Darlene dreams of a bigger life. Not the self-combustion. Of people living in dead ends. Skin and bones consuming. Stuck. Rude hicks whack stuff, pour fuel into metal drums. Light a match to hell with the consequences. Them pack animals going insane. Interminable dry land defeats reckless men swatting insects. Men transfixed by emptiness searching for treasure. Lost.

Lightening Stone Ridge. Makes no effort. Flat on its back spitting opals at miners naming the black gems Emperor of The Outback, Black Prince, Pride of The Desert. And colourful opals, Light of the World, Flame Queen. The biggest, Sunset Princess weighs ten ounces cut into two pieces according to the Haws, produces volatile outcomes out out cripes one flesh sparkle, one body glint at. Stuart ready and waiting with his hundred-mile stare. Long seventies hair hides pimply complexion. Gloom face and hazel eyes stony rolling plains expression hides terror whistles. Oklahoma. Innocent hawk makin' lazy circles in the sky. Cracks his knuckles. Grinds his teeth. Grabs a toy gun. Nope never does the job right. Stuart a bumble bricklayer specialising terrible in crazy paving curved terracotta tiles creates a pattern of flower petals, unintentional depiction of a woman's external genital organs big as a playground. A rude passer-by says, That looks like a twat.

The shocked customer panics.

Rip it out. *For God's sake.* It isn't what we had in mind. Darlene hears the sound of clay breaking. *He will do.* Not quite. What she has in mind. Girl of twenty calculates her worth. Too homely. Not chosen Opal Queen. Quiet. Marvellous dimples. Pert mouth, pouty smiles. Horrible memory how in high school a slobbering boy kisses, his furry teeth wrapped in twinkling metal braces. Darlene the now and the one to come. Virgins thinking. Life. Happens like second hand excitement.

Reverend Potter says Amen ahem relief finally *finally* the service ends. Old battle-axe Mrs Munro leaps up in her Hallelujah floral frock worn since God created the world in seven days, God shouting,

Supper is served in our Sunday School Hall.

Sunburnt relics crunch across the gravel. Old sexless women compare hysterectomies and harsh hairstyles. Blokes recall gaunt times, world wars, jobless haggard packing a swag droughts worse, men skint on the breadline, fingers fray to stone. Mince and stale cake and memories trailing away waiting for the water to boil. Lipton's strong. And a bullish younger generation. Opals. Difficult to find. Hide a shotgun under the bed. Land Cruisers rumble through rock n roll, large belt buckles, wide-brim hats, grill chops, this steamed ginger pudding life whatever.

Darlene sidles close to Stuart nervous by the exit, a shy cup and saucer wobbling in one hand. Speechless. His mouth full of Mrs Munro's homemade scones. Sings in his mind, my honey lamb wind sweeping down the plain the waving wheat sure smells sweet. Watches Darlene help herself. Orange cordial, not fizzy. Bright colour almost blinding. Darlene a tad show-offy, flicks her ratty hair she always rinses in lemon juice. The dear smirk. Sugar girl bites lip coy mimics a husky voice eek going for sexy, comes out squeaky,

Hey Stu, guess what twinkles?

Hands clasp behind her back. Shows her small breasts more prominent. Bra lace saucy wide blue eyes rounder than a cracker biscuit. This hard nipple a forlorn performance. Plays the devil with Stuart's nerves, neck turns a shocking pink. Adam's apple bobs up down choking he swallows a whole scone. Doughy bits between his teeth. Darlene grins.

Opals. Lightning. Me. We all twinkle.

Her fingertips make little starburst gestures. Stuart steps back. Blinks backing away.

Darlene silly weak at the knees. Flees from blinding orange, doughy bits, apple breasts, tea scalding her impudence ahh not the small-town flirt she hopes to be. Dashing. Dash home sweaty lies on the floor. Has a good cry. Remembers her Pa saying *Hooly dooly here come the waterworks.* Pa calling her, *my little sunset princess.* Pa the widow grocer. Froth of ginger hair and her mother, serene woman good country, grubby aprons, always a clothes peg between her teeth went sooner. Asthma attack. Remember Nan's swollen eyes. Your mother couldn't breathe. She's gone forever. Darlene eight years old held her nose to suffer what without breath feels, how it's meant to be. That year, 1960, monsters chop down The Tree of Knowledge standing proud at the intersection of Drover's Pass. Her Nan complaining,

Those bloody butchers.

While old timers scratch at their beards. Mutter,

Strewth. A flaming shame.

And Pa rearing Darlene, weeps for death, loss, the muddle of his life and Nan saying, there there. As puberty changes Darlene humming, *where the bee sucks there suck I.* Sings, *in a cow's lip bell.* Ignoring sudden boob plum lumps. Surprise magic pubes appear like a fairy rhyme. Airy-fairy Darlene says,

Don't care.

Her body the wrong magical. Never tries to look at touch secret places. Why that unconscious throb. Don't ask. Hungry for a stronger hand. Breasts appearing puts her Pa in a panic. Stern this fear preserve chaste like raspberry jam. Pa strict no fun for Darlene. No lipstick, Go Go boots, false eyelashes, cigarettes, shaved legs, the frug, the twist. Sour

Darlene twiddles her thumbs. He outlaws entire decade of the sixties. On the *Lord's* day tight jeans cotton top shows cleavage. Threatens to smack Darlene. He warns,

Listen, pet. Men can't control themselves.

Darlene horror wonders. What an uncontrollable man might do. Like mad Bluey the barman, running amok hangs like a bat from the rafters in a shed behind the pub. Her Nan explaining,

Batman Bluey won't ever calm down cause he needs a rest and a woman.

Her Pa's heart stops in 1971. Well that's it then. How to survive. The sadness of waxy hollow honeycomb. Feet twitch. At a future managing the grocery store crammed with excess tubs of margarine, weevils in the rice bubbles, cream going off. And at twenty well Darlene might light up a smoke. Go wild in hot pants. Wear a see-through blouse. Brighten the house. Paint the front door psychedelic cherry, put in a peep hole.

Her Nan feet hobbling sore from bunions. Half-crippled with arthritis. Flicks a duster across shelves. Boils a pot of beans add a spoonful of bi carbonate soda for the green. Hugs Darlene,

You alright?

Darlene opens a window.

Yep. I need some air. Can you lend us a quid?

Every morning dawns all sun. How to get her hands on. Stu.

Will do. Darlene ripe age goody-goody old maid musty, husband hunter. Her whim scribbles a short note on rose-scented stationery line of love hearts. The gist. *Love, love me do.* Same as the song. Ending with, *I think I love you.* And signing it Sunset Princess with a kiss.

Stuart reads the note, puts on his best shorts quick as. Washes the mud off his gumboots. Races straight over to. That weatherboard cottage where she lives. One street behind Stuart's squat brick house four rooms low rent. Lawn the size of a pocket-handkerchief. His mother Edna the seamstress plants sunflowers, grow to great heights. Then collapse. Edna raises chickens filthy. When the rooster crows, Darlene's ears flame.

Stuart asks,

Wanna go for a walk?

Darlene thinks. That's pretty cheap. Still she paints her lips scarlet as a toffee apple. Wander past the Digger's Rest hotel. Sound of rowdy yobs mongrel pissant bludgers. Sparra roaring,

Youse shitheads.

And Snowy brainless maudlin. Life not worth living. Dickhead Clancy cracks a fat. Beer mugs overflow awful rough. How about Mario's Milk Bar? Blackboard chalk *SPECIALS hot chips, hamburgers with the lot, sauce extra, milkshakes all kinds.* Rows of jars full of anise rings, sherbet grubs, jersey caramels, musk sticks, Fantales, cobbers, freckles, Minties. Darlene's mouth waters. Mario twists his curly moustache. *Take Your Pick*. Scoops candy into a paper bag for Darlene and Stuart chooses a caramel strawberry milkshake. Sickly. So thick impossible to suck through a paper straw.

Outside the caravan park. A neon sign flashes. No Vacancies. Permanent residents weld to aluminium deckchairs. Pissheads gape at the heavens. Heathens rave at the sky. A horrified stratosphere looks back at them. Don't dare go near that lot. Listen. Hear the whack of the Headmaster's cane. One-room school half a block away. Oh it doesn't sound good. Remembers the ghost of herself tiny child holding out a quivering hand. To be struck. Walk the dirt track beside Crook's Creek. Look at the exposed roots of a gumtree. Where Gwen Wilby got shot dead. A woman goes without a cry. Darlene knows. Ten years ago. Overhears two young housewives all this gossip. That Wilby woman. Loose tart, rouged cheeks, cocksucker, loaded pistol, jealous rage. Darlene's confusion.

What's a loose tart sock sucker?

Her Nan shock covering Darlene's open mouth.

Never you mind, stickybeak.

Darlene and Stuart stare at the murder ground. His hand itching groin always. Expect maybe. Soil hiding a skull, bones, guts. Darlene shivers, a tree's sloping sighs the narrow stream. On purpose. Stuart slides his arm around her waist. The scrub, the saplings close in on a wilderness. Cockatoo screeches something naughty. Jags of yellow crest curl in obscene arc. Darlene glows below. Ah-ha. Minor thrill, gently slaps Stuart's face. He ducks.

Hey what's that for?

You got a mozzie biting your cheek.

Cheeky.

The kiss comes wet. And her lips. Pucker up. Without any tongue this smacker. Teeth bang together. Pash, giggles Darlene, a silent tickles the rub of innocence. What must there be. Well. Tongue. Darlene knows this much. But not much else. Except lovemaking the salt of life. A tongue-shrivelling tang. Now this taste not tangy. Tongue doesn't work. No tongue. Something wrong. Cannot put her finger on it. Each grope and fondle. Her chest tightens thinking of Edna the seamstress afraid of combustible girls. Stitching Darlene shut with a sharp needle and thread.

So how about a drive.

Stingy again. Parks his Hillman Minx beside an old fossicking field. Fumble on the back seat. Gear stick a problem. No one guesses anything going on. Which isn't much. Drive to the public pool fifty metres long twelve metres wide of a luminous blue glow. Darlene tells Stu,

It's visible from the Milky Way.

Stuart laughs.

Yeah right, *Darl*.

Darlene frowns.

Don't call me Darl.

Righty-oh. Hows about a swim in the nuddy?

Someone might see.

She leaves him holding his bewilderment hard-on. Under a streetlight. *Love, love me do.*

Secret visits to the local library. Researching sexual acts Darlene discovers. A lot. Some. Peculiar variations. 'The A-Z Fool's Guide To Fornication.' Alphabetically listing skills. Frotting, fingering, foreplay, pegging, penetration. Christ. How revolting. Drops the heavy volume on the carpet. Next. 'Instructions For Young Women.' Darlene doesn't get far. The opening paragraph. *Men must be denied or they will demand 'intimate relations' every day. Women should give little. Give rarely. Give reluctantly. The wise woman allows two brief encounters weekly while planning to make every effort to decrease the frequency.* Darlene sniffs.

That can't be right.

She thumbs through 'Storks Deliver Babies.' Idiotic paperback.

So petting. Nature's trap lures girls into actions propelled by lust. Best kept for honest lovemaking leading toward marriage followed by mating. A girl must be prepared. Kissing is loaded with dynamite.

Darlene smiles.

Okay. Dynamite.

This load of dynamite. A bone-dry sunset. Green gardens turn brown. The heat bakes snails in the soil. Unbearable itch gnaws at stifling conformity. Of nothing street. Ostrich neighbours peer over back fences. Wind chimes rattle mating. Inside Darlene's tinderbox house. Rattle rattle rattlesnake. On the settee clumps of stuffing burst from a hole in the vinyl. Missing buttons leave indentations in cushions. What remains. Strands of cotton. Silent television. Knick-knacks. Fake boomerangs. China ducks flying nowhere up daisy wallpaper. Souvenir teaspoons not worth keeping. A dish of bananas gone bad. Gradual. Stuart shifts across to lure. Drowsy hot repeats,

My honey lamb. My honey lamb you sure smells yum.

Honey lamb wonders. Is he dreaming of a Sunday roast? Clamps both elbows to her sides. Worries armpits leaking perspiration. She balances on the slippery end of the couch and waits. For it. Swears now. Fuck it. Creases the pleats of her skirt. Oh damn and blast. Everything creases in the Ridge. Too many opposites. Darlene set in stone. Darlene chock full of lightning. Darlene on the edge waiting for Stuart to finally do the job right. Thumping heartbeat his heart somehow wallops against her breast. His head moves close. Her face blushing what if he starts a bastard baby. Happened to the hairdresser, slutty Tracy May drinking bleach to get rid of it. Her Nan will kill him.

Excuse me. Quick. The bathroom. How does she look. Spins around in front of the mirror. Flat boobs, just bug bites. Fried eggs. Pools of mercury bouncing. Stuffs toilet paper inside each bra cup. Pale shoulders. Spotty Clearasil skin. She believes. Freckles come from lightning. Slim figure. Not random or weird like the map of Australia. Remembering as a child with a set of colour pencils neatening the corners and smoothing the rough outlines of the lucky country. Gives the land a colourful surface. Shall it resemble an animal, a piece of fruit, something real.

Darlene creeps back into the sunroom and switches on the telly. The Flintstones. Stuart fidgets with his zipper. Her surreptitious watches Fred bully Barney. Wilma worrying, *if Fred doesn't come home soon dinner will be ruined.* Betty chirps, *sometimes I just don't know what's the matter with men.* Same, thinks Darlene, uneasy about cartoon characters not wearing underpants under short jagged loincloths. She declares,

Cartoon characters should be required to wear underwear.

Stuart's excitement at the mention of underwear. His hand approaches. Darlene slips the toilet paper out of her bra. Oh crap. Blood gushes from Stuart's nose. Nosebleed stains his flannel shirt. Throws his head back. Pokes a wad of tissues into each nostril. Tissues protrude like tusks soaked in red ink. Darlene cannot bear to look at him. She just doesn't know what is the matter with men. Stuart carries on seducing thrusts his face of blood-spatter tissues. His fingers wiggling. Clumsy caresses. The devil's voice in her ear. The devil's fingers wiggle down there. Satan on horseback yelling, giddy-up whoa love me babe.

A nuclear cloud rips through. Invisible thing nobody tells. She doesn't understand what. Zings her body. Mushroom electricity tears out her hairclips. Tramples airy fairy dark secret spots now cavernous. Showers of sparks burst. Every pore of her skin. Each follicle, fingernail. Her ears on fire. Nipples hard as pearls. And this groan. Unleashes. Comes animalistic. Guttural from her gut. Growls. Unstoppable. Goes and goes and comes and comes. Why does she think. Of her mother lips gone blue without breath. With the death of it. Her father's heart crashing. Grief heartache aches itself so bad, it caves in. Why think of the dead. As a magical beast streaks through her like a. Seizure. The moans echo more beautiful than death. Deep from within the gaping hole she doesn't know exists. Delirium like a gun shot, shattering porcelain ducks, bad bananas, senseless teaspoons remembers. Tarts sucking cocks, no socks, how a jealous man kills a woman. The sudden of sudden. Of. Cockatoo squawking. Darlene wails panting bird pants. This ridiculous Cockatoo inside her claws through her whimpering. Nerves tingle. Toes curl. Bird's *wark wark wark* matches her throb. Grunts. Spine arches. Flings her head back to. What swears she saves for the now shriek.

Fuck me. Fucking wow. Bugger bloody hell. What in the name of Almighty God. Was *that*?

This loss of herself. Cockatoo takes fright flies away. Stuart jumps up.

Jeez Darlene, you scared me.

Down there, sopping pink. In the shape of wings. Flaps of

skin split apart. Red sea parting. Strange ruptures her body splitting Sunset Princess in half. Into two of herself. Two separate bodies. Two faces of double Darlene's. Impossible. Yet happens. Which is real. Who is the true self. A chance to escape. The first Darlene slithers off the settee. Abandons the other Darlene lying on yellow linoleum. That creamy colour of sick fainting. Nauseous semen. The other Darlene calls to her disappearing self,

Don't go. Stay and watch me.

To be her own audience. She needs. She wants. All four eyes. To see the spectacle of herself. The other Darlene robbing herself of dirty jokes, stealing that solitary orgasm.

The first Darlene, this woman comes to life. Free from restraint. Regaining her voice. Races for the door. And runs and runs a zillion miles. There. The big smoke. City of. Going further. To prove just reach the horizon. Fall off. Live a lovely life. Awaken a mighty revelation. She doesn't know what yet. Maybe transform into. Queen of the night. Gold-digger. Grass widow. Lewd lascivious whip-smart beauty. Chocolate damsel in delight. Greatest woman born from a romantic novel

She looks back only once. Blood drips from Stuart's nostrils. He fiddles with damp briefs. Zips his fly. A mysterious wet patch on the front of his jeans. Shock. Stuart peed his pants! For the love of God. Sometimes. Darlene knows the truth about men. She knows more than she lets on.

The other Darlene, the girl that settles. She is. But does she know what twinkles? Always. It is her. Twinkling down a weeping stream. Last shudder on a cold floor. The other Darlene, the final Darlene ends with a hiccup, a swear, shit hic, wipes tears. Stuart asks,

What's wrong?

Nothing. Bloody well nothing. How's your nose?

Still bleeding. Slower now in drips. This other final Darlene weaker than blood from a stone. Slows. To avoid the beginning of real life. These drippings. Stick. Never let her go. Amen. Pigs fly. Hell freezes. Hiss and yawn. At the same time. Running from her shadow. An echo without a voice. Every impossible understand why. She has nothing better to do. *He will do.* Just like that. She begins a fucking surrender.

Honeymoon at Richterswil Harbour

Suzanne Joinson

She stood on Richterswil's harbour and watched Hadid swim in the lake with the mime artist who was rapidly losing his make-up with each dive under the water.

The mime artist's eyes became black circles. The red lipstick smeared at first, and then disappeared, leaving pale flesh. He turned away from Hadid and came back towards Clara, swimming as a dog does: body submerged, chin uncomfortably high and the sense of struggle beneath the surface of the water. When it was shallow enough, he waded without grace and Clara held out her hand towards him.

'Come, Mimi,' she said. He ignored her and hauled himself up on to the jetty.

Together they sat and watched Clara's husband-to-be continue his determined breaststroke out towards the heart of the lake. Soon enough, he was no longer her husband-to-be but a black mark. The lake was deep and still. It was indecisive weather; the sun came and went and lit spots of the water in temporary patches. She had wanted to say *don't swim*, but Hadid had insisted. He came over child-like and enthusiastic.

'Too tempting,' he'd said, taking off his shirt. At some point during that week she had touched each segment of his spine and its dip. Black shadows disturbed the flat water. The stones making up the shoreline looked like paperweights.

Clara had her Kodak with her, but she did not take a photograph. The sky was too vast, and the lake appeared to be swallowing it. There were no edges and so nothing to frame. This is our honeymoon, she thought. They were not yet married, but this day and this moment with Mimi dripping on to the stones next to her and the temperature just right, this was theirs.

Photograph the space. The thing that exists between earth and sky. That is what Hadid told her when they first started to work together in darkrooms. She had looked down towards earth, then up to the sky. How does the thing integrate into the sky? What is its relationship with the sky? Let's find how the light builds architecture. A woman can only fall in love with a man who will teach her things. Later, on the evening of this honeymoon day, they would decide to move to Alexandria together. Yes, they agreed: that would be the thing.

'Was it neutral?' she asked him.

'Not really, but still.'

In the Zürich darkroom Hadid taught her about light and how it moves. She was greedy for knowledge: about the shutter speed, about stepping into the picture, about stepping out of it again. Also, about Alexandria. She had, of course, seen Hadid's pictures of the city. Perhaps, when she got there, she would be able to put into context his obsession with the framing of things.

'Will you stay, Mimi, or try to leave the country?' He was damp and shivering on the deck. She would offer him her scarf which was purple with miniature emblems of lions embroidered on with gold thread, but she knew he would not take it. He was gallant and sweet and made her think of the sort of man who might have a diagonal scar on his person as a residue from a duel. The air smelled of fresh spruce, or pine.

'Of course I will stay. Where would I go?'

He patted her hand, gave a clown's unhappy smile.

In the studios of Zürich Hadid held her hand but did not pat it like Mimi. He squeezed it and stroked it and when she stood next to him immediately her balance and the centre of things was thrown. She squinted into the lake-light.

'Can you see him?'

'He's there, look. I don't know how far he's going.'

Hadid was an enigma, this concentrated person, this self-taught photographer from Alexandria. Who comes from Alexandria?

'That isn't a real place, you can't be a real person.'

It is and I am.

Still squinting, she could see the head: a black dot barely seen. Mimi's eyes, panda-smudged and melancholy, were watching his friend carefully.

'Is there a secret tide, a pull underneath that we don't know about?'

'He's a strong swimmer,' Mimi said.

Hadid had taught her about light and then, as if that weren't enough, he taught her how to waltz. They waltzed in a club called The Dead Cat, as if he did not come from Alexandria, nor her from Wales. Pentrehobyn, to be exact, near Mold.

Wales?

Hadid said it like a dream and a question. You say Alexandria is a mystical otherness of a place, what is this Wales? As far from the desert as is possible to get. Rain, clouds, the flint and the chop. Clay and limestone and the rubbing down. Wet Sundays. Nothing Alexandria about Mold.

'I wouldn't get romantic about Wales,' she said as they waltzed, as a concertina player stretched the bellows so that they might burst.

'Let's dance, and not think about why we are here.'

'Let's do that.'

Madame de Meuron at the wall, watching. She was the link between them.

'Let's waltz,' he said, 'and soon we will go to the lake and forget all of this.' Hadid was employed by Louise Elisabeth de Meuron to take photographs of Amsoldingen Castle for Clara's father. The curves, its cellars, its garden were of a style that her father craved for Pentrehobyn Hall. Clara had begged her father to be allowed to go, to learn a little about photography.

These are not the times to travel.

Switzerland is neutral. (Is Alexandria neutral?)

He agreed, but only because his brother was travelling there. The journey was uncomfortable, awkward for them both, and at Ziirich the churlish, unhappy Uncle Andrew withdrew almost immediately. Clara was left to become the assistant to a young man brought in to photograph castles.

Madame de Meuron, who only dressed in red and black, despised her husband who was her cousin, but rather liked Hadid. She did not like this Welsh assistant with brown-red hair, with red apple cheeks, who came from nowhere and was being taught about light.

Hadid worked on the commission for his photography master, Keller, who couldn't stand photographing Swiss castles. It made him sick to be photographing crumbling castles. He would rather be photographing soldiers. The war was happening, and they were on neutral land. A scrap of make-believe. Guilt came from all corners.

Clara and Hadid waltzed at the cabaret with the mime artist and the woman who claimed to make love to parrots. A beak leans in and delicately plucks at an eyelash, she would say. They drank and drank the wine until some of them were asleep under tables and Hadid admitted to photographing Madame de Meuron, naked, in the Ball

Room of Amsoldingden, capturing the concertina fan of lines on her face and the rings that sliced her neck skin like the trunk of a tree.

In this Ball Room, by this time, the German Officers moved in a line with beautiful women at their arms, they danced in a corner, they sang, and they drank jugs of beer. Clara picked up a button from a German officer's coat and put it in her pocket. When the third of their friends, a painter called Stael and his model were both killed in an unexplained incident near their studio, Clara had said,

'Can we go to the lake now?'

'Of course. We'll bring Mimi with us.'

'Let's forget.'

Mimi, huffing to himself, pretending he was a starfish. He liked to make everyone laugh. He was dry now, he was clothed, but he did not bother to reapply his make-up. At the dances, at first, he had walked behind the German officers mimicking the formal stamp, making them look like fools but very soon he stopped that. Now he preferred to mime rather than speak; he wasn't of the correct race. Now he no longer mimed, nor clowned.

Clara had an insect bite on the top of her foot. She rubbed it and made it swell further, she pressed on it, irritated, and she tried to wipe it off. *Come back, my love.* He did not come but kept on swimming. What was he trying to reach?

After his confession of photographing Meuron, Hadid had been drunk for some nights in a row while Clara remained in the darkroom. He explained it as a fever that must be got through. She tried to understand, but working alone in the darkroom her thought, at the time, was precisely this: *except the blank intervals when he disappeared into his darkroom his nearness made the light grow lighter.* Drips from the photograph paper, painting with light.

Hadid tried to convince her to come dancing with the parrot lady who lived in the same apartment block, who kept summoning him down at midnight. *Come down for fun* and Hadid went to her as if towards a magnetic pull. Let's drink.

'Why not come?'

'I don't like the soldiers. I don't feel safe.'

Zürich is neutral. They said it again and again. As neutral as Wales.

'What would make you feel safe, Clara?'

'That you will love me forever, that I will have enough food, though I will remain thin, that I am in a library surrounded by books, the pages are curled and the ceiling is covered with maps, the blue lines on the maps link from one page to the other and there is no separation, no end to all the countries and connections in the world and men in overcoats following orders they don't agree with will not kill children.'

He had looked at her, strangely.

'I don't want to bring children into a world where soldiers kill them,' she'd said.

He continued looking.

'Also, I don't trust the parrot lady. There is something strange about her shoes, they are boots. Men's boots.'

This happened yesterday:

Hadid again left at midnight, disappearing through the door, moving, slipping down slowly and then running down the wooden stairs. She said to herself: it is not that he wants to be away from me, and the darkroom, and our bed, it is that he needs to be out there. In life. With wine in him.

She thought she understood.

When the door closed behind him, she stood against the wall. Unsure noises in the room: the flap of a bird's wing and the crunch or rumble of a stomach or a light pummel, like a piece of dough being tortured into the correct shape. Once she registered these sounds and accepted them, she returned to the darkroom. Silhouette of the pine. The outline of a rampart. The beginning of a door. She thought of her unfortunate, ill-mannered uncle who had left her here and did not care for his return. If she dreamed of her father, he was always growing the horns of a stag from his forehead.

Hadid came through the door before dawn and fell face-first onto the bed.

'I just want to sleep. I just want to sleep.' His face was swollen, she crouched over him to examine his cheek.

When her finger touched his skin, he groaned. She washed where there were scratches, she kissed the bruises.

'Let's forget. Let's go to the lake.'

He was coming back towards them, swimming slowly, like a turtle. She could smell from the trees a soft woody smell. He had wanted her in the morning, despite his aching and his injuries: this marvel of a foreign girl who will sleep with him before marriage. Chin in the curve of her neck and she had been next to him, facing the blinds, letting him turn her in half.

'He's coming back,' she said to Mimi and they were silent and watched. It took him forty-five minutes to swim back to them and when he came, the rain started, a light rain. He came out of the lake like a member of another species, he was slithery, his bruises swelling and the marks on his chest bright red. His left eye was spectacularly black and purple.

'The water helped.'

'Hadid, we must go.'

'Yes. We'll go to Alexandria, but first, we must marry.'

This was when he'd said: letter from my aunt's cousin. She has died, the house then, despite the family moaning about it, is mine. It is full of cousins and uncles and family, but he will kick them out, remove them, and it will be for us, if we want it.

'Let's go, let's go.'

It rained the whole way home from the lake, and it occurred to her that she had taken no photographs all day.

There had been a night in the room of one of the artists on the run from the frontline; several men, many of them French—an aristocratic French prince of something or other and some Poles—were surrounding a sofa. In their centre was a young woman from Skopje. They were taking it in turns to stroke her ankle with just one finger. First an elderly French man, his knees snapping as he crouched down, and then a younger man, an Austrian. The girl's face did not shift as the stroking went on. She was younger than Clara, perhaps twenty, and of a higher social class than the men other than the aristocratic prince. She was unmoved, if her face was to be read, and Clara had leant towards Hadid and said, 'That would be a photograph.'

'I was thinking the same thing.'

I must tell Mimi. Start to gather your things, I am going to enquire about the passage. It is time now.

Alexandria is a ladder, an axis mundus; it leads to a blissful place. Yet, if it were such a city of reaching to the sky, of moving upwards to Heaven, why could she not see up? Why did the closed tunnels and stairwells shut her down when she thought of it? A field, in Wales, lying on her back amongst August poppies. Her feet, when she ran, had crushed numerous snail shells. High summer. Insects buzzing: the low slunk of a cloud. A light she had never known. Nobody says, 'Come with me to Alexandria! We can set up our own photography studio!' That isn't a real person.

He had taught her about light and that was the important thing and they would go at the end of the week.

The steps on the stairs to their rooms were boots, but not Hadid's. She knew they belonged to the parrot lady whom Clara did not trust. There were three large bangs on the door. There was talk in the stairwell, voices unkind. It was not Hadid, it was not Mimi. The lake was gone. She did not answer. They were looking for him, but he wasn't her. They were shouting his name and banging. Clara applied black mascara to her eyes, slowly, with precision. The mirror was dirty, she wiped it with her sleeve. When it was done, she wiped her eyes and blurred the make-up so that the blackness came down in circles around her eyes, so that her lips were pale. Through the window sunlight lit upon her in patches, so that she might live through her honeymoon one last time.

The Hands of the Andes
Niall Bourke

Pepe flipped the beer mat over and back while he waited. He slid it forward with his thumb until it overhung the counter edge and then flicked it up from below with the tops of his fingers so it hopped into the air. He always managed to catch it before it landed.

When his drink came, he laid out the beer mat before pushing the usual handful of dollar bills across the lacquered wood and then sipped his beer in small mouthfuls, watching as the foamy white rings banded the inside of the glass like a coati's tail. The barman knew to keep serving until the money was up.

The other miners heckled Pepe now. A scab, they called him, a Judas and a turncoat, and so Pepe had picked this bar because it was quiet. The taverna where the other miners still drank was raucous and the barman there served quickly, tossed shakers over his shoulder and opened bottles behind his back. This barman was different; he was awkward and slow and his rusty movements seemed to drag out the evenings interminably and Pepe liked that just fine.

Pepe drank in silence as the frothy head of his beer dissipated, arranging itself into shapes which floated on the yellow body below: a map of Bolivia, a sleeping fruit bat, a toy car. When the glass was empty, the barman served up another and then asked, as was now the routine, what was the news? Usually Pepe met this with a grunt or some comment about the weather—at most a muttering about the declining price of silver. So why did he decide, on this night, to tell the full story? Maybe the barman seemed, just then, peculiarly insistent.

*

Pepe told him he had grown up in Uyuni, a town at the edge of the high salt flat. It was a town, he said, of the decaying skeletons of train locomotives, the corroded tombstones of a bygone prosperity from when this part of Bolivia still had access to the coast, of tourist hotels and street-corner chalk boards and metal-grilled cambios for relieving visitors of solid dollars in exchange for fragile bolivianos. It was a gateway town, a town that guarded the vast expanse of the salt.

The high salt flat sat on the Collao, the plane that crested at over four thousand metres between the two largest Andean ranges, and to live here was not easy. If Pepe had money, he said, he could have made more of it. Could have bought a Toyota Land Cruiser and taken groups on tours of the salt where they would pay handsomely for photographs; eight tiny people standing on top of a giant bottle framed by an immense mirror of white hexagonal plates. Or he could have illegally bought up dollars to sell to the Argentinians who scuttled over the border to be rid of their toxic pesos. Or maybe even opened a taverna or, better still, bought a hotel. But Pepe did not have any money.

He said he'd borrowed some once, enough to buy a second-hand delivery truck. It turned out to be a lemon. The salt kicked up from years crossing the plains had corroded every last nut and bolt and, after the third clutch went, Pepe had left it to rot alongside the other hulks in the iron-shod mortuary at the edge of town. No, Pepe did not have any money. But neither, he said, did he have a taste for working out on the flats, digging and bagging salt in the spears of cold until the glare of the sun burnt out his corneas. So he left for the Cerro Rico, the largest silver mine in all of Bolivia.

It was in the Cerro Rico that he learned to drive the huge supply train that transported the carts of galena and argentite down to the waiting river boats, a train that ran along thirty-five kilometres of track and descended over four thousand metres. It was a track that bore right through the heart of the mountains before falling down to the flat and soft lands of the jungle; fifty-six hairpins and each one cut just long enough to allow the fully laden train to complete its white-knuckle turns. On one side ran the mountain so close that Pepe said he could still brush the yellow flowers of furze exploding from the rocks, still hear the shrieking of the condors as his swaying carts groaned in the mouth of the wind.

Pepe drove for three years under the tutelage of Eduardo, a gnarled and nine-fingered bachelor whose bawdy humour heated the cramped cab more than its little iron stove ever did. There was not a woman Eduardo had not fucked, Pepe said, not a man he had not fought or a lie he had not told over those three years. But Pepe said, for all that, Eduardo taught him well to feel when the brake was being overworked or when the train was gathering too much momentum, when it could in fact be pushed on a little more. And the most important thing Eduardo taught him? Always drink a capful of singani, the oily brandy distilled from Muscat grapes, before each journey began. Drink yours first; it might be your last. Then pour a second, tip it on the slopes and watch it bead into rounds of dust on the thirsting rocks— *Pachamama*, a blessing to Mother Earth that you might make it down one more time.

Four more years, Pepe told the barman, and he had driven his perilous cargo alone. But every year they loaded a little extra into the trailers, pushed drivers to take just one more carriage down. Each extra kilo was a victory for the hungry gullet of the mountain, helping it suck the train into the hairpins just that little more quickly, making it just that little bit harder to stop the whole load derailing. Too often he had seen carts decorating the bottom of the valleys, unhitched carriages glinting up at him like jewels from an unstrung necklace.

One afternoon, exiting the final hairpin, the overloading finally caused the brakes to fail. An acrid plume of melting rubber engulfed his cab and ten thousand tonnes of train went careening down towards the port until at last slowed by the mercifully rising gradient. And had it happened one hairpin higher? So Pepe said that is why he refused to drive again. Why he refused to drive until he got assurances that the trains would be safer, the loads would be lessened. That his family would be provided for should he not return.

★

Three weeks later, Pepe said, he was picketing the mine's southern gate when he saw the large man approaching, his chin sunk into his bomber jacket against the wind and looming larger and larger set against the frozen mining locomotives. He reached Pepe and stopped. Then he began punching.

These were not punches of anger, said Pepe, not the amateur windmilling of a whiskey brawl or overzealous ones snapped off below the elbow. They were controlled, lazy, thrown up from the foot so that each fist landed on him carrying the entirety of the large man's weight; the difference between being hit with a rolled-up magazine or with a stone swung in a sock. They were aimed not at Pepe's head but at a spot some two feet beyond, so each straightened pole of the large man's arm pushed right through the line of Pepe's skull. Every punch arrived from an angle outside his vision so the first he knew of each crashing fist was the flower of a white firework in the dark behind his eyes.

The last punch was an uppercut. This one seemed to carry not only the large man's entire weight but also the weight of the mountain on which he stood, and landed on Pepe's jaw so his molars chipped as they clacked together and the ground spun up to meet his body. It was a punch born in the fighting pits of El Alto; a hand of the Andes, he said, a shot to wake the dead.

A boot pressed down on Pepe's face. *The fucking train runs tomorrow.*

Pepe was silent. The boot was thick-soled and had deep and diagonal treads, the sort that gave good purchase when walking the rocky trails criss-crossing the mine. There was leaf litter and small stones wedged between the wide treads, sharp pebbles that would go unnoticed on the mountain tracks but would scrape jarringly when back walking on asphalt or concrete paths. Dog shit covered a square under the ball of the foot, pressed in so deep it would require a suitable twig to de-foul it.

You always were a stubborn fuck, and the large man dropped down on Pepe, one knee landing inside his pelvis and the other heavy on his chest. The force made Pepe's head lurch up and the large man's knuckles cracked just where Pepe's septum met his lip, rocking his head back against the stones.

Pepe felt his front teeth loosen and his eyes began to fill with water. Something warm gathered on the back of his head where it connected with the sharp-edged shale. *They say you're a selfish little shit because when the mine is closed the whole economy suffers.*

Despite his welling eyes, Pepe said he could see the large man's face more clearly now that it was no longer silhouetted. It was a face built by the ferocity of the high mountains. The glare of the cloudless days had darkened the skin a deep brown and the savage cold of cloudless nights had flattened and widened the nostrils. The skin was karstic with the lines of life in the mountains and red blossoms hung on the cheeks from the years of drinking singani. It was a miner's face, said Pepe, not so different from his own.

The large man stood up, once again shadowed against the haloed sundogs, and sank a toecap into Pepe's ribs. The weight of the boot made his foot swing pendulously before hitting Pepe's side with a noise like a mallet sounding out a cavity wall.

Does that fucking train run tomorrow? the large man said. Four more weighted digs. *Does. It? Does. It?*

Pepe was still silent.

Fucking Christ. The boot was raised and held high above Pepe's face. Pepe gauged the full weight of what was going to come down on him: the tread and the stones and the shit, the heft of the man behind. He broke.

Alright, tomorrow. I'll drive tomorrow.

The large man leaned over and hauled Pepe's flopping body up to sitting against a flat-faced rock. Dusting off a boulder, he sat down opposite and watched Pepe finger the battered shell of his face, checking the anchoring of front teeth between index knuckle and the pad of his thumb.

That would have given me no pleasure, said the large man before unzipping his jacket and reaching inside. Against the quilted orange lining Pepe saw the black sheath of a bowie knife and for one stuck-limbed moment waited for the blade to emerge—but the large man's hand came out holding only his wallet and an etched leather hip flask. He placed the flask by his foot, tilted to rest against his ankle, before opening the wallet and taking out a photo.

I have two girls now.

He held the photo out for Pepe to see, round-faced twins of three or four with plaited hair and dark eyes like hungry mouths. The large man replaced the photo and turned his attention to the flask. He spun off the silver cap and took a long draught, sucking in air through the husks of his teeth when he was finished. He shook his head to settle the singani and then poured a second measure into the cap which he emptied onto the rubbles of earth. Pepe watched it split, the drops scattering like insects amongst the cracks.

Pachamama, the large man said, and then offered out the flask.

I never meant for a strike, said Pepe wincing as he received the flask. *I never thought the others would follow me and the whole fucking mine would close just because I stopped driving.* Pepe slumped back against the rock cradling the flask.

The large man reached into his jacket again and this time pulled out a wad of dollars as thick as a fist. He held the green curve of bills out at arm's length between forefinger and thumb so Pepe could take in their full weight. Under the heft of notes Pepe saw a familiar sight jutting out, the bulbous pod of a truncated middle finger round and smooth as a stone.

This is what I was paid to deliver my message, the large man said.

With a cruel and deliberate slowness, he licked first his thumb and then his forefinger, peeling off just under half the bundle and throwing it down so it landed just in front of Pepe with a dusty whump. The rest he returned to his jacket.

I'll pay your family's assurances myself. No child should risk their father every time he leaves for work.

Pepe stared at the money but said nothing, instead tracing out the raised detailing on the hip flask with his thumb. With a deliberate slowness of his own he lifted the flask to his mouth and pointed his chin skyward, throat bobbing as he swallowed. He screwed his eyes shut until he felt the brandy heat his oesophagus, wiped his mouth with a wrist and re-threaded the sliver lid. The large man rolled his eyes.

Leave it for the mountain then, if you'd prefer. God knows we take enough from her. But either way, you drive that train tomorrow. Then he shrugged and stood up from the boulder, fixing to leave.

I hoped for better, Pepe said at last. *That was my mistake.*

The large man re-zipped his jacket and sank his chin back down into his collar. *It's no mistake to hope for better,* he said, *only to expect it.*

Pepe drew his knees under his chin and wrapped his arms around his shins. He buried his head into his lap and was still a moment, but then began shaking. Gurgles of laughter trickled out of him and the large man looked down, bemused. Then Pepe's laughter subsided until the air was as still as salt. He looked up.

Tell me one thing before you go, Eduardo.

The large man nodded. *Okay,* he said, *one thing.*

Then tell me this. When the mine's closed the economy suffers. But when it's open we suffer. So why is it we're we not the economy too?

The large man split a ragged smile. Now it was his turn to laugh, the coarse brays of a heavy smoker.

That one's easy, Pepe. It's because we're miners. The economy? His arm cut a wide swathe across the blue-domed horizon. *Who the fuck knows. That's out there somewhere.* He gave Pepe another splintering smile. *You can keep the brandy,* he said and turned on his heel, crunching over the rocks as he picked his way back through the frozen locomotives.

Pepe told the barman that he sat alone for a long time after that, said he drank in sips, staring at the fold of dollars lying on the stones as bloated as a goitre. Then he said he got up and went home, leaving the money festering in the mountain dirt.

At least that's what Pepe said.

Rough Spain

Catherine Talbot

Out past Alicante airport rising from ochre flatland a
billboard instructs 'Smile You Are in Spain'. Ray smiles,
he can't help it. Every summer the same. His rental Fiesta
is small and cramped, but at least it's white. He has read
somewhere that white is a safe colour.

Beautiful Spain, ready to settle him, to warm his sun-
greedy face to banish from memory his recent DIY fiasco—
the sheet of MDF falling on his foot, his toenail turning
blue, then black. Beautiful Spain, lulling him into believing
that the heat of the Spanish sun will dry out the blood that
has gathered underneath.

A most precious place, where he can swim in tepid water
just before nine in the evening, when the sea takes on a
shade of blackness and he gets a slight thrill worrying about
living things, like small harmless Spanish sharks that he
cannot see. Where he can envy the fishermen as they set
up for the evening, their tins of sardines and their modest
beers, their grass, their packets of deep-fried corn and their
empanadillas, filled with tuna and tomato or morcilla that he
is quite partial to—the Spanish pudding that has a different,
more slimy consistency than the Irish offering, speckled

with barley. The full darkness will come quickly and he will not think of his toenail at all. The feeling that there is something almost enviable about the social behaviour of the Spanish man. The cadence of voices of the fishermen going on late into the evening, how he wishes he could join them.

He knows the roads well, can handle the roundabouts, to give way to the left, to shirk in his seat as large trucks pass him by. To not show fear. Molly has warned him that she will not get behind the wheel. He will be doing all the driving. It seems a waste, considering she doesn't drink.

And he is determined to have a good time.

There's an exotic heat in the Fiesta, one that he'll get used to. Molly is figuring out the air conditioning and the radio. It would be nice to listen to euphoric music, something from Elbow maybe. He loves their orchestral stuff. Feels like they could go on forever and that he wouldn't care. Terrible Spanish chart music is what he gets. He looks at Molly and notices that her face is pale as she hums along to the radio. Bleached to him. Washed out. As if she's sick. A sick girlfriend on holiday isn't ideal.

In the afternoon Ray suggests the boat club for lunch because he goes there on the first day of his holiday every year. This year will be no different. As they walk along the paseo Molly looks even paler than before, now that she is actually out in the Spanish sun, but this can be easily explained by contrast—the Irish, wan beside the Spanish.

At the club they sit on white plastic chairs at an outside

table overlooking the magnificent yachts and the RIBS and the motor boats and wait for their drinks. There's a red plastic ashtray on the table and he tries not to think about having a cigarette. The dress code is casual. A waiter brings him an ice cold beer and Molly a Coke and they drink quickly the way children do conspiring to get a second fizzy drink in before their meal arrives. The waiter places the menu on the table and talks about the lunch special—pork stew with apricots. He has a way of talking with his hands that makes Ray stare at him and think about words like animation, sallowness and fluidity.

Ray opens the menu that reminds him of the dissertation he sweated over in college. He gives the pork special some thought as he reads. He can smell fish being fried in scorching olive oil from the kitchen and the pork is forgotten. He talks about the burning point of olive oil and how it isn't ideal to use at high temperatures as it smokes more easily than other oils, say sunflower or vegetable, and yet the Spanish use it regardless.

Molly sits leaning towards him listening, just listening. He asks her if she feels okay because she's quiet and still pale and she tells him that she has a headache and to stop going on about it. He asks her again—this time he phrases it differently, he says 'how's the pain?' and she says that it hasn't changed much, that it's still there but perhaps not as acutely as before. He talks about the physical presence of headaches and how it can make you want to vomit. He talks about his childhood migraines and how he couldn't stand the winter light and she says that she feels the same way about the sun. And he remarks that he is curious as to why she would agree to come to Spain with him knowing that the sunlight would affect her in this way. She tells him that she hadn't thought about it and assures him that she will be fine and that they should order lunch.

Will we try the shark? he asks.

The look as if he is suggesting that they eat a rotten carcass.

Jesus Christ, Ray. Next thing, you'll be forcing me to eat miniature battered fish, their eyes, guts, their very innards, she says.

He decides that he doesn't give a fuck what she thinks and he orders the fried fish for two.

He doesn't tell her that the fish is shark.

He spends the day showing her around and settling her into the apartment that's been in his family forever. Molly reads a copy of *Vogue* that she bought at Dublin airport and he sits down on the wicker chair, a cold beer in his hands. There is a certain satisfaction in simplicity. His old copies of the *Hardy Boys* series lean slightly to the left on the shelf in the living area. He pulls them out one by one and rubs a layer of dust from their tops. Dust that seems welcome and warm and friendly to him and he's unsure how the presence of dust can do that. The shelf was covered in laminate with a fleur-de-lis pattern a long time ago by his mother who had assured him when he was a kid that it was fashionable. He's aware that he's free to change it now. She won't know any different with all that soil on her head in Deans Grange Cemetery, but he doesn't feel that it would be right.

Later on he tells Molly that he is going to the bar by the pollo asado place to get Wi-Fi. The waft of the chicken as it turns slowly on spits isn't something to miss. The place is normally full of grown men and women with chicken oil on their chins as if proving that greediness cannot be reserved solely for children. Molly tells him that she's ready and grabs her handbag. Her face falls a little as he explains to her in his offhand way, developed as a child, that he'd prefer to go out alone for a while, he needs a bit of space, that he usually spends time on his own on the first night. He tells her that he'll be back to take her out to dinner. People eat so late in Spain he assures her.

A mosquito buzzes about her face as he speaks. It seems to be clinging to her, adhering to her scent. She wears Trésor. Ray stretches his arms towards her as if to suggest an embrace —the perfect hasta luego hug. She leans towards him believing that he's trying to touch her but he doesn't follow through. When he says goodbye it's as if he is extracting himself from her hurt.

A bit of time alone. Plenty of time for embraces. But for now his haven, Bar Javier: the bar with Wi-Fi and girls. Girls that are full of life. Pretty waitresses too.

He takes a seat outside the bar and he asks a waitress for

a Martini Rosso and he makes sure that he smiles as he says *por favour* because she is pretty fine. Across the inland sea of the Mar Menor the long narrow isthmus of La Manga is bathed in late evening sunlight glinting on the high rises and the rest of it. There's a promise of churros in the air.

The martini arrives in a tall, thin glass overloaded with conical-shaped ice. The pleasure. Ray laughs at the price, takes a good swig. The heat of the evening intensifying, his hand glides down the glass, a wet mark on the glass and on the table. A small bowl of toasted almonds in their skins placed next to the glass. It's perfect. He eats them slowly, sucking the gritty sea salt off each one.

He opens his laptop. He deletes all the circular emails from the tennis club that he left almost a year ago. He nearly misses a request from his agent Kieran to write a colour piece while he's on holiday. He begins to work on a physical account of the area, describing the smells and the heat and the way the sand on the beach is lighter and less grainy than in Ireland. He's a long way away from being homesick. He doesn't write about groceries—how they are much cheaper in Spain, deliberately doesn't mention the price of a beer because it's predictable and he doesn't want to be predictable. He uses bullet points to get down as many initial ideas as he can and he promises himself that he will work out how to expand them into something decent later. This is one of the thrills of being a journalist. He drains the martini.

He orders a beer. Scooters whizz by. Children pull at

mothers' arms demanding ice cream while mothers struggle to open up fresh packets of cigarettes. Everybody smokes. This fact stops his guilt. His feet are uncomfortable in his moccasins, the skin feeling thinner than normal from the heat, and his black toenail is on his mind.

He thinks of Molly and how he didn't tell her that he ordered shark at lunch. His niggling guilt.

And he thinks how he'll go back to the apartment soon.

Some children play on the metal swings on the beach. People still move in and out of the water, the Spanish women slowly, as if they're in no rush to go anywhere. Content to stand around and chat to one another, they don't ever seem to actually swim. Ray enjoys listening to their gasps of astonishment at the temperature of the water as they scoop palmfuls, splashing their arms and their shoulders. He imagines them in the Irish Sea or the Atlantic. Spanish women screaming in icy waters.

The number of palm trees on the paseo has been significantly reduced in a year. Once the red palm weevil has got its hold, everything is too late. A sort of silent damage and the trees that are not completely dead have produced dates that are turgid and wrinkled. Somebody should do something. Ray looks away, tired of Spanish complacency.

Glasses clink. Children shout. His arms are bare and he looks at them for a moment. His chest is heavy already from smoking harsh Spanish cigarettes. He kind of figures this feeling is worth the low price. A sudden wish for rain passes.

The almonds are almost gone, he chokes on the last one. The waitress tries to help but he does his manoeuvre on his own. He doesn't want to appear completely helpless in front of her because she has a very nice arse. On the paseo a boy hits his dog. The action is violent, he repeatedly swoops at the animal. The boy says para, para with each strike. But nothing stops, not the dog and not the boy.

He'd worried about bringing Molly to Spain. How she might change his feelings about the place, his memories. She'd made it clear that she didn't want to mix with the people that he knows here, friends from his childhood summers. He wouldn't mind bumping into Miguel or Alejandro, in fact he would love to see either one of them. They still keep in touch, they know the dates he comes to Spain, always the same, the first two weeks in August when the weather is sometimes beautiful in Ireland and sometimes not so beautiful.

He becomes slightly nostalgic and wishes with a heightened passion one feels when consuming alcohol that either one or both of his friends might by some chance appear. That they will sit with him and drink cañas until the magnificent deep orange sun drops from the sky in one fell Spanish swoop and the blackness of the night comes in and they are told by the waiters that it's last orders. And the waiters will allow them to finish their last drinks in peace while they stack the plastic chairs into the corner of the outside eating area by the cigarette machine. And then finally the waiters will say that the night is over, their tone jocular and Ray will fall home happy.

They are not coming.

Miguel and Alejandro are not coming.

He begins to feel peckish and he orders mussels because he wants to. Molly's probably not that hungry in any case after their lunch. He remembers that she had a Crema Catalana for dessert. He orders minute squid—chipirones. He can't resist small bits of seafood, heads intact, scorched in fried oils. He eats as much as he can and then he smokes because there is no one to stop him, because she is not here to deny him his small pleasures. He has his fill of beer. He switches back to martini, the sweet and cloying heaviness of it. It hits his throat as it is meant to, fiery. Molly doesn't really drink because she worries about her figure.

Molly has a nice body. His hands have been all over it. He has felt keenly how quickly it responds to his touch. It is laughable. She is incapable of holding out. A fast physical mess in front of him as though offering herself to him, alone. A cut of meat and him her butcher. This is their sex. She has a varicose vein. It will throb mindlessly in the glare of the sun, the heat will bring it to life. He is vaguely repulsed by the sight of it. She will attempt to cover it with a sarong, he will tell her to let it be.

He looks over to the boy still loitering by the wall. The front of his hair is dyed straw-yellow with toilet bleach, he has dark-leathered skin. There is a stain on the crotch of his shorts.

Quieres otro? the waitress asks.

Sí, he replies.

He drains the long glass and sucks an ice cube until his lips hurt.

Señor, uno otro? the pretty waitress asks him. She has a tattoo on her wrist—a twisted mean-looking snake.

The music is louder than before and so he has to shout, Caña por favor.

Vale, she says and by God is she attractive.

It arrives promptly this last drink. He doesn't need it and yet he welcomes it. Craves it, the salty-sweetness. He looks at his arms, in a matter of days he will bronze deeply. The moon is orange and full, polluted magnificently, blurry with the dust of the arid landscape. The moon and his body. Goodnight moon. Sleep tight moon. The waitress empties his ashtray and she smiles at him. She has a little golden ring on her lower lip which she is able to manoeuvre easily, elegantly. He is in some flush of happiness. Molly and their dinner plans are clearly scuppered. He pushes the promise of duty away from him. Spontaneity his new friend but he must remember to bring his laptop home with him.

He rouses and tries to work out where he is. The girl in bed beside him murmurs something in her sleep, cryptic soft Spanish. A blue T-shirt with Bar Javier printed on it hangs from a brittle cane chair beside the bed. An empty bottle of

Luzón on the floor, crushed-twisted empty cigarette packets, fuma mata warnings strewn about as if untidy picnickers had unthinkingly left their litter behind. A cockroach scuttles by a rum bottle. He holds down bile, recalls that a cockroach can live for a number of days after its head has been chopped off. Coagulated spittle, he spits it into his palm, a minute speck of blood in it. Any amount is too much. The place is stuffy, a basement apartment. Wrought iron bars on the outside window, a withered basil plant on the windowsill. An acrid smell of failure in the room. Let there be sun. The TV flickers in the bedroom. The springs in the mattress dig into his back.

He touches the sleeping figure beside him gently. He leans into her face and feels a sweet and warm breath on his face, her breasts move through her inhalations. They appear small, most of the flesh is spread out and lost to the sides of her body. A bizarre phenomenon. Two mosquito bites on her tanned shoulders. Juice on the sheets.

On the floor beside him a loosely knotted condom, a torn foil wrapper.

He looks at the TV. A train crash in Madrid. Blood-soaked staunch emergency workers clawing through the twisted steel wreckage. Severed limbs. The veritable grimmest of work carried out in excruciating temperatures. Bodies rotting expeditiously. Fragments of limbs, ripped-apart flesh and sol. The reporter's dress is a deep red—scarlet—and it is somehow inappropriate for the occasion, as if it is mocking the passengers covered in blood.

And the dead.

His mouth rancid, he props himself up bearing the brunt of his weight on his right arm and tries to recall her name. He only knows her as his bar girl from the night before. She continues to sleep despite the TV, he names her Esmé. He searches the floor for his boxers. His movements wake her.

She smiles at him and asks, Desayuno?

Sí, he answers.

He locks his eyes on to her. She makes her way to the small breakfast bar and he follows her with a gait of shame. She chops tomatoes into small pieces and she spreads them onto toast and the tomato juice soaks into the bread. She pours a fair amount of olive oil and a pinch of salt on the tomato. Olive oil tastes different in Spain. The saline and the coffee bring him to life. For this he thanks her. He chews thoughtfully looking around the cramped place. A pile of children's toys are skewed in a corner of the living space but he sees no sign of a child.

He's not here, Pablo, he's at his father's, she says as if she can read his mind.

Oh, you have a son, that's great, muy bien.

She wears sky-blue shorts with white polka dots and she tells him that her son is six and that he's a wonderful child and Ray doesn't care. He doesn't want to listen to a woman telling him how good her child is at any time and not at this time because he's deteriorating and his head is developing a steady throb. He's dreading the sunshine outside. A T-shirt corsets her stomach. There's a touch more girth on her than he remembers from the night before. A Spanish hangover. Hard to know if there is any worse kind. The heat exaggerating every symptom. She moves to him.

Toca, aqui, she pulls his hand to her face. Touch me.

He touches her face, her lips. It is only then that he thinks about Molly.

Más pan con tomate? Café? she asks.

Sí, he says.

She gets to work. Refills the silver coffee maker with Mesclas coffee. Aromatic air. Coffee smells different in Spain.

They fuck—up against the fridge a delicious sexual-balancing act. When he comes alphabet magnets dig into his back.

It's for you, this holiday. Everything is always for you. Will you let me in, Molly, for fuck's sake?

The door is shut fast. He has a key but it won't work. She has placed a barricade behind it. She has locked herself in and him out. He hammers on the door until she opens it.

I waited for you, she says.

Things got away from me. That's all.

I made breakfast. She points to the table on the balcony.

He isn't hungry but he takes a croissant. His mouth is dry from booze and the croissant is cloying on the roof of his mouth. Molly is sulking with each morsel he takes.

They are due to leave Spain in thirteen days.

I bumped into Miguel and Alejandro, we had a lot to catch up on and I crashed at Miguel's place. We got pissed and I forgot all about dinner with you. Miguel sends his best.

He doesn't know me.

He knows about you. I've told him about you.

A flicker of a smile, it might be enough. He's pretty sure that she believes him despite the fact that no man would ever send his regards to a friend's girlfriend. They play Uno in the afternoon like a pair of kids hiding in the shade. They swim together. He lifts her up in the air in the water like a synchronised swimmer and she laughs and it is beautiful for an instant out there in the calmness of the azure blue waters. And in this moment they are happy and he senses forgiveness. Her smudged mascara is heroin-cool on her cheekbones. She is fluorescent. Beautiful. He is charmed and the small white jellyfish with the purple centres don't cause him any angst.

This his game. He is careful with her all day long and well into the early evening. He fixes her a Coke with extra ice the way she likes it. He sips beer alongside her. The balcony is cramped what with his legs and the rest of it but it's the sort of place that doesn't feel inadequate if two people are happy. She allows him to hold her hand, but briefly and loosely and under the table and he swears that she's prettier when she's not angry.

She was rarely angry before. So pretty the day he met her. Two years ago. She wears the same T-shirt now that she did then. It was mild and humid for a day in November in Stephen's Green Park for that is the beauty of November— its unexpected warmth. She was hunkered down not feeding the ducks but looking at them as if she was trying to read their thoughts. She seemed completely lost in a world of her own and in a way he almost felt bad for taking her from it. He wondered stupidly if ducks had any thoughts of their own and it occurred to him it was something he could investigate, but not immediately, not just then. Lovers were perched on park benches, their hands held together in silence. There were scant children about, it was the wrong time of year. He brought Molly for a sandwich in a pub and they both chose tuna. It was a strange thing to eat on a first meeting. She went back to her work in the Graphic Studio Gallery crammed full of prints by Irish hopefuls who thought that life was for the taking.

He'd missed this. Climbing back into the safety of a cosy bed after his weekend morning run. The comfort of placing his legs under the warm duvet. The muffled noise from the M50, droves of people ferrying kids up to Carrickmines shopping centre. The insanity of unnecessary consumerism, it never leaves some people. Friends compliment him on having a lovely home. This in itself encourages him to be happy because he agrees with them and he has bought everything that he needs for it. Molly comes into the bedroom and he continues to read a copy of *El Mundo* that he has brought home from Spain.

Ray, I was just thinking, she says.

He is quiet, she's always thinking.

Children, Ray, do you want a child?

An image of the condom wrapper in the apartment in Spain.

Penetration performed. The verdict.

Chewing parsley after eating garlic, rubbish times.

I don't know, he says.

She asks him if he heard about the poor children slaughtered by their own father in Shankhill. He asks her why she wastes her time with tragedy. She tells him that she cannot help it. She wants to know why he's looking at her strangely. He mocks her, for her disaster stance, her poised back. He tells her that it demeans her and she asks him about his writing.

They'll take me on, couple of stories here and there, just for now.

That's great, she says.

He reaches out to touch his CDs stacked at an angle.

Why do you bother with CDs?

He doesn't answer her.

He writes mainly in their bedroom now—stories,

reviews about interior design, trends, and oddments. Molly brings in most of the money to the house. This causes him pain but it is moderate. He often falls asleep over his stories in much the same way that he falls into an old person's coma as soon as they begin to watch a film together. At night he stops writing to go for a piss, washes his teeth and then reads in bed. His slumber is light as though he is an old man suffering from insomnia, with a fuzzy head on him in the morning time.

Coffee helps. Breath, breathing uncomfortable after an uncomfortable night. Dreams turning into nightmares, her requests to go back to Spain, to have a child. An immense tiredness feels like it's climbing into the socket of his eyes. In the garden a warmth a gentle breeze on his collarbone, memories of Esmé, memories of his lost toenail.

The editor of the magazine changes words like less strong to weaker in the edits of the first story he agrees to publish. Ray doesn't mind, not really. His lips benefit from the strawberry balm he places on them while he thinks what to write. He goes into the kitchen and looks at Molly's collection of herbs on the windowsill—sorrel, sage and basil. Noise from the television in the sitting room, he inhales the scent of pastry baking in the oven.

Esmé, her warmth and her clinging to him. He cannot remember how he knotted the condom after he pulled out. Esmé's child Pablo; he recalls now that Pablo was spelled out in the magnetic alphabet letters on the fridge. Memories of

Spain. On Sky News, reports of a crazy woman sacrificing her child on the steps of the altar in a church in Elche.

He never wants to have a child.

Molly flicks channels with the remote control and settles on a repeat of *Location Location Location*.

Do you have to watch that? Those people are deeply uninteresting. Look at them. Walking about in Barbour jackets as if buying up London is entertainment.

He goes upstairs to their bedroom to write a story based loosely around the pointlessness of the property market. Instead he finds himself staring at the map of Alicante that he has pinned to the wall.

Highgate

Ian Green

They stand separate in front of Marx's tomb, mud-stained boots static on slick stone. Standing close, but—taut, too new to each other to know what is right, unsure what distance is safe. WORKERS OF ALL LANDS UNITE, writ large in gold beneath an imperious brow, a bellicose beard, a philosopher's unkempt mane. Cameron looks at the graves encircling the main event, the apostles of the apostate, pretends to read names, and runs his thumbs across his fingers in his pocket nervously, and he bites his cheek, and he tries not to stare at her. He wants nothing more than all that she is, but it's too soon. Hannah sways in the breeze and gazes into stone eyes. Thin trees devoid of leaf or life strain against the wind and high above them the sky churns.

'They used to paint the eyes,' he says, 'on old statues. Like Michelangelo's David, the Elgin Marbles, you know? That's why there's no pupil or iris carved on. They would paint the eyes. All the rest of it too, I think. I mean, this is more recent obviously. So I don't know why the eyes are like that. Maybe it's a thing.'

Hannah looks at him impenetrably and he feels his cheeks flush. She checks her watch.

'It's time,' she says, and smiles.

They leave Karl with a brief salute each and together exit the East Cemetery and cross the narrow road, join the short queue. It is the first tour of the day. As they wait he is trying to memorise the way she stands, the way her hair falls across her face. A small man drowning in a wax jacket and dense jumper takes their money and lets them through the wooden doors and into heaven. After five minutes he closes the gateway and seals them all in. There are six other people on the tour, but Cameron notices nothing about them; he is too busy noticing everything about Hannah.

As his eyes flit from hair to feet to hands to legs to eyes to smile he fingers a hole in the sleeve of his jumper, thick black wool, and tries to think of something to say, anything about anything but the long-dead Left. Last night he slept on her floor, this morning they drank black coffee and talked about black coffee.

Before then, she passed him by.

He lacked the vocabulary to engage with her. Dialectical materialism and *Das Kapital* were words in a foreign tongue; economics was witchcraft; political theory so much white noise. He went to the meetings because he knew she went to the meetings, and listening to her voice was like listening to Duke Ellington. He had no idea what any of it meant, but it made his heart pump sunshine. He would sit at the back with his more militant friends and close his eyes and listen to everything she said and understand none of it. Her voice was water over rocks. Until, until; last night there was the pub and luck and chance and fate and they ended sat in her room, taking turns choosing songs to play through her old computer. It was Lenin & Stalin during Lennon and McCartney, but when he put on Paul Simon's 'You can call me Al' she smiled beatifically and said 'I love this song,' and stopped talking about Trotsky, about action, about Brecht, about unions. She slipped off her Doc Martens and they spoke properly and when she thought he wasn't looking she pretended to play the drums.

She said, when the song finished, 'I just wish everyone wasn't so serious. I miss dancing, just dancing and not thinking and not having to think about everything.'

She said, when the second wine bottle was empty, 'Sometimes I don't know what I'm doing. Everyone I know spends their time finding ways, finding philosophies, finding methods to look at the world, to understand it. I don't just want to understand it. I don't know if you can understand it. I'm sick of arguing. I want to *do* something.'

She said, as the skies grew light and she pulled on a jumper, 'Do you know what you want to do? Who you want to be? Isn't that terrifying, to have a philosophy, a truth to live your life by?' As she said that her mouth smiled but her eyes were dark, unknowable.

Now he is biting his cheek and trying to think of something to say. Last night he slept on her floor, her jacket folded under his head. It smelled of old leather and perfume.

Last night he slept on her floor and this morning they drank black coffee and spoke about black coffee, about food about France about travel about croissants. He could not bear for it to end—and so, to Highgate. The cemetery is his place in London, sealed behind high walls and guarded by immortal historians. For a fee they would admit the congregation, they would lead you through the forest and tell stories, list facts, point out the oddities amidst the crypts. Here was the owner of the menagerie with a lion atop his tomb, here the bare-knuckle boxer guarded by his faithful hound. They would explain the symbology of death, angels and urns and pillars, heads down, heads up, palms raised; the fashions and fads of tragedy.

This is not why Cameron comes to Highgate.

Years of neglect has admitted the chaos of life, each tomb entwined and snared in greenery, all of it connected through grave and sepulchre and catacomb—a pulsing life, a silent gasp and exhalation amongst the decay. The cemetery is home to a green beast made of tree and bush and vine and creeper, an amalgam of limbs and roots and shoots that permeates everything. Cameron comes to Highgate to see humanity's works undone.

It is winter now. The beast sleeps; he cannot think what to say.

They walk slowly behind the group and do not listen to the guide, do not look at the other patrons. High above them the sky is full, the clouds fighting for position, charred

Titans warring in the heavens. Cameron points out where the ivy has broken stone, where roots push through brick. He loves this intervention, but he cannot articulate it. Hannah points out a squirrel, a robin. He is hungry but he does not say anything about that. He watches her mouth as she reads the names of the dead. They are surveyed by endless eyes, marble angels and whorls in tree trunks scrutinising every movement.

'Do you think everywhere will be like this one day?' he asks, and he means it as a joke. The next time the group stops she stands a little closer. Separately and in unison their stomachs quietly grumble, their bodies harmonising discontent.

In the cold of the catacombs she stands on her toes and leans up to his ear and quietly says, 'This was a really good idea, thank you.' Her breath is hot in his ear. He needs to say something, something perfect, something to make her realise what he is and what she is and what they could be. Last night he slept on her floor, but that could be an ending. He needs to say something. The miracle that pervades each inch of the place is subdued by the season brown branch bones climbing high over their scattered flesh, green turned to gold turned to brown—and he draws strength from the frailty of all of it. He needs to say something, but their vocabularies barely overlap.

He opens his mouth to say: *Mankind will not be free until the last king is hung with the entrails of the last priest.*

Or maybe: *The philosophers have only interpreted the world in various ways—the point however is to change it.*

Thankfully he doesn't say either of those lines.

High above them, a prelude to thunder whispers amidst the clouds. Cameron closes his mouth and shakes his head, watches her watch the sky and grips the ends of his sleeves, flexes fingers against fabric. He starts humming 'So Long, Frank Lloyd Wright'. Each footstep is precious as they tread towards the ending of the tour, the ending of the moment. Each instant is a chance to say the right thing, and all around them the trees murmur and moan as the wind finds strength. Cameron turns to her and she smiles, and he cannot find a phrase to explain his love for the place. They are by the gates. High above, amidst the tempest, the tension is too much.

In a moment the world is water, turgid heavy drops bombarding. Their guide opens the gates and before she can say anything or hesitate in shelter Cameron grabs Hannah's hand and he smiles.

'Come on,' he says, and they run into the park. The rain is unstoppable now and already there are rivulets running down the path, off the grass. The world has been waiting for this and it exults. The horizon is lost in water as they run up the hill to a tree, and there they sit, wet and cold and scarcely sheltered. Hannah opens her mouth to speak, but she doesn't say anything.

All around them the world is drowning—but he is still

holding her hand. High above them, the thunder rolls on and on and on.

Burn

Mandy Taggart

Midsummer Night, and not the Shakespearean kind. At the final dropping of darkness Billy McLaughlin sprawled face down on the wooden deck of the bridge in Donnelly's Park, whilst yahoos of the borough stumbled and roared their way homeward up to the Heights. Beneath him slid the spumy burn, less of a meander than an invitation to drown yourself.

A sour, leaking, handful of a place was Donnelly's Park, cupped within the foggiest and most sodden hollow of town. Founded by a local unworthy a century ago, it was formerly the ditch beneath beleaguered ramparts, still earlier a ferny basin of pagan repute.

Billy was thirty, by now fully adept in the reverse miracle of turning wine into water. Six weeks later he would be obituarised in the *Herald* as a *well-known local character*: a dignified term for being mocked by children for chanting to yourself and spinning twigs into the burn. An old-fashioned drinker, whilst his contemporaries had raved from glue to speed and on to prison, or else mortgages and decency. Now, with trousers soaked and his cheek stubble scrippling slime, he paid mind to rare wisdom from his mother. Maurie, solid-armed, bitter, widowed at forty-two.

'Once you're on your arse,' she said, in his head, 'you'll never rise again. Not till you've taken stock of what put you down there in the first place.' Maurie herself had been put down by a joiner's van before she'd seen fifty.

Billy took stock. On the bridge deck there brooded a unique species of mouldering slime, composed of trodden dogshit, green algae, extrusions of slug, the piss of man, bird and beast. The only grade of grip presented to boots and tottery heels was in the narrowness of the planks: a tickering under pram wheels, a trip-trap under the feet. It was the best sport in town during those three wilderness years that hang between earnestness and irony in the deployment of council play equipment. The children had it polished to a lethal shine.

He'd hit the bridge at a reel, scoring a calligraphic gouge across the slime. Had narrowly missed clanking the railings with his forehead, or sliding between them into the scum and beckoning water weeds. He was nearly skinny enough.

But he didn't find it unpleasant, in that state of drink where the chill was welcome, the slime velvet and intimate. The bridge lay tender under his cheek, arched like a stretching animal. You could nearly hear the groan out of it. The stench in his nostrils was closer to the sea than he'd been in a while.

Billy grimaced. He put out his tongue and stroked it along the deck in front of him, tasting Buckfast and primordial swamp. He'd once spent an August night on the grass not far from here, beneath the syphilitic ash locally dubbed Baldie's Tree. Fallen asleep with terrible poetry in his soul and woken with the arse eaten off him. He should move. He shifted his hands to shoulder level, took stock a moment longer, then braced to shove himself upright. Spied as he braced a shaft of clear daylight streaming upwards out of the burn, through a chink in the boards three feet ahead of him. The shaft simmered with bitie-flies, ravenous for arses, and around it nothing but the night.

Billy wriggled sealwise towards this phenomenon, caught the twittle of birdsong. At the join of two boards he spied a pale peeled crack the colour of straw, by a stiletto heel that evening freshly split. He spat out slime, fitted his eye against the crack. Was blinded at first, then his sight adjusted.

And then Billy no longer heard the yawl of the yahoos beyond the railings, because he was yawling to beat the lot of them all by himself.

*

The next morning a figure was observed, trolling with intent the burnside in Donnelly's Park, a good three hours before he was usually abroad. Billy couldn't remember how he'd got home, but it had been at speed. He'd lain haunted half the night by the vision. A storybook Devil, with horns, goatish beard and hind legs, had peered up through the crack and beckoned him, whilst litter eddied and caught in its dingy black tailcoat.

Now, by the burnside, with the folded-knee look of a skinny man, Billy brooded. On the grass where the bridge base met the bank he frowned through the barrier into the weedy darkness where the burn disappeared. Three weeks' beard on him. A wee cap and fishing rod would have set him off rightly.

Yonder slime was powerful stuff, if it had you seeing the Devil. He'd make his fortune, if he could find the knack of it. The yahoos would love it. Trip of a lifetime, boys. Have yis swinging your pants in no time.

He'd have been up there harvesting already, if it hadn't been for a childed young pair casting themselves into some fuck-perfect little scene, flicking twigs over the railings, skittering across to watch them spin away. Performing for each other whilst the child lolled dribbling in a buggy, more interested in mulching its mouth around the sleeve of its cardigan.

The child began fretting and the couple flung a final twig, dragged back to reality. The woman fussed with the buggy straps. Billy stood, feeling last night's drink churn inside him. Waited while they cleared the deck. Cracked from Baldie's Tree a twig for the scraping, and felt the ground bend under him while he did it.

Up on deck he knelt and keeked again through the crack, but saw only the pitch and shimmer of the burn. A passing pair of young fellas dared each other to boot him in the hole.

'Mecca's the other way, Mohammed. Ai-yaai-ahh—'

Fumbled in his pocket now, tugged out the scraping-twig. Billy began scoring it across the beslimed planks, tapping the scrapings into his palm again and again until he'd curled off a hearty amount. There was the job. He took a lavish lick along his hand, felt himself change as the salty slime melted over his teeth.

★

He is himself, at three. A wee snot of a thing, stupid navy woollen coat on him. On the grassy slope, a girl with trailing hair straddles a pair of lazy denim legs. His chin is rashy under the coat, too warm and heavy for this weather. A slope for rolling down. Tumble and bump and over and under, grass and sky and daisies and sky, until he drops half a foot and is suddenly engulfed, cold closing over the crown of his head. One more vast turn underwater with thunder in his ears, and then no up and no down for long seconds, until his feet find purchase and he heaves himself to a miraculous, dripping stand.

'Ma.'

It creeps out as a weak whisper. Parked on a bench at the head of the slope, Maurie uncrosses her legs, tighted calves swishing one over the other. Turns a page of the *Herald* that riffles in the breeze and feels up her forearm for sunburn.

The current threatens his balance, forces him sideways,

water weed lascivious on the backs of his knees. Immobile in his wrappings like a comedy baby: the coat has taken on half the burn. On flattened ground halfway up the slope, the old roundabout shudders around with nobody on it. Alongside him the underparts of the bridge loom and ooze, cold as a bat cave. He spits bitter burnwater, struggles to wade. Turns helplessly with the driving current, losing his feet now. And under the bridge he sees the goaty Devil.

The Devil winks, and points one fingernail up the slope towards Billy's useless Ma. Billy finds his voice. Opens his mouth and howls until the long-haired girl leaps off her boy and charges, screaming, towards him.

He rises from the burn as if baptised.

*

The vision dispersed. Billy took his twig and flung it into the burn, still licking around the inside of his mouth. Felt within himself other visions loosen beneath the clag and silt that covered them.

Fortune or not, he wouldn't be wasting this one on the yahoos, that was for sure. Billy crouched a good while longer on the bridge, and the burn flushed on.

*

This whole valley was about the drainage of land, the burn a glorified ditch like all watercourses from Donnelly's Park to the Nile Delta. Trickle or surge it had run since prehistory, down from the boglands where people lay disappeared in ditches, gathering as it went bone and seep from the Mount, sharded delft patterned with fragmented flowers. Dregging down what it lacked the strength to carry forward. Sending up vapours, drinking them back, steaming them upwards again. Here and there along its flatter courses it was dammed, long ago, into dank pools for the retting of flax. All abandoned afterwards, to lurk behind the fences of low-lying householders and threaten them in wet weather.

They dredged it when Billy was eight, hauling up trolleys, putrid trainers, weighted sacks of tiny, feline skeletons. One day a rusted bicycle lay on the bank, one pedal up and one down, as if an invisible man were bracing his foot to ride.

'There's the water cycle,' said Maurie, who'd been educated.

'What's that mean?'

'Carry this.'

From between her fingers he took the plastic fishmonger's bag, cold with trout skin.

Three miles down from Donnelly's Bridge the burn joined the main trunk river and within it powered ahead. Through the flood barriers out to the estuary, where tourists laughed and pointed at an otter ripping the head off a salmon at the crossing of two waters.

★

Fit for work. It was a fucking joke. But that was how it went now, with diseases of the mind. It had been a bitter morning. Billy kicked and swore his way up the street, took malevolent joy in shattering the puddles that lay glaring like fallen angels at the sky that had flung them out. He cut across the railway line, doubled back through Donnelly's Park. It was where he'd always been headed.

No denim-clad courting here these days, if you didn't count the two Jack Russells riding each other up by the roundabout. Earthworks performed for the Centenary had sanitised the place, shallowed the slope, barred the banks to stop any more untended woolly eejits flinging themselves in. The shrubby ground at the head of the slope was gentrified now by pergolas and trailing foliage. Wedding couples sometimes came to have their photographs taken. There was another fucking joke. This hollow had never been any place for weddings, unless it was over the brush you were going.

To delay the pleasure, he broke off a twig, let himself feel the crack and peel of it. Turned and examined it, nubbed and grey. Ash trees drop their summer twigs already brittle. In winter there would be blown keys from Baldie's Tree; in spring, rotted florets that Billy had thought were broccoli for years. And in October a giant fungal growth, dark and bulbous, big as a head, would bob in the central fork.

Billy retched. He tossed the twig into the water, imagined

a grey hand that rose and plucked it away with the grace of an Arthurian illustration. The Gentleman of the Burn. He inclined his head at the receding fingers.

A stone smacked him on the leg. A skitter of bastards from the Heights whooped and clattered away. Only wee ones today, and Billy ignored them. He could put it off no longer. He climbed to the bridge deck, scraped with fingernail and sucked.

A whiff of burn stink from under the bridge, blood and sulphur. The clouds separated. Light cracked through like the white of an egg.

★

Eight or nine. Back seat of the Honda, head heavy with stale smoke. Maurie parks on a double yellow by the park railings and they sit for a grey half-hour, waiting for Da.

'Can I play in the park?'

'The rain's coming on.'

Half an hour more and Maurie heaves herself out, knots a plastic hood under her chin.

'I'm away to find him.'

'Ma. I need the—'

But she's left, and locked him in. Splatches of wet darken her coat as she stumps away, one shoulder higher than the other.

Water hammers the roof of the Honda, swept-up river

silt and microscopic fossils skittering down the windscreen. To his left, the park railings. He's desperate, kneels up and watches the sky blow sideways to distract himself from thoughts of pee. Louder still the rain, in waves now, while gutters dribble and gulp down by the car wheels. Billy presses his nose and huffs the runnelling window, trying not to think about other things that splatter and flow. He wipes away fog, and in the dark nook of the bridge sees the Devil waving.

His loins spasm. The Devil grins, springs up, unzips and pisses, long and lavishly, a low arc that catches light and plunges deep as water slides over his hairy, goaty knees. Billy can stand it no longer. He seizes the window lever and churns it down. Wriggles his skinny self outside, unzips at the last second and sends pissdrops scattering along the railings while the rain blatters down on his head.

And here comes Maurie at last. Here comes Da. Archibald with a stagger, shamed out of the Forge in front of all his cronies, a brown tweed cap planted flat and furious on his head.

Billy's hauled by the arm and his shorts yanked down. Bare-arsed on soaked concrete with blows raining down on shoulders, legs and back.

'Sorry, Da. I'm sorry!'

The cap falls off Archibald, leaving his head as pink and naked as Billy's arse.

'Filthy wee bastard's what ye are.'

... And then Billy catches a briny taste around his lips. Swallows deep, twists the memory and pulls it around.

'Stop hitting me.'

'What?'

'Stop hitting me. It wasn't my fault. It was *your* fault!'

... The taste fades. He still gets battered, but the blows fall on squared shoulders.

'Sure, that's enough, Archie. That's enough.'

Not Maurie's mercy intervening, but the sight of a traffic warden striding towards them. Billy is bundled into the Honda and they skid away like TV detectives. Receding in the rear window, the Devil shakes off, zips up and blows Billy a kiss.

★

It was gone, and a new sun was evaporating puddles all over town. Back to clouds at last, souls of water rising.

He knew he'd only altered the story, not the truth. But what was the difference, after all? Better to pick and choose what you carried along with you. The kid who spoke up for himself. The lucky boy, springing undrowned from the burn.

★

As July opened, Billy squatted in his fetid living room,

tongue out over a writing pad lifted from the 99p store, striving to render the Devil in splinter-leaded colouring pencils.

'You'll never make an artist,' said Maurie in his head, in the harsh voice she'd developed by the time he was eleven. Gall in her now, sick of Archibald's taste for the devilment.

She was always just coming in when he got home from school, and more and more there was a smell of fish off her. She filled the sink with dull scraped scales, cut tails like halved mermaids flung down for the cat. Slick hinged mussels with insides like the sticky magazines up amongst the bushes in Donnelly's Park.

'The fuck is that?' Archibald poked a thick finger.

'The only thing on offer,' said Maurie.

Upped and slammed out before he could answer, left nothing behind but the flat hanging stink. Billy and Da with their four arms the one length sat stranded at the table.

Archibald fumbled about with the tweed cap, shoulders twitching with the want to be away.

'You're a good boy, son.'

'Am I?'

Cap going on, now. Situation resolved.

'So I know you'll be grand here on your own. Won't you, now?'

The door closed behind him, opened again a second later, the capped head dipping through.

'Clean them fish pans before Mammy gets back.'

Away at the devilment the both of them, leaving Billy up to the red elbows in foulness and grease.

Maurie only left off the fish on the day she was widowed. Screamed in her neighbour's kitchen years later, when a freshly floured trout leapt up in the pan.

★

In the middle of July, the council came and hosed down the bridge, amid dire talk in the *Herald* of broken ankles and litigation. Billy huddled on the bank and prayed to the Devil for dank weather, as flies doted over the burn. Shivered with longing, wept like a poet into the water while the young boys chalked pentagrams under the pergola. Stronger on him even than the pull of drink.

Billy was blessed with smears of green on the seventeenth day. He dropped to his knees and took it, freshly tongued off the spine of a groaning bridge.

★

Fourteen, shuddering, desperate for allies. Gus the razor-scalped leader of the Hellburners takes the measure of Billy, sees him skinny but strong. Gus was a Gary until he took to the mushrooms one fair October night and bit a policeman on the leg. Fungus the Bogeyman ever since. A fast-laughing mania to him, his father a rabid street preacher of brimstone and fire.

Billy comes to him rank from a run across town, after being met by Maurie from school, hauled into a flat above a fish shop and introduced to some trout-mouthed fucker she called his Uncle Ken.

'Fuck that. Where's my da?'

Shrugging off her hand, feeling himself lithe like the young buck in a Western. Forgetting the end of young bucks everywhere.

'Sure I'll be yer da, now.'

His voice like a hand on Maurie, his hand like a fish on her. Steam and stench through the window from the gutters below, where cats growled over slithery innards. She'd brought him to the source. Young buck Billy twisting away from the hands and stink, setting himself for the door. Ken the Literal Motherfucker trying to square up to him.

'You'll stay here.'

'Where's my da?'

'Do what he says, Billy.'

Billy darted his eyes, looking for the gap to dodge through and run away.

… And then licked his teeth, and found a salty tang.

'Make me.'

Saw his face on the level with Ken's. A pike rose and snapped, sudden teeth in the shadows.

'Make me.'

Said it again, just for the sound of it. Drew back his arm

in slow motion and felt the jaw crack under his fist. Saw the admiration in Maurie's face as he turned and stalked away.

★

Billy lay on the deck and roared with satisfaction. Flipped round to his belly and scraped right down the plank with his teeth, nipped and lapped it like a lover.

★

Acne cheeks grin down at him now, more Hellburners slink up from nowhere.

First they all crouch behind the gasworks, where Gus shakes tobacco over leaves of white paper and seasons it with drops of a sharp-scented oil. It is rolled and passed like a sacrament from fingers to fingers. Then Billy with velvet skin and rolling vision stands chin up, feet planted, while Gus whirls a fighting stick over his head. Still as a winter ash he lets it whisk the hairs across his crown. Passes the test.

'Last wee fucker took a whitey,' says Gus.

He's nearly disappointed when the next stage is nothing more than holding his palm over a lighter flame. Lasts well by pretending the hand belongs to somebody else. Gus jerks his chin to show approval.

'Mon tae fuck.'

Away now, just the two of them, a ragged ramble round

the hard shoulder of the ring road telling each other who they'd fuck out of the four McNeill sisters whose knickers hang on the line across the road from school.

'I'll take their ma,' says Billy, and wins a laugh out of Gus.

Scrag end of the year, first ice in the air, a leaking sky, the moon like oil dropped in water. Billy strokes at burn blisters inflating across his palm, tries to still his head. Doing well.

Across the Poorhouse Graveyard Gus tells of the headless horse he met by the gates one night, dragging a cart full of bodies. They stand pissing against the memorial stone, daring the souls of the wretched. On round the back of the hospital, the sudden loom of a digger behind flimsy steel barriers, scramble and hoist into the driver's compartment. Billy closes his eyes and cools his temple against the window, feels the slashing of the seat beside him and lets Gus hear his chuckle of approval. Takes the offered knife and makes three long, incantatory slashes. The heavy rip of vinyl, foam puckering under his raw knuckles.

'Attaboy, Billy. Good man.'

And at last to the head of the slope in Donnelly's Park, where the Hellburners stand waiting. Gus gives his deputies the nod.

'Just one more thing.' Razor-headed smile.

A girl steps forward. Gus's cousin, Leanne with the harelip, reaches wordlessly for the fly of Billy's trousers.

'The fuck?'

He casts about, looking for the trick of it.

'Do you not want it?' Gus with the threat behind the teeth. Trap or not, he's fucked. The childless roundabout creaks and turns.

Gus and his deputies evaporate. The same bravado that stilled his hand over the flame holds Billy now amongst autumn-rotted bushes, twigs rasping his arse and his head roaring, a girl's hair chilled with night sweeping his thighs.

Just as he claws his fingers deep into the muck, Leanne turns and judders away with a scream, leaving him straining forgotten into empty air. He scrabbles at his trousers, lurches up and after her. What the fuck did he do wrong?

He catches her halfway down the hill, grabs her and she wheels round shrieking into his face, a sudden smell of piss off her. Babbling that she looked aside and saw the Devil, jerking like a madman, flailing over the grass with his coat tails flipping.

Billy turns her loose and lets her run. Staggers back and crouches in shadow as Gus and the Hellburners erupt from the bushes and rave down the hill like the blue-arsed hordes of fuckery. Charging after the wails of Leanne, miraculously thinking Billy is chasing her. He croaks to himself as they thunder over the bridge. Clatter and thump of bodies scaling the railings, dropping to the pavement on the far side and raging on, away up into the Heights. And then silence.

A queer one the Devil to be saving your virtue, and if that doesn't sum up Billy's life, nothing ever will.

★

He'd been too caught up in the moment to doctor the memory. Could hardly blame himself, Leanne his one and only time.

So close. Billy whimpered and lapped again the paltry slick of green, scrabbled it like a digging dog. But there wasn't enough. He felt his senses heighten, but the vision was formless as a bag of kittens. He reeled down off the bridge to the bank, scrambled over the barrier, fought his way through knee-high tangle to the chattering lip of the burn. Pitched and splashed his way under the bridge and crouched in gloom where the chattering deepened to a hollow rush as the burn surged riverwards.

Feet clattered above him. Voices, wheels. A twig sailed, dropped and was carried, rocking, past his knees. The childed couple at their games again.

He flailed about for an implement, saw what he needed being borne towards him along the burn. A half-rotted piece of timber, stained in Forest Oak, the remnants of somebody's garden fence. The water carried it straight into his hands. Of course it did. And maybe he saw grey fingers slip from round it as he hauled it out.

He held it caberwise and gave three mighty knocks on the bridge's wooden underside. Heard screams above him, a sudden run of wheels, the trip-trap of retreating shoes.

Billy hugged his knees and rocked under the bridge, laughing like a drain.

★

A black Saturday near the end of July. The rain that had heaved down the whole day had blown out over the coast, leaving the evening stunned and heavy: more to come later.

The bridge was furred lightly, like a coated tongue. Billy came to it with the taste of Buckfast sweet on his lips. Body and blood. They do say a drinker will look for any excuse.

★

With the simmer of slime in his throat he mounts the slope to the bushes, beats about for his bearings, then shuffles around and puts his head as close as he can manage to where Leanne had hers. Bobs his face like an inexpert girl, peering to the left and right. And sees something there indeed, a black and revolving thing, down by the ash tree near the bridge.

He forces himself up, and forward. First a low object, dark and round against the tree. Now he makes it out. Archibald's brown tweed cap, leant like a memorial against the trunk.

A slow rise of the eyes. Take your time, Billy.

Archibald's boots at belly level slowly swinging. Higher,

the contorted hands. Higher still, the dark tilted head, the unspeakable eyes. Billy collapses at the foot of the ash with his nails clawing down his face.

... And now he rises to his feet. Reaches with calm assurance. Lifts up Da's cap and plants it on his own head. Produces a knife, stolen perhaps from Gus in the digger, and cuts down the body of Archibald. One noble tear runs down his cheek. He can't save Da, but he can save himself. Lays his father gently on the grass. Good man, Billy. Walks away with straight back, to find a house with a telephone.

... But that isn't what happened. He feels the slime falter just at the tip of his reach. He seizes the cap and vomits into it. Drops it and runs with piss down his trousers, right up into the Heights, where he flips the finger at Kieran McKendry outside the off-licence and gets a broken nose for his alibi. Leaves Da hanging there to greet what the *Herald* will call *a member of the public*: some poor wee doll doing her Walk of Shame at five o'clock tomorrow morning.

A groan sounds from beneath the bridge, and on the tree every twig titters like a hanged soul.

*

Prostrate on the deck, Billy licked and writhed and howled for the Devil. He didn't turn when the yahoos arrived behind him. Ryan, son of Gus, fathered at fifteen, put his foot on the bridge first.

'The fuck? Look at this bastard.'

The laugh rose in Billy.

'Giggle-headed fucker so ye are.'

Billy stopped laughing, wriggled to his knees, slowly raised his hands.

'Sing us a song, Billy.'

Almost with joy he lifted his voice in music.

'A-as I was walking down the rooaad…'

'On yer fiddles, boys!'

Ryan and the yahoos lifted their arms, sawed and twinkled fingers over empty air. Without emotion Billy watched Ryan raise his boot.

'So early in the morr-ning…'

Thump. He felt his forearm crack.

'You got a note wrong.'

'I me-et a young girl…'

Thump.

'Start again.'

On the third bar of his sixth time around they cracked his face to the ground. Billy stopped singing. He ran his tongue along the green a final time, turned a broken cheek upward.

'Sure I'm your Uncle Billy, boys. Sure I'm your Uncle Billy.'

Ryan son of Gus raised the heel of his boot, and all that had made up the living Billy McLaughlin distilled into the drop of blood that oozed over the crack and down through it. The Devil blotted him up with a finger and licked him away.

★

First, a long calmness, then a jolt awake, a slow understanding. The head on him. Billy McLaughlin arriving drunk to his own immortality.

'Haven't seen you in a while, Billy boy.'

A chorus of voices, for the Devil is legion. His gang, his company at last.

'So Hell's in the burn, is it now?'

'Attaboy, Billy. You could break the jaw of a fishmonger with spirit like that.'

'Is this the afterlife?'

'Only if you wants us,' says the Devil.

He scoops a palmful of burnwater, leans over and shows Billy a host of figures shifting within the reflection. Archibald's face, all white and whole again.

★

Happy under the bridge he waits, listening to feet and wheels. Revelling in the plurality of himself, an eternity's worth of stories. The Devil has a long memory, like flypaper, with the same sorts of things stuck across it.

He plunges his face underwater and inhales deep. Rises,

dripping, and breathes murk upwards like a carnival water-eater. Fingers of mist rise through the crevices and plaster slime across the deck. Somebody new will come looking, one of these nights.

Billy crouches, chattering spells to bring the eye to the crack, to spin the cycle of life and water.

Balloon Animals

Laura-Blaise McDowell

Those who foolishly sought power by riding the back of the tiger, ended up inside. —JFK

'You know those clowns who come in here?' I ask Rhonda.

'Sure,' she says.

'Are they from Kennedy's Circus?'

'Sure are,' she sighs, her Bostonian accent echoing. Sure ahh.

'Their tent is after catching fire,' I tell her, holding out my phone for her to see.

Rhonda jerks her head up from straightening the lapels of a freshly cleaned coat, and peers over its shoulder at a photograph of a huge tent, its red and white stripes blackening and disappearing in great gulfs of blue and yellow flame.

'Jesus Christ,' she breathes.

'It doesn't mention anyone being injured,' I say, scanning the article. 'But I guess they'll have to kick the habit now.'

'Whaddaya mean "habit"?' she snaps.

I had been working in White Sheets dry-cleaners near South Circular Road only a couple of days before I found out what was really going on.

'What?' I say. 'Did you think I'd assume you were leaving little bags of washing powder free of charge in people's coat pockets, so they could do it themselves next time?'

Rhonda eyes me from underneath her black beret, taps a heeled boot on the tiles.

'Look,' she says, dropping her hands from the coat and reaching out her right arm to lean on the counter. 'Honestly, I hired you because you looked boring. Not like, boring in the sense that you'd grass me up, but boring in the sense that you wouldn't want to be involved, per se. I hope I was right about that?'

'Jesus, Rhonda,' I say. 'I'm hardly looking for a cut of the action. I'm just surprised you thought I wouldn't notice.'

She shrugs.

'Is that why you call it White Sheets?' I ask.

'Pardon?' Paahdan.

'White Sheets. It's a joke, isn't it? Like a hint? Cocaine? White...?'

'Aren't you sharp?' she says, narrowing her eyes.

'Well anyway,' I say. 'We probably won't see them for a while, I'd say they'll need to pinch their pennies after this.'

Rhonda doesn't say anything.

'To be honest,' I go on, 'it was that lot who gave you away. The last fella was rifling through the suit, had his finger in his mouth before he'd even paid.'

He had stood there in front of me, looking me in the eye

as he rubbed his finger so hard over his gums it looked like he might press his teeth out.

'Fucking Malachy. It was Malachy, wasn't it?' says Rhonda, shaking her head so that strands of her black fringe move side to side. 'The one with the scar.'

It had indeed been Malachy. The clowns usually left their suits in to be dry-cleaned every couple of days. They invariably had paint encrusting the lines of their faces, seeping into their crow's feet, red circling the curls of their nostrils. There was always some around the scar that dragged the left corner of Malachy's mouth down towards his chin. They never said much, only handed over their dockets and stood twitching, wide-eyed in the bright lights. One time, when I returned with his suit, Malachy thrust a balloon animal at me. It was in the shape of a tiger, with the stripes crudely scribbled on in permanent marker. It hadn't felt like a friendly gesture.

As Rhonda taps her heel, I notice the tiger, deflated on the floor in the corner, all bent out of shape.

'I hope you're right, kid,' she says. 'If I ever see that sorry bunch again, it'll be too soon.'

'Why?' I ask. 'I thought they were your best customers?'

She shifts her weight from one foot to the other, rests her hand on her hip.

'Okay. We had a thing going. I was their sponsor. I'd wash their costumes, uh, etcetera. In return, they advertised my business. Used to have a big White Sheets banner up inside the tent and at the entrance. Set me up with customers for dry-cleaning, and ya know, the bit extra. But just last week I pulled my sponsorship. Ended our relationship completely.'

'Why?' I ask.

'Those clowns,' she leans forward, 'are bastards.'

'Bahstads?'

'Bastards. Sure are. Can't say I feel sorry for them. See, I'd never actually gone to see one of their shows, y'know? All our business was conducted outside of the tent. So I go along last week, they bring me backstage, I think we're gonna have a party, a good time.'

She breathes out, shaking her head.

'No pahdy?' I ask.

'I'm tellin' ya. That was no party. I couldn't believe the way they treated that tiger, the size of the cage. All those clowns out of their minds, tormenting him.' She shudders. 'I pulled my sponsorship right away.'

'The article says the tiger was lost in the fire,' I say.

'Poor tiger,' she says.

'Poor tsigah,' I agree.

The next day, we're working late. I'm in the back, sorting orders when the door flings open, the bell bashing wildly. I turn to see through the plastic-wrapped coats and dresses that it's Malachy. He's wearing a moulting neon-green wig, a black suit jacket over a blue and green checked clown suit. Face paint outlines his features but the flat expanses of his cheeks and forehead are clear and pale. His eyes are black, and before Rhonda can say anything, he pulls a handgun from his inside pocket, points it at her and shoots her twice, once in the chest once in the head.

She lands almost at my feet, hitting the bottom rung of the clothes rail. It shifts on its wheels as she lands; the garments sway on their hangers. The bullet has blown two strands of her fringe in opposite directions, like curtains opening on a show. I look up and Malachy is staring right at me, though he can only see my eyes above the rail. I duck and feel a bullet howl over me. The door flings open, the bell bashes again, then silence. On my knees, I look at Rhonda, her head all dead and upside down. Her eyes are open, her beret blown clean away. There is blood on her chest where she's been hit but her face is intact, apart from the hole. She has a tiny piece of lettuce stuck between her two front teeth. I wish I'd told her when I had the chance.

The bell clangs again and I jump up. This time it's not a clown, though these two men also have guns.

'You!' says the smaller one, pointing the gun straight at me.

'Don't bother,' I say. 'It'll be more trouble than it's worth.'

'Get out from behind there,' says the small one, who's from Dublin. 'Let us see ya.'

I step out, and towards the counter. 'Do you have a docket?' I ask him.

'Did the clown see ya?' he asks.

'Yes,' I say.

'You have to come with us.'

'No,' I say. 'I work here. There'll be no one left if I leave.'

The two men look at each other, then separate and walk around either end of the counter. The taller heaves Rhonda over his shoulder while the smaller one grabs me, his gun to my back, and drags me out of the shop.

'No messin',' he says.

When I said it would be more trouble than it was worth, what I'd meant was my parents would kick up an almighty fuss. It probably sounded self-deprecating, but it wasn't really. Those men, weedy enough behind their barrels, didn't stand a chance against my mother and father, fierce and feral when it came to their offspring. One time at home, when some local gurriers hopped on my younger brother Cian, Mam and Dad drove around town for hours with him in the back, a tissue up each nostril and an icepack affixed to his head with one of Mam's aerobics headbands, till he spotted the perpetrators loitering outside a newsagent flicking matches at each other. Dad got out with a bat and the intention of beating the living daylights out of them, only the guards happened to cruise by at the right time, so Dad handed the culprits over to them. Either way those little shits got their comeuppance, so you can only imagine what might befall two hapless eejits, dim-witted enough to murder their daughter in her first year away from home. University life ahead of me. And I their oldest. Not a chance they'd let it lie.

There is a Micra parked outside.

'A Micra?' I say.

'Shut up,' says the taller, as he bungs Rhonda's body in the boot and climbs into the driver's seat, knees practically up around his ears. He's a northern accent and he's wearing a black beanie.

'Are you in the Ra?' I ask. 'Is that what this is?'

'Shut up,' he says again.

The other sits with his arm around me. His grasp would almost be romantic were it not the embrace of a kidnapper. I glance down at the hand holding my arm. Nails bitten to small islands floating in the middle of fleshy seas, coasts of dirt lining their circumference, tips white with the pressure.

'Relax, would you?' I say.

'Shut up,' he says and I smell his breath.

'Tayto for dinner?'

'Shut up,' he says.

He's up against the left-hand door, and I'm in the middle. I notice the gun on the seat next to him, but when I look down at it, I realise it's plastic. Then we take off, and he lifts his other hand to cover my eyes, though I can still sort of see through the cracks. His fingers are skinny and don't touch even when they're pressed together at the joints.

'What kind of criminals are ye,' I ask, 'that ye forget a blindfold?'

'Shut up,' he says. 'Or I'll make you a gag as well.'

I go quiet and we shudder along. It's dark, so I can't make out anything recognisable through the gaps between his fingers.

'Why did he kill Rhonda?' I ask after a few minutes.

'Shut up,' says the one holding me.

'Well you're going to have to tell me at some stage,' I say. 'Since you clearly know.'

'Shut. Up,' he says.

I sigh. We're stopped at traffic lights, and I decide to make a break for it. I wrench myself to the left. They didn't lock the door and I'm halfway out before the one beside me tackles me around the waist and drags me, kicking, back into the car as the one in the front takes off at full speed.

'Jesus fucking Christ,' he says.

'Jesus Christ yourself!' I say. 'I could have been fucking killed!'

Your man raises an eyebrow at me.

'But I suppose that wouldn't have bothered ye too much, would it?' I try to laugh, but the adrenaline is pumping in my ears. I hadn't even managed to see where I was when I'd leaped out, but it had been pretty quiet and I don't think anyone saw. At least, I didn't hear anyone, no one shouted. Your man is sitting fully on top of me now. I'm stomach down and he's straddling the small of my back holding my arms down with his hands. There's nothing over my eyes but I'm flat to the seat and can't see out the windows. Your man driving doesn't even look around.

'You're some pair,' I say, my voice muffled slightly against the old car seat. 'What are your names?'

'Neck,' says the one on top.

'What about your pal?' I say.

'That's Tongs.'

'Those are fairly gas names,' I say. 'What do your mothers call ye?'

'Would you ever shut the fuck up, would ya?' Neck growls. He's pressing hard on top of me and my neck is starting to hurt.

'Neck. My own neck is beginning to get at me a bit, would you ever leave off and let me sit up, I won't try anything again.'

He doesn't respond.

'You clearly feel an affinity with necks,' I try again, 'so I was hoping I could appeal to that—'

'I'll bleedin' break your neck if you're not careful,' he says.

'That's what I'm afraid might already be happening though,' I say. 'Your enormous weight and masculine strength are a bit much for my tiny woman spine and—'

'Jesus, fine, if I let you up will you shut your poxy mouth? Fuckin' hell.' He leans over and manually locks my door as I clamber up to a sitting position.

'Here lads, are we in Phoenix Park?' I ask, looking around.

'For fuck's sake, Necker!' says Tongs without looking

back at us. 'Don't let her see where we are, ya fuckin eejit.'

'Ah it's too late now, lads,' I say. 'I know Phoenix Park like the back of my hand, sure don't I come for runs here on the weekend.'

'Fuckin' hell,' says Neck, rubbing his forehead. We keep driving. Neck looks crestfallen.

'Ah I was only joking, lads,' I say. 'I don't actually run here. Sure I live over on the other side of the city. I only recognised it from going to the zoo last year.'

Neck doesn't say anything but he looks a little cheered. We're silent for a few minutes as Tongs keeps driving deeper into the park.

'Ye'll forgive me for my endless curiosity,' I say, 'but what the hell is going on?'

'Just fucking tell her,' says Tongs. 'Tell her anything to shut her up.'

'Is this to do with the Ra?' I ask again, imagining Tongs all plastered in Republican tattoos beneath his jacket.

'No, it's not to do with the Ra,' says Tongs.

'That sounds like something a militant would say.'

'Aye, well I'm not a fuckin' militant, alright? That's very offensive.' Tongs turns around for the first time and as he does so, doesn't he hit a fucking deer. The poor thing ricochets off the front window, shattering it. Tongs swerves off the road and into the undergrowth, but thankfully misses the trees, stopping neatly between two pines. I end up in Neck's lap, his body flung over me.

'Jesus, everybody alright?' says Tongs, whose airbag has inflated and is pressing weakly into his chest.

'Yeah,' Neck says.

'Peachy,' I say.

Neck gives me a look. Tongs gives the airbag a few whacks to quicken its deflation and opens his door. He's gone a minute and then arrives at my window with the deer over his shoulder.

'You're not putting that in here with me!' I say.

'Yes I fuckin' am,' he says. 'Unlock the door.'

I look at Neck, appalled, but he reaches over me and unlocks it.

'What the fuck are you—' I start to say, but I'm cut off when Tongs dumps the lifeless, bleeding carcass next to me.

'No room in the boot,' he smirks, and slams the door. The smell is overwhelming and I gag a little bit. The deer is a young female. She's contorted, her neck up against the back of the seat, body sliding down in a backwards S shape, broken legs everywhere. Blood glistens around her nose and drips from a large wound on her side. She's facing me, looking me right in the eye. It reminds me a bit of when someone falls asleep next to you on an aeroplane, mouth gaping, dribbling on your shoulder and you're powerless.

'Wanna swap places?' I ask Neck. He doesn't respond.

Tongs has found himself a rock and is busy smashing out the rest of the windscreen. Once that's done, he climbs back in the front and attempts to reverse out of the undergrowth, arm flung over the passenger seat, craning his neck.

'Here, I can't see anything through the back window, will you push the deer down?' he says.

'Are you joking?' I say. 'I'm not touching that.' I'm already pressed up against Neck, who is in turn flattened against his door, in order to be as far from the carcass as possible. I don't even like prodding snoring neighbours on aeroplanes.

'One of you push her fuckin' head down before I batter the pair of you.'

Neck gingerly stretches out a hand and using one finger, applies the tiniest amount of pressure to the still-warm head. She slides down a little.

'Pair of fucking pussies, you are,' says Tongs as he revs the engine and manages to get us out of the undergrowth. We drive along a little way in silence again. I'm still practically in Neck's lap.

'I'm a weekday vegetarian, you know,' I say. 'So if you're planning on feeding this one to me for dinner, I'm afraid ye'll have to make other arrangements.'

'Nah, she's not for you,' says Neck, with the vague hint of a smile curling the corner of his thin little mouth.

'Oh, she's not, no? All for the boys, eh?'

'Not for us either,' says Neck.

Something about the way he says it makes me uncomfortable. There's a change in the atmosphere in the car. I shift on the seat so I'm not touching Neck as much, so

I can't feel his Tayto breath moving my hair.

'What's it for so?' I ask.

'Ho ho,' says Tongs. 'Just you wait and see.'

It's freezing now that there's no windscreen, the only heat coming off the steaming deer. I suppose I could leap straight ahead of me, out the front and over the bonnet, but I'd likely impale myself on the jagged glass still left around the edges.

'Lads, will ye just tell me where we're going? Or else let me go, I'll not tell on ye. Sure I don't even know your real names, do I?'

Nobody says anything. I read somewhere that humanising yourself to your kidnapper can sometimes endear you to them, make them more sympathetic. Apparently, there was once a serial killer who paid for a potential victim's flight home because she told him her dad had cancer.

'I've a nickname, too,' I say. 'It's Lopey. My name's Penelope because my parents had notions back in the day, but I was never called Penny, I was called Lopey because I was forever moping and loping about the place.'

Again, neither of them say anything.

'Did ye get your nicknames from something ye did or... or how did they come about?'

Jesus, they're making me feel like I'm inflicting myself upon them, trying to sit with the cool kids at lunch.

'Neck,' I say. 'Is that just, like, a sort of D4-type way of saying Nick? Did you actually grow up real posh and now even though you've escaped your yuppie past, everyone still calls you Neck?'

Neck unzips his black fleece so that I can see his throat. He runs his finger across a long scar above the twin points of his collar bones.

'Jesus, what happened to you?'

'That was meant to be a threat,' he says, drily.

'What was? It's not me with that scar.'

'No, but...' He tuts and shifts in his seat, rolls his eyes. 'I'll fuckin', like, do it to you if you don't stop nattering on.'

'Nattering?' I say. 'I'm hardly here by choice. Just trying to...' I glance at the deer, open-mouthed and glassy-eyed next to me, '...lift the mood.' Neck looks out the window.

'What about you, Tongs? Were you birthed using a pair of tongs in lieu of forceps? You know, I heard about that happening to someone, I think my second cousin? Came early and was born on the kitchen floor, and her elder brother had to haul her out with the tongs from the fireplace. Don't know if he ever recovered. Can ye imagine having to extract a baby from your own mother's—'

I realise we've left the road. We're driving through undergrowth and then the car stops suddenly, sending the deer lurching forward, only to land with a whack against the seat, sending globules of blood flying onto my face. I wipe them away.

'Have we arrived?' I ask. Neck's arm is back around me, as tightly as it had been at the start. He flicks the handle of his door and kicks it open, dragging me with him.

'Best to stay quiet,' he whispers, and it's not menacing, I just sort of believe him.

I don't know what part of this vast park we're in, don't even know what time it is; it's pitch black, and it's sort of hitting me that Rhonda is dead and these guys know something. Now that we're out of the vacuum of the car, the night seems huge and the weird atmosphere that arrived after the deer seems to have escaped out into the world because I can feel it still. I'm almost glad of Neck's arm around me.

Tongs hoists the deer out of the car and over his shoulder, then takes off into the woods. We follow. Rhonda is still in the boot. Neck keeps his arm around me. The ground's uneven and it's too dark to see what's underfoot. It occurs to me to try and make a break for it, but I don't know how I'd find my way out of here and I'd make an unholy racket crashing through the undergrowth. If Neck has any speed on him, which by the looks of him he does, he'd have me back in a minute.

Suddenly we're ducking under a large sheet hung between two trees that I hadn't even seen coming; it had been totally camouflaged. Behind the sheet is a clearing in which sits a pair of tents, the gazebo ones you see at festivals. Tongs heaves the deer off his shoulder and throws it on the ground. He rummages inside the entrance of one of the tents before returning with a small axe, and commences hacking her into several pieces. I look away, the sound of it turning my stomach. Neck steers me into the tent where the axe had been.

'Now don't get any ideas,' I say quickly, seeing the sleeping bags on the floor. 'You better not lay a finger on me, now or—'

'Would you relax?' says Neck. 'I'm not gonna touch you. You weren't part of the plan in the first place.'

'Well I can see that, ye didn't even have a blindfold for me. I'm just saying, don't think—'

'I'm not. Give us a bitta credit, ya mad thing.' He laughs a little and picks a dark green hoodie up off the floor. 'Here, stick this on ya. It's fuckin' freezin'.'

I slip it on and as my head pops through the neck, I hear it. The tearing of flesh. Gnawing coming from the tent next to ours.

'What the fuck is that?'

'That is why this whole mess happened in the first place.'

'It sounds like a fucking werewolf or a tiger or something?'

Neck gives me a somewhat surprised look.

'Do you watch a lot of nature programmes, do ya?' he asks.

'Watch a few, like. Enough to know the sound of something being devoured. Jesus. It's not...Tongs... Tongs isn't a werewolf, is he?'

'No, Tongs isn't a fuckin' werewolf. But you were half right.'

'Half right? He's a whole wolf?'

'No! The tiger bit.'

'He's a tiger.'

'No! But that is a tiger you're hearing.'

'Fuck off!'

'Serious!'

'Where did lads like you get a fucking tiger? No offence.'

'We rescued him, didn't we?'

'Ye rescued him.'

'Yeah. From the Kennedys.'

'Sure I read about that. But when the news said they'd "lost a tiger" I didn't think they meant they'd fucking *mislaid* one.'

'They told the cops the tiger was definitely in one of the trailers that was burnt to smithereens, think they mighta thrown a dog carcass or something in there to convince them. Wanted to hunt us down themselves.'

'And you burnt their circus down?'

'We did what we had to do. Couldn't leave a lovely creature like that in the hands of those coked up mad yolks. They didn't treat him right. He was half starved.'

'Well, what's his name?' I ask.

'It was Kennedy, he was their mascot, like. But we renamed him Leonard.'

'Leonard?'

'Yeah, after Leonard Cohen. Wanted to imbue him with a bitta dignity, after the mortification of life in the circus.'

'Yeah alright,' I say. 'But like, why do ye have him here?

Why did they shoot Rhonda over it all? I'm more confused than I was at the start, Neck. And why did ye bring me here? You're hardly planning on my being Leonard's next meal... are you?' I begin to panic, but Neck puts out a hand. 'Would you relax?' he says. 'He's very civilised. He'd be insulted if he heard you going on like that.'

'Would he?' I say.

'He would of course. C'mere till you meet him.' He takes me by the arm.

'Eh, you're alright, I think I'll stay here,' I squeak, digging my heels in, but Neck drags me out.

'He's mad friendly, so he is!'

Tongs is standing outside Leonard's tent having a smoke.

'Leonard's delighted with himself,' he says, smiling a little. He's lit a fire in the centre of the clearing.

'Tigers can eat up to twenty-five pounds of meat a day, you know.'

'So I've heard...' I say. 'How long will that deer last him?'

'She was small, only about three days,' he says. 'I'll stick the rest of the meat in a couple of freezer bags. But he'll need something else by the end of the week.'

I shift from foot to foot.

'How long have ye been here?' I ask, looking around. I notice that they've hung sheets between trees all the way around us, forming an enclosed circle. The sheets on the inside facing us are white, but where they fold over the ropes I can see the other sides are expertly painted like leaves, trees and undergrowth. The sound of the deer being ripped and torn still emanates from the tent.

'Few months,' says Tongs, exhaling.

'And where did ye get the camouflage sheets? They're class.'

'I painted them meself,' says Neck, proudly. 'Rhonda gave us some she had spare.'

'You're mad talented.' I tell him. 'Did you take art classes?'

'Just paint what I see,' he says.

Just then, there's a rustle from Leonard's tent and I leap up. Tongs and Neck chuckle as an enormous head peers out from the tent. The tsigah. His broad, beautiful shoulders are almost on a par with mine as he emerges and pads towards us, blood around his mouth and on his paws.

'Jesus fucking Christ,' I say.

'Don't be bleedin' rude,' says Neck to me. 'This is Leonard. Leonard say hello.'

Leonard sniffs me. My arms are clasped up around my face and I'm paralysed.

'Good boy, Leonard,' says Tongs. 'Good boy.' Leonard flicks his tongue and licks around his mouth. He gives my leg a lick as well. His tongue is so enormous it feels like a gloved hand rubbing up and down my thigh. Neck sits down by the fire and Leonard ambles over and lies down next to him, big bloody head in his lap. Tongs sits down as well and after a minute I manage to unclench my body and perch gingerly across from the others. They're like a happy little family. Leonard is purring, all sleepy after his meal.

'So. You went to the circus, saw that, eh, Leonard, was being mistreated, and just decided to liberate him?' I ask.

'Not exactly,' says Tongs. 'There's more to it than that, but what would you have done?'

He is looking for something in his pockets and after a moment, produces a deflated white balloon. He begins to blow into it, his cheeks round and pink underneath his straggly facial hair.

'Well, I mean, probably like, reported it to the authorities,' I say.

'Ach,' scoffs Tongs, inhaling deeply as he ties a knot in the balloon's end. 'They'd've done sweet fuck all. We needed to take action. Couldn't have a troop of deranged fuckin' clowns tormenting this prince one minute longer.' He leans over tickles Leonard's ear affectionately, then returns to the balloon and begins twisting it.

'See,' says Neck, 'we used to do a bitta work for Rhonda. Shift a bitta blow here and there. We'd even deliver to the clowns now and then, but we'd never been inside the tent, seen what went on in there. Never even occurred to us that maybe we shouldn't give it to people who were in charge of wild animals.' He laughs. Leonard slobbers happily on Neck's lap.

'So one day, about last week,' Tongs continues, not looking up from the balloon, on which he is scribbling with a marker. 'We call into Rhonda to pick up, and she's in a wee state. We ask her what the matter is and she tells us.' He pauses and holds up the balloon, which he has mangled into something resembling Rhonda with a little black beret and black boots. As he talks, he waggles the balloon Rhonda from side to side. It is eerie in the firelight.

'Tells us she'd been to Kennedy's and she was withdrawing her sponsorship. Said they were abusing a tiger, every one of them absolutely outta their mind during the show. Said she couldn't bear to stay.' He cleared his throat. 'So I said, "Rhonda, give us a wee pair of tickets and we'll go down, see for ourselves." Fuckin' grim, depressing freak show, it was. This lad being made to jump through hoops, hit with a whip, shouted at by fuckin' Malachy, the fuckin' creep. Not a chance, not a chance in hell we could let that go on. Not a chance.' He shakes his head. 'Not a fuckin' chance.' He pulls another balloon from his pocket and begins working on it.

'So after the show, we torched em,' grins Neck. 'Burnt them to the bleedin' ground. It was whopper. They saw us taking off with one of their trailers, with Leonard inside it. Didn't catch us, though.'

'Jesus,' I say. 'And where's the trailer now?' I want to interrogate everything they've just said, but this seems like the most sensible question to ask.

'Ah, we torched that too, once we had Leonard safely here.'

'And no one saw?'

'We left it out on the side of motorway miles out and scattered. The clowns won't find it, or us.'

'Won't you need it to transport Leonard?'

'He's not going anywhere,' says Tongs. 'He can ride in the back of the car if he needs to, sure.'

'Sure,' I say, mesmerised by the numerous balloon creatures that are fluttering from Tongs' busy hands like petals. They glisten all amber through the flames.

'Those poxy clowns would be hard pressed to find us here,' says Neck, 'but we'll find them.'

'Aye, that's it,' says Tongs. 'We came back to White Sheets to check on Rhonda as soon as we had himself established here in the tent. We thought they might have gone for her after what we did. But we were too fuckin' late.'

'You only missed Malachy by a minute,' I say.

'Aye,' says Tongs. 'I know. We have to make it right. So our Leonard is gonna eat well from now on. A clown a week. Isn't that right, pal?' He tosses a balloon version of Malachy, scar and all, into the fire where it explodes with a bang.

'It is. A clown a fuckin' week.'

Bang, bang, bang.

We sit around the fire for a long time. Neck gets up and brings a bottle of whiskey from one of the tents, gives me a plastic cup full of it. It burns, but I'm thinking about Cian with the tissues in each nostril and how Mam and Dad hunting down those gurriers had been the biggest news in our family in a while. I wonder if I'm on the news yet; if my phone's ringing on the shelf behind the counter of White Sheets. I look at Leonard, all lit up. His strong, lithe body. Faint scars running against the stripes of his back. Neck's hand stroking his fur, gently, over and over.

After a while I get up and walk into the tent with the sleeping bags. Nobody says anything and I climb into one, let the heat from the whiskey pour into my hands and feet. I'm asleep almost straight away.

In the morning, I wake and I'm alone, though the bags on either side of me look to have been slept in. Birds trill and I can hear the roar of the city in the distance. I struggle free of the sleeping bag and crawl to the door. Looking out, I see Neck piling sticks and leaves into the bonfire pit. Rhonda's lying on a white sheet on the ground, Tongs standing over her. I climb out and approach them.

'What are ye up to?' I ask.

'Ah, just getting poor old Rhonda ready,' says Tongs, nudging her corpse affectionately with the toe of his boot. Looking down, I see that in addition to the bullet hole in her forehead, Rhonda's throat has been cut.

'What the fuck? What happened to her?'

'Just took a little offering,' Tongs says. 'Rhonda died in the name of saving our wee Leonard. Her strength is gonna be in all of us when we go after those clowns.'

He points at the bonfire pit. I look around and see by the stone circle the three plastic whiskey cups from last night, plus a fourth one, each half full of black blood.

'It'll probably have congealed a wee bit,' says Tongs cheerfully. 'Had to do it last night before it dried up inside her, you know? Besides, it'll be less messy now when I have to dismember her.'

'Dismember her?'

'Aye. I know it sounds rotten, but sure we can't let her go to waste. We don't know when we'll catch the first clown, can't have Leonard going hungry while we track them down, can we?'

'I think I'm going to be sick,' I say.

'Well, don't do it in here, if you are,' says Neck, tossing another bundle of sticks into the pit. 'Go outside the sheets if you have to. But I want nice loud vomitin' so we can keep track of you. Don't think about runnin' away. We'll only hear you and have to bring you back.'

I look back at Tongs. He's moving around Rhonda, looking at her from different angles.

'Have you ever done this before?' he asks Neck.

'Nah, mate. Not like that.'

'What's the best way to do it, would you say?'

'Fuck knows. How'd you do the deer?'

'Badly. I'd like Rhonda to have a damn sight more dignity than fuckin' Bambi though. Fuck it, let's toast to her first. Before anything else.'

He turns and picks up two of the cups, handing one to Neck and one to me. The cup is cool.

'Leonard!' calls Neck, walking around the other side of Rhonda. 'Lenny boy. C'mere. There's a good fella.'

Leonard comes padding out of his tent and over to where we stand. Tongs takes the fourth cup and empties it on the leaves in front of Leonard's paws. Leonard leans forward and begins lapping it up, his shoulder blades like fins beneath his fur.

'To Rhonda,' says Tongs, raising his up above Rhonda's body.

'To Leonard,' says Neck, following suit.

They look to me and there is nothing I can do.

'To justice,' I say, and down the cup of blood, metallic and slick in my throat.

NIALL BOURKE has an MA in Creative Writing from Goldsmiths University (2015). His poetry and prose have appeared in publications including *A Bowl of Mysteries* (Poetry Ireland), *The Irish Times*, and *Magma Poetry*. His debut poetry collection, a perverse novella in verse called *Did You Put The Weasels Out?* (Eyewear, April 2018), was longlisted as a Poetry School book of the year. He was selected for the 2017 Poetry Ireland's Introduction Series in 2017 and has been shortlisted for the Costa Short Story Award, the Over the Edge New Writer of the Year Award, the Cambridge International Short Story Award, the Mairtín Crawford Short Story Prize, and the Hennessy New Irish Writing Award. Originally from Kilkenny, Niall lives in London.

JUNE CALDWELL worked for many years as a journalist before becoming a writer of fiction. She has an MA in Creative Writing from Queen's University Belfast. Her short story collection *Room Little Darker* was published in 2017 by New Island Books and by Head of Zeus in 2018, *The Times* described it as 'an unflinching collection which thuds with life and kicks with horror'. She is a prize-winner of The Moth International Short Story Prize and has been shortlisted for many other awards, including the Calvino Prize in Fabulist Fiction. Her debut novel *Little Town Moone* is forthcoming from John Murray.

LUCY CALDWELL was born in Belfast in 1981. She is the author of three novels, several stage plays and radio dramas, and a collection of short stories. Awards include the Rooney Prize for Irish Literature, the George Devine Award, the Dylan Thomas Prize, the Imison Award, the Commonwealth Short Story Prize (Canada & Europe), the Irish Playwrights' and Screenwriters' Guild Award, the Edge Hill Short Story Prize Readers' Choice Award, a Fiction Uncovered Award, a K. Blundell Trust Award and a Major Individual Artist Award from the Arts Council of Northern Ireland. She was elected a Fellow of the Royal Society of Literature in 2018.

JAN CARSON is a writer and community arts facilitator based in East Belfast. Her debut novel, *Malcolm Orange Disappears* and short story collection, *Children's Children*, were published by Liberties Press, Dublin. A micro-fiction collection, *Postcard Stories* was published by the Emma Press in 2017. Jan's novel *The Fire Starters* was published by Doubleday in April 2019. Her stories have appeared in journals such as *Banshee*, *The Tangerine* and *Harper's Bazaar* and on BBC Radio 3 and 4. In 2018 Jan was the Irish Writers Centre's inaugural Roaming Writer in Residence on the trains of Ireland.

JUDYTH EMANUEL's debut novel *YEH HELL OW* is published by Adelaide Books. She was one of three winners in the 2017 Victoria University Short Story Prize for New and Emerging Writers. Her story 'Treacle Eyes' can be found in *Joiner Bay and Other Stories*. She has short stories in literary journals *Overland, Electric Literature Recommended Reading, Into The Void, Hobart, Literary Orphans, Verity Lane, Intrinsick, Fanzine, STORGY, Connotations Press, Jellyfish Review, Adelaide Literary Magazine, Thrice, Malevolent Soap*. Her second novel, *wing me over the sea to see,* is due June 2020.

WENDY ERSKINE lives in Belfast. Her debut collection of short stories, *Sweet Home,* was published by The Stinging Fly Press in September 2018 and by Picador in 2019. Her writing has appeared in *Being Various: New Irish Short Stories* (Faber and Faber), *Stinging Fly Stories, Winter Papers 4* and *Female Lines* (New Island Books), and on BBC Radio 4.

LOUISE FARR lives in Bangor, Northern Ireland, where she works full time as an English teacher in Alternative Education. In 2018, she won the Benedict Kiely Short Story Competition and the Trisha Ashley Award (Exeter Short Story Prize), In 2019, she was a finalist in the Doolin Writers' Weekend Short Story Competition and the winner of the Ink Tears Short Story Competition. She recently completed a novel for young adults, which was shortlisted for the 2018 Exeter Novel Prize.

LAUREN FOLEY is Irish/Australian. Her stories are published internationally. Lauren has Systemic Lupus Erythematosus (SLE) and is disabled, owing to this the majority of her writing is dictated. Her short story, *K-K-K*, won the inaugural Neilma Sidney Short Story Prize with *Overland* literary journal and was shortlisted for the Irish Book Awards Short Story of the Year. She was shortlisted for the Hennessy New Irish Writer of the Year and was a recent Pushcart Prize nominee. Lauren is an Arts Council of Ireland 2018/9 Next Generation Artist.

IAN GREEN is a writer from Northern Scotland based in London, with a PhD in epigenetics. His short fiction has been widely broadcast and performed, including winning the BBC Radio 4 Opening Lines competition and the Futurebook Future Fiction prize. He has been published by Londnr, Almond Press, OpenPen, Meanjin, Transportation Press, The Pigeonhole, and more.

DANIEL HICKEY is from County Mayo. He is a winner of the 2019 Escalator award, presented by the UK National Centre for Writing. His poetry has been published in the *Mayo Anthology of Poetry* and his short fiction in the online journals *Apocrypha* and *Abstractions* and *Eastlit*. He currently lives in Norwich, where he works as a journalist for the *Eastern Daily Press*.

MICHAEL HOLLOWAY was born in Liverpool in 1985. He studied English Literature and Creative Writing at the University of Central Lancashire until 2008 and got his

Masters in Writing at Liverpool John Moores University in 2012. He currently works as a library assistant at Liverpool John Moores University and the University of Liverpool. He was shortlisted for the Sunderland Short Story Award 2018 and he is working on his first novel.

SUZANNE JOINSON is a prize-winning novelist, creative non-fiction writer and Senior Lecturer in Creative Writing at the University of Chichester. Her novels include *A Lady Cyclist's Guide to Kashgar* (Bloomsbury) and *The Photographer's Wife* (Bloomsbury). She regularly reviews for *The New York Times* and writes for many publications. She teaches creative non-fiction, memoir and the crossover areas of fiction and non-fiction.

NIAMH MACCABE was born in Dublin and lives in North Leitrim. She is published in *Aesthetica Magazine Anthology*, *The Writer Magazine*, *The Bristol Prize Anthology*, *The London Magazine*, *Bare Fiction*, *Bath Flash Fiction*, *Wasafiri*, *The Honest Ulsterman*, *Retreat West*, *The Lonely Crowd*, *Structo*, *Tears in the Fence*, and many others. She is a Best in British and Irish Flash Fiction nominee, a Pushcart Prize nominee, has won the Allingham Flash Fiction Award, the Wasafiri New Writing Award, the Molly Keane Award, was finalist in Glimmer Train Press Contest, R.A. & Pin Drop Award, Costa Short Story Award, Books Ireland Award, Galley

Beggar Press Prize, the Anton Chekhov Prize and the New Ohio Review Editors Prize, among others.

LAURA-BLAISE MCDOWELL graduated with an MA in Creative Writing from University College Dublin in 2016. Her poetry and prose have appeared in *The Honest Ulsterman*, *The Galway Review*, *Headstuff*, and *Junior Press* among others. She was shortlisted for the Maeve Binchy Travel Award in 2016 and the Doolin Writers' Weekend Short Story Award in 2017. She is currently working on a novel.

GERARD MCKEOWN's work has been featured in *The Moth*, *3:AM*, and *Litro*, among others. In 2017 he was shortlisted for the Bridport Prize, and in 2018 he was longlisted for the Irish Book Awards' Short Story of the Year.

MANDY TAGGART lives near the North Coast of Northern Ireland. Her short fiction publications include *Crannóg Magazine*, *Honest Ulsterman* and *Incubator Magazine*. Her work has been shortlisted for the Bridport Flash Prize, Lightship One Page Prize and the KWS Hilary Mantel Award, and she is a previous winner of the Michael McLaverty Award for her story 'Ways of the North'.

CATHERINE TALBOT lives in Dublin and recently graduated with an MPhil in Creative Writing from Trinity College Dublin. She is currently the Literary Fiction Editor of the TCD literary journal, *College Green*. Her short story, 'Richard's Grief', was shortlisted for the Fish Prize 2015 and published in *Banshee*. Another short story 'Shrinking from Life' was longlisted for the inaugural Colm Tóibín International Short Story Award and the Fish Prize 2014. 'Rough Spain' was shortlisted for the UK Short Fiction Prize 2018. Catherine's debut novel, *A Good Father*, will be published by Penguin Ireland in 2020.

SAM THOMPSON was born in London, has spent time in Dublin and Oxford, and now lives in Belfast. He is the author of two novels, *Communion Town*, which was longlisted for the 2012 Booker Prize, and *Jott* (2018). His short fiction features in *Best British Short Stories 2019*. He has written for the *Times Literary Supplement* and the *London Review of Books*, and has taught at Oxford University, Oxford Brookes and Queen's University Belfast.

JOANNA WALSH is the author of seven books including the digital work, *seed-story.com*. Her latest book, *Break.up*, was published by Semiotext(e) and Tuskar Rock in 2018. Her writing has been widely published in anthologies, newspapers and journals including *The Dalkey Archive's Best European Fiction*, *Granta Magazine*, *gorse*, *The Stinging Fly*, *The Guardian*, *The New Statesman*, and *The Los Angeles Review of Books*. She is a UK Arts Foundation fellow, and the founder of #readwomen, described by the *New York Times* as 'a rallying cry for equal treatment for women writers'.

DAWN WATSON is a PhD candidate at Queen's University, Belfast, writing a prose poem novel and researching prose poetics. Her poetry pamphlet *The Stack of Owls is Getting Higher* was published by The Emma Press (June 2019). She completed a Masters in Poetry at the Seamus Heaney Centre in 2018 after winning the Ruth West Poetry Scholarship, and has a story in the anthology *Belfast Stories* (Doire Press, June 2019). She was a 2018 Poetry Ireland Introductions Series poet, and won the 2018 Doolin Writers' Poetry Award. Her writing has been published in journals including *The Manchester Review*, *Blackbox Manifold*, *The Stinging Fly*, *The Moth* and *The Tangerine*.

ELEY WILLIAMS' *Attrib. and other stories* (Influx Press, 2017) was awarded the Republic of Consciousness Prize and the James Tait Black Memorial Prize 2018. With stories anthologised in *The Penguin Book of the Contemporary British Short Story* (Penguin Classics, 2018) and *Liberating the Canon* (Dostoevsky Wannabe, 2018), she is a Fellow of the MacDowell Colony and the Royal Society of Literature.

ACKNOWLEDGEMENTS

This book would not be in existence without the help and support of many people: Ian Sansom and the kind folks in the Seamus Heaney Centre at Queen's University, Belfast for idea bouncing, technical expertise in podcasting and free coffee; Conor Graham and Michael Darcy for the most practical support within the world of publishing and book distribution; Emma Warnock, you know why; Stephen Connolly, for the important, and aesthetically crucial, job of typesetting; all the staff in No Alibis Bookstore for their advice, enthusiasm and support. Bob Price, cover design extraordinaire; June Caldwell for her amazingly buoyant and inspired introduction. And finally, to all those who submitted stories for this anthology: you are what this is all about: storytelling.